ALL MY HUSBANDS

Book One: The Challenge

Dr. Patricia C. Churchill

Outskirts Press, Inc.
Denver, Colorado

All My Husbands
Book One: The Challenge
All Rights Reserved.
Copyright © 2008 Dr. Patricia C. Churchill
V3.0R1.1

Contact Dr. Churchill by e-mail at happy@soundofwisdom.com. Visit her web site, www.soundofwisdom.com and post your comments on the novel or other inspiring insights.

Outskirts Press, Inc.
http://www.outskirtspress.com

ISBN: 978-1-4327-2536-5

Library of Congress Control Number: 2008933113

Outskirts Press and the "OP" logo are trademarks belonging to Outskirts Press, Inc.

PRINTED IN THE UNITED STATES OF AMERICA

Table of Contents

Prologue

You are about to read Book One, the first of two volumes on the fascinating life of Lila Mae Thornton. There are six intertwined stories here, two of them told by Lila Mae and four told by men who love her. These men help to shape Lila Mae's complex and challenging life experiences. As they speak, they reveal strengths and weaknesses of their own personalities.

Lila and her husbands talk to you, the reader. You become a character in their stories, someone they know. Expect to be drawn into their world with all of its joys, sorrows, hopes, fears and uncertainties. If I have succeeded as a writer, you will become intimately involved. You may wonder how others would tell *your* life story.

The folks in this novel enjoy good eating. Here, you will find food for thought; spiritual nourishment; pleasure for the palate; the nectar of laughter, and a dash of spice for good measure. Favorite recipes of the characters are in the appendix.

Lila, Jimmy, Henry, Ezra and Buster channeled to me their own stories, to be shared with you. You will find a handy chronology of their adventures in the appendix. Enjoy!

- Patricia C. Churchill

Lila Mae – Young Adult

Life is the game that must be played.

-Edmond Rostand

Men appreciate me. If you really want to know Lila Mae, you have to understand that. Like the tall guy who looked me over as he walked out of here a minute ago.

I've been thinking about my life. About how I happen to be sitting in this hotel bar in Atlanta on September 17, 1964, sipping on a virgin pina colada and waiting to catch a train up North tomorrow. Since it's just the two of us in here, let me tell you my story from the beginning.

I was a World War II baby, born to Lucius and Alma Thornton. If my daddy had been drafted, my story might be different. He wasn't. With help from his father, he purchased our eighty acre farm near Macon in 1935 and did pretty well with it. Even during the last vestiges of the depression, the family ate well and had the basic necessities covered. Some years, the weather didn't cooperate, the crop yield dropped and Daddy didn't make much money. When that happened, we had to cut back on expenses.

For example, when I was eleven I had to stop taking piano lessons for a while. My older sister, Gwen, never wanted to practice, so my parents let her quit taking lessons soon after she started. I loved music. I would sit at the old upright and try to teach myself since neither of my parents could play. I even composed songs, which were really variations of tunes I heard on the radio. Gwen sometimes made up

1

words to go with the melodies. They sounded silly. First she would sing and then I'd join her, harmonizing with my alto voice. Sometimes I would add words for a second verse. The words were so ridiculous that we would fall out laughing.

To my parents' delight, I learned to play hymns and gospel songs by ear. If I could hum them, I could soon pick out the notes and play them. Mama said that was a gift. In all, I took piano lessons off and on for six years. I'll never be a concert pianist, but I can entertain myself and my friends.

You could say we were a middle class family on a slippery slope. To stabilize his income, eventually Daddy got a job at the post office. It was about the only place a Negro could get a decent job in the Deep South in those days without a college degree. Getting hired by the federal government was a prized achievement. Mama managed the farm workers after Daddy started his post office job. I have to say, I had a pretty decent life growing up in rural Georgia, compared to some folks. We had a two story house, and I shared a large bedroom with my sister, Gwen. My younger brother, Terrell, had his own smaller room and my parents had the main bedroom. I never felt poor. Kind of isolated, but not poor.

Nothing special about that, huh? But there are some unusual things about Lila Mae. I'll start with my theory about the way men respond to me.

In a way, I'm like a long-stemmed daisy -- graceful, tantalizing and beautiful. When I sashay down the street with my naturally swaying hips, the fellows turn their heads to stare or to catch a quick glimpse. Attractive women who don't get the same response from guys are puzzled by this phenomenon. Babies are fascinated too. In a crowd, they will stare at me and smile.

I believe that forty percent of it is in the vibrations I send out. On a good day, my vibes radiate with great energy in all directions. They feel like sparks spontaneously popping outward from my center. Men and babies must have special receptors to grab that energy. They get it.

Good looks account for another thirty percent of my gift of attraction. I'm pretty, but I'm not a high maintenance woman. I straighten and curl my own hair, manicure my nails, and sew some of my own clothes. I can crochet too. I'm not bragging. I was blessed to pick up some skills from Mama, Aunt Minne and my high school home ec teacher. I can customize my appearance on a budget.

Other than attracting men and babies, I'm a born daydreamer. Since I was knee high to a duck, I have dreamed up all kinds of adventures. For years I never knew where those images in my head were coming from.

When I was three years old, I would pick up a stick in the yard and pretend that it was a steering wheel. My mouth became a motor as I vroomed down an imaginary road. I was quite the entertainer for my parents and big sister, Gwen.

My mama would say, "Where are you going, Missy?" She later told me I'd answer, "To Douglasville." Mama would shake her head and mutter, "Douglasville? Wonder where you got that from?" She used to tell me, "You've got a big imagination." She didn't know, and neither did I, what stimulated my creative play.

Another strange thing started happening when I was a kid. Once in a while, I would hear a lady talking like over a microphone, only it was in my mind. She would say just one or two words or one sentence, giving me advice. She was always right, so I started thinking of her as my second mother, kind of a Supermama guiding me.

She might say, "Stop!" when I was getting ready to do something stupid like sass my teacher. She was so firm that I knew I had to listen and act accordingly. The few times I ignored her, things did not turn out well. I got used to her showing up once in a while. It didn't seem like my imagination, though. It seemed real. I can't explain it in words.

My creative energy stayed with me as I grew up. Jimmy, the handsome man I married, has been in love with me since I was in first grade. He always had his own strong energy. No other man can touch him in my eyes. We got married in June of 1960 at Mt. Carmel Baptist Church.

We planned a simple wedding, but things got out of hand. By the time my aunts, my mother, Jimmy's mother and some of the church ladies got involved, Jimmy and I were lost in the shuffle. I had to remind them that we were the ones getting married. It was our day.

After a while, I just wanted the ceremony to be over so that I could be Mrs. Jenkins. Jimmy was more sentimental about the wedding than I was. My mind was racing ahead, thinking about our married life. I imagined myself serving him his first breakfast as his wife. Breakfast in bed on a beautiful tray, like the ones I saw in *House Beautiful* magazine. I asked Gwen to buy us two trays as a wedding gift. I could hardly wait.

Mama designed and created my bridal gown, floor length with a full skirt featuring hundreds of sequins sewed on one at a time by hand. It had a five foot train in the back. Mama really is talented. She never got a chance to go to college, but she is one smart lady. She makes her own clothes, the curtains and drapes, bedspreads, throw pillows and everything in the house related to fabric. She made most of my clothes when I was growing up. I didn't want to learn how to sew, but when I was ten, she sat me down and taught me anyway. Now, I'm glad she did.

You see, I daydreamed about having people sew for me, cook for me and clean for me. In my imagination, I was going to be rich. I would ride horses from my stable, have tea in my mansion, eat at fancy restaurants and travel all over the world. I asked people for their old magazines and cut out pictures of things I'd like to have and places I intended to visit. I pasted the pictures in a homemade dreambook and hid it in the closet. It was for my eyes only.

One of my favorite magazines was *National Geographic*. My Aunt Minnie never left the South, but she subscribed to *National Geographic*. It had pictures of people and scenes from all over the world. I could see myself walking on the beach in Bermuda and dancing with the Masai in Africa. Every time we visited Aunt Minnie in Waycross, I would ask for some of her old copies of that magazine. I never told her I was making a dreambook.

Now, here's the reality. I grew up in the country and married my best friend, Jimmy Lee Jenkins, or JJ as I sometimes call him. He was the only guy I ever loved, and he was crazy about me. When we married, I had never left the state of Georgia except in my imagination. For two years, I worked with my husband on our small farm and helped out part time at the church nursery school. I did what I could to decorate our little house and make it a real home. Jimmy's affectionate ways made everything all right with me.

One day, after a brief rain shower, I stepped outside the house and walked to our peach orchard. Gazing upward as the sun dismissed the clouds, I spotted a gorgeous rainbow. I wondered, "Where does its mystery lead?" I wanted to climb aboard that arching multicolored sliding board and ride it to its end. As I looked around the orchard at the still green peaches, I began to feel closed in. Then, refocusing my attention on the endless sky, I felt myself opening up and connecting to the world. I wondered how many people in South America or Africa or even California were looking at the same sky.

That afternoon, I took my dreambook from its secret place. I touched the face of a Chinese peasant and the furry parka of an Eskimo child. When I heard Jimmy come through the door, I quickly dropped the book inside the closet and went to greet him. While I was making dinner, Jimmy found the dreambook and flipped through the pages. At dinner, he asked me about it.

"I found an old scrapbook of yours in the closet. How long have you had that thing? It's full of pictures of people in different countries. Was that part of a geography class project?"

"No. It's my dreambook. I've had it for years. I used to wonder what people were like in other parts of the world. When I found a picture I liked, I pasted it in the book. Then I'd imagine visiting those places and talking to those people."

"Lila, you always had your head in the clouds. This is our dream, Babycakes. Being together on our own land and planning a family together is a dream come true."

"I know that, honey. I'm happy here, and I love being your wife. You're the kindest man I know. Daydreaming is just an old habit of mine. I don't understand why faraway places pop up in my head. But I guess there's no harm in fantasizing about stuff."

"You are the center of my life, Lila Mae. I can't keep you from dreaming. Just take a short peep and come back home. I want your feet planted in our little world. Our private love planet."

"Mmmm. We do have a beautiful world, JJ. We've got each other and plenty of food from our own piece of the earth, like the sweet potatoes in this pie I'm getting ready to serve you."

"Yeah, Babycakes. Bring it on. We work hard for this food. The earth isn't handing out charity."

I laughed, and then leaned over and kissed my husband. When our lips touched, his vibes warmed my insides. The rest of the world melted away. That night, we made love in Jimmy's slow motion style, his hands circling up and down my torso. He went out of his way to wake up my whole body, every single satisfied cell. Not a trace of wanderlust was left that night.

Over the next week or so, Jimmy apparently thought about my dreambook. He tried so hard to please me. We were outside inspecting the peaches when he opened the conversation.

"Lila, I know you get a little restless sometimes. I think you need a change of pace. You've been talking about going to Atlanta. We can do that in a couple of weeks. We can go out to dinner or something, though I'm sure your cooking beats the food in those restaurants hands down."

"Jimmy, I'd love to go."

"Yeah, I know you by now. You have to have a little adventure now and then. I've been thinking. For our fifth wedding anniversary, we could take a trip to New York and see a play on Broadway. Tyree's cousin is visiting family here. He works as a stagehand at a Broadway theater and he was at the pool hall last night. He talked about how exciting New York is. I got to thinking about how you write little skits for the Sunday School children for Easter and special occasions. I made up my mind right then to take you to Broadway."

"Oh, JJ!" I hugged him enthusiastically. "We'll have so much fun in New York."

"I thought you'd like that. It'll take us a while to save up for those high priced theater tickets. Anyway, it gives us something to look forward to."

"I'll put it in my dreambook."

"They say it's crowded up there and people race around, but it'll be a nice change for a couple of days."

"Only a couple of days?"

"It's expensive up there, Lila. It's not practical to stay too long. And who would look after the chickens and the cow more than a couple of days?"

"You're right, JJ. I see that you've thought this through. Thank you, darling, for paying attention to me and thinking about what will make me happy. And thanks for being patient when my restlessness pops up. I don't know where it comes from."

"Maybe, you're wanting to have a baby like your bid whist buddy,

Leola. That will happen, Lila. We'll have our own little bundle of joy."

When I said my prayers that night, I asked the Lord, "Why do I get so restless sometimes?" As I lay next to my sleeping husband, an answer came. It was one of those guidance thoughts that I get sometimes. That female voice – maybe an angel – said, "One part of you wants to be practical, but another part wants to fly." I was puzzled by that answer and I had no idea how to handle it. How could I want to go in two different directions at once?

Jimmy kept talking about wanting children, but I didn't get pregnant. He seemed to be driven by thoughts of a sister who died when he was young. Something he never resolved and rarely mentioned. Finally, I decided I should go to work full time to help save some money for whenever we did have children. Kids are expensive.

At age twenty-one, I found a full-time job at the Piggly Wiggly grocery store on Rocky Creek Road in Macon. There, I met an older man named Neil Rivers. He was about thirty-six or thirty-seven years old and fair skinned for a black person. He was tall, like a basketball player. Although he was nice, sometimes he talked crazy. He was definitely different from anybody I knew. He helped me learn the job and we became friends in the first six months I worked there. Both of us liked music, so that gave us something to talk about.

Neil had moved to Macon after running his own five and dime store near Atlanta. He lost everything in a fire, and the insurance company wouldn't pay up. They said his premium payment was late. Neil said they cheated him, but he couldn't convince the powers that be. He gave up and moved to Macon to live with his sister and start over. He had lived in Macon a year and a half when I met him. He was full of ideas about starting another business, but I think he was too scared to try.

Neil stocked groceries and other items. I did that sometimes, but I also helped to keep the records. I was good with figures. Neil and I had the same lunch break as Sarah, who worked in the deli section. Sarah didn't talk much. She mostly listened with various expressions going across her face. You could just about tell what she was thinking by the way her eyes and her mouth moved.

Although Sarah usually ate with us, this particular Wednesday she had to go pay her light bill. There I was, eating my egg salad sandwich, making polite conversation and mostly minding my business. At first,

7

Neil started talking about one of his ideas for starting a new business. He said a friend in Atlanta had contacted him about opening a night club. It turns out that Neil did have some money put aside. He was driving an old car and living with his sister to save the money he needed to start over as a businessman.

"Right now, I'm researching the night club business to see if we could really make a profit. I don't mind taking a risk, but I want to have a good chance of succeeding. I've been imagining what the club would look like. I have a mental picture of the people socializing and dancing to soul music."

"Neil, you have a big imagination just like I do."

"Well, you've got to dream if you want to have something. You have to have some idea of where you're going and also where you've been."

"Where you've been?"

Neil leaned forward. With his steady, hazel eyes staring into mine, he asked, "Lila Mae, do you know where you came from?"

"Now you're being weird. I came from right here, Bibb County, Georgia. I was born on July the 4th in 1941 on a farm just outside Macon."

"No. I don't mean the place where you were born. Where did you really come from?"

I was getting annoyed. "I came from my mother's womb. Originally, I came from my parents getting together. You know, like they teach you in the health education part of gym class. Did you come from somewhere other than that? Maybe another planet?" I couldn't resist laughing.

Neil smiled. "Do you believe in eternal life? A lot of people say they do, but they are only referring to the future. Eternal life goes in both directions. Did you ever think about that?"

"Frankly, no," I said. "I'm too busy thinking about work, home, church, my husband and family, and how I happen to be in this room listening to somebody who sounds like he's talking out of his head."

"No, not quite. Just exploring the origins of people's souls. I can help you find out where your soul started out and where it has been over these thousands of years."

"I have never heard of anything like that in all of my twenty-one

8

years. My soul is right here with me where it started out when I was born," I replied. "And I go to church to save it so that I can end up in heaven instead of that other place." After a pause I asked, "Are you on medication or something?"

"No. I'm perfectly all right, but I have ventured out where some folks are afraid to go. It's called past life regression and I dare you to go there." I almost choked on my sandwich. I didn't know what he was talking about, but shivers went down my spine.

"I don't want to go there if I end up talking like you." Neil ignored my response. He said, "I could put you under light hypnosis and you would discover some of the other personalities your soul has lived through, the people you have been."

"I know I have been just one person, Lila Mae Jenkins. I was born Lila Mae Thornton, but I am a Jenkins now," I said. "Lila Mae has enough to worry about with one life. Why would I want to clutter up my mind worrying about a hundred other lives? If I had them, they're over and that's that. I don't get in God's business."

Neil smiled. "Your past lives are influencing this life. You just don't know it. But you could easily find out." All my senses went on alert. If this guy put me under hypnosis, there's no telling what he would do. And I wouldn't remember any of it. No sir. I could see right through that scheme.

I said, "This is not for me. My father is a church deacon and he didn't raise me to believe in stuff like that. That's as bad as all these people trying to go back and find out who their ancestors were. They all think their great-great-great grandparents and grandcousins twice removed were kings and queens."

Neil's brows knitted. He said, "This is real. I had my first glimpse of some of my past lives about five years ago. Mr. Edmond Cox, a fellow from Maryland, stopped through Atlanta one Saturday morning on his way to Florida. He was sitting in the Top Cut Barber Shop bragging that he could help people see their past lives. Most of the guys thought he was crazy. Nobody else wanted to try it, but I was fascinated. Malcolm, the barber, dared me to go ahead with the regression and report back to the group.

"Yeah, do it," one of the customers joked. "Maybe you used to be Jonah in the whale."

Another guy shouted, "Naw. He was Frankenstein." Everybody had a good laugh.

Malcolm offered to cut my hair for free if I took the dare. Being a frugal and a curious man, I did. The men started to take bets on what I would discover, though most of them believed it was a trick.

"After Mr. Cox and I had our haircuts, we went to the back storage room of Jackie's Pool Hall next door to do the regression. There in the stale summer heat, among the boxes, the mops and the dust, I was introduced to my eternal soul. Mr. Cox was calm as you please as he spoke softly to me. He said I was hypnotized, but it felt like I just had my eyes closed. I was aware of everything that happened. What I learned amazed me. I was a white woman in my last life. Naturally, I didn't tell the fellows that part."

I replied, "Are you trying to tell me you're one of those funny guys? Why would you be a woman?"

Neil patiently explained what he meant as I sat there holding my half-eaten sandwich inches from my mouth, unable to take another bite. "I'm not queer. We can change sexes between lives depending on what our mission is in the next life."

I said, "Well, Mr. Past Life, I'm a woman and I always have been." He went on to say, "I had two more regressions within a year, then I got the regression training in Atlanta. I wanted to help other people get a look at their soul's history. People like you." I took a long swig of my root beer, thinking, "Not hardly." I glared at him.

After taking a deep breath, he threw out something astonishing. "When you first walked into this store, Lila Mae, I recognized you. You were a tall, good-looking stock car racer in your last life and we were in love." I choked, spilling root beer on my blue blouse. I felt like I had just swallowed a sword, cutting loose something I had tied down.

As a child of five or six, I kept dreaming about a white man racing in a fast car. It always ended the same way, with him crashing into a concrete wall on a steep curve. I felt a shock go through my body every time the car hit the wall. The first few times I dreamed it, I screamed out. Mama came rushing into the room to see what was wrong. I told her about the dream, and she explained that it was a nightmare. She told me not to worry about it. Everything was all right.

Of course, it was not all right. The dream came back every month or

10

two for several years. I learned to stop screaming when it happened, but I was still upset. I had trouble going back to sleep. I wondered why the man in the car felt like me. For one thing, we did not have a television at that time and I had never seen a real race car. I had only seen pictures of them in a *Look Magazine* feature story on race cars drivers. Those cars were low and sleek and they raced on beaches. They didn't look anything like the race cars in my dream.

Anyway, I finally managed a response to Neil's matter of fact statement that I had been a male race car driver and he had been my woman. "If I was that good-looking, why would I want you?" He laughed. "Oh, I was very pretty and sassy too." Just then, Sarah came in the room and we stopped talking. That's the only way I got to finish my egg salad sandwich, one of my best recipes.

Somehow, I got through Wednesday afternoon. The following day, I took sick leave. I had to have time to think about all this. As I straightened the little four room farm house I shared with Jimmy, I asked myself, "Do I really want to know more about past lives? Could I solve the riddle of my childhood dreams? I could be dealing with the devil himself. Neil doesn't look much like a devil, but Satan comes in slick disguises. That's what Daddy always said. This whole thing is peculiar."

Back in the country where I grew up near Macon, everybody more or less believed the same thing. If you went to church, you were a Baptist, a Methodist, or a sanctified holy roller, and nobody believed in past lives. In fact, if anyone had mentioned such a notion, he would have been suspected of either going off his rocker or practicing witchcraft.

When I kept talking about the race car driver in my youth, my mother looked me over and declared, "You are an odd child. Very odd. You remind me of my brother, Curtis." Curtis was dead and I had only met him once. He had lived up North. I got the distinct feeling that it was no compliment to be compared to Curtis. I never mentioned the race car driver to Mama, Daddy or my sister, Gwendolyn, again.

At the most unexpected times growing up, I seemed to have racing in my brain. We had a farm horse named Maggie. Daddy let me ride her now and then, under his supervision. Sometimes, I would run outside, climb on bales of hay, mount Maggie and ride her bareback. If

11

no one was looking, I tried to make her run. I wanted to go faster and faster. It gave me such a free feeling.

One May afternoon when I was nine, I mounted Maggie and rode toward the shallow stream that ran through our property. I signaled her to go faster. She broke into a flat out run while I held on for dear life. As Maggie approached a narrow section of the stream, I thought she would either run through it or jump. Wrong! She came to a sudden halt and I went flying to the other side of the stream. I thought I felt someone's arms pushing me toward a pile of hay. That's where I landed.

Willie, one of the field hands working nearby, saw the whole thing. He carried me to the house on his back. As he relayed the story of my adventure to Daddy and Mama, he said, "Lila Mae sure is lucky. I thought she was going to land on the hard ground, but the wind must have changed. It carried her over to the haystack for a softer landing."

Daddy was upset. He had caught me riding Maggie once before and told me not to ride unless he was there. He said, "Thank you for helping Lila Mae, Willie. Please go find Maggie and put her back in the stable." Then, he turned his attention to me.

"Where does it hurt, Lila?"

"My ankle hurts." He put some pressure on the ankle and I squealed.

"See if you can wiggle your toes." I did.

"I don't think anything's broken, Mama. She probably sprained her ankle. We'll put some ice on it." Mama went to get the ice and Gwen and Terrell came downstairs to gawk at me.

Daddy started fussing. "Girl, are you crazy? I told you to leave Maggie alone. You'll kill your foolish self running that horse. If you can't mind me, you're going to be stuck to your mother like glue all day while I'm at work. No playing outside. This is your last warning. No more riding unless I'm out there with you."

"Yes sir." That meant no more racing.

When I was settled in my twin bed that night, with Gwen putting on her nightgown a few feet away, I struck up a conversation.

"This sore ankle is really going to slow me down."

"You need something to slow you down. You take too many chances. I was looking out the window and saw you riding that horse."

12

"I was having fun. I didn't know Maggie was scared to jump the stream."

"Even if she wasn't scared, you could have fallen off if she jumped. The trouble is you don't know danger when you see it. You think you can do anything you want and it will be okay. I'd rather be safe than to try the stuff you do."

"Being safe all the time can be boring. How can you learn anything that way?"

"You can learn not to crack your head open taking chances."

"I thought you were my friend."

"I am. Get the safety pin off the top of the dresser. We'll stick our fingers and mix our blood. Best friends forever, even if it means I have to save you from getting killed." We pricked our fingers, mingled our blood and pledged to stand by each other no matter what, and to keep secrets for each other."

Climbing into bed, Gwen muttered "I hope I don't live to regret my pledge."

"I'll try not to take too many chances."

She laughed. "I can see you now, tied to Mama's apron all summer, dragging along behind her."

"Humph!" I pulled the covers over my head and refused to say another word to Gwen. That night, the race car dream returned. I shivered, but I didn't scream.

Over the years, I forgot about the race car driver until July 6, 1960 when something surprising happened. I remember the date because I had just turned nineteen. This was long after the nightmares stopped.

I was driving my first car around a steep ramp exiting the highway. I had inherited the 1956 Buick Roadmaster from Granddaddy. I used to help him wash it and polish the chrome when we went to visit him and Grandma. Anyway, I was moving a little too fast that afternoon, daydreaming about my upcoming marriage to JJ.

As I rounded the tight exit ramp, fear rushed over me. I felt like I was losing control of the car and that it would run right off the ramp and crash onto the ground about ten feet below. My hands started sweating and a lump formed in my throat. My adrenaline was pumping. I held tight to the steering wheel, downshifted, and lightly pumped the brakes. The tires stayed on the ramp miraculously. By the time the

Buick came to the stop sign at the end of the ramp, I was trembling. I had escaped the danger, but how?

Turning toward home, I tried to figure out what had happened. Just as I seemed to be losing control, it felt like something or someone else took charge of the driving. I can't explain it, but I seemed to turn into that race car driver. I felt like he had rescued me. How, I couldn't tell. It was like his skills kicked in at the critical moment. Anyway, my fiancé, Jimmy, was waiting for me at my house and I got involved in talking about wedding details. I never told anybody about the near accident or the strange sensation I had. JJ and I were getting married and I did not want him to think he was marrying a lunatic. I pictured us growing old together and having three or four children.

Driving to work on Friday morning, I made up my mind to avoid Neil. I decided to go to Marie's Barbecue for lunch rather than eat in the back room of the store. There is no way I wanted to get into anything as strange and scary as a past life regression. I started to tell Jimmy about it, but I knew how he would react. Jimmy is jealous. He would automatically assume Neil was trying to get next to me. Jimmy is a good husband, but he isn't too sure of himself where I am concerned. I can tell by the remarks he makes after guys stare at me a little too long. I am shaped like a Coke bottle and my naturally sexy walk gets lots of attention. I don't try to be sexy. I just am.

Jimmy once asked, "Can't you walk straight instead of swinging your hips from side to side?" I practiced walking straight right in front of him. After seeing how artificial it looked, he said, "You look like a robot. Just do your regular walk."

"Jimmy, you should know by now that my hips have been swaying every since my butt rounded out. It's just the way I'm built and I can't help it. I can't make myself into somebody I'm not."

When I returned to Piggly Wiggly after polishing off some sho'nuff ribs, Sarah told me Jimmy had called. I phoned him at the Feed and Seed store on Hawkinsville Road where he works part time, but he had left for an emergency. When I reached him at home, Jimmy said his mother had called him at work. Jimmy's step-father, Mr. Wright, was in the hospital and the doctor thought he had had a heart attack. Jimmy said, "I'm driving up to North Carolina as soon as I finish throwing some clothes in the suitcase."

Jimmy is his mother's only living natural child, although he has an older step-sister. His parents left Georgia a year after our wedding. They moved back to the Wright family farm in North Carolina after Mr. Wright's parents died.

"Jimmy," I said, "Let me go with you. It's a long drive. I can get off work." He replied, "No, Lila Mae. You've been coaching the kids at Sunday School for their play this coming Sunday. You should stay here." I thought about my obligation to the children, but I really hated for him to go by himself. Finally, I relented after he insisted that I stay behind.

The rest of the afternoon, I felt empty and frustrated. I thought, "Jimmy loves children and wants to be a father. We have been married for two years. We have not used any birth control, but I haven't gotten pregnant. We talked to the doctor about it, and he was no real help. My cousin, Tillie, was married five years before she conceived. Maybe we just need a little more time. Maybe we're too anxious."

Anyway, when my shift ended at five o'clock, I picked up my paycheck and clocked out. I rushed to the Buick outside and turned the key, but it wouldn't start. It had hesitated several times, but it always cranked up after two or three tries. This time it didn't. I started back toward the store to ask Sarah to take me home. Then, I remembered she had left an hour early for a doctor's appointment. Neil came out to the parking lot at that moment.

I thought, "I have some choices here. I could call a cab, but it's six miles to our farm. That's going to be a big cab fare, and I spent my spare change on those barbecue ribs. I do have some money in the emergency jar at home, but suppose Jimmy took it for the trip?"

I was thinking of other people I could call when Neil approached. "Why the frown?" he asked. "It's a beautiful afternoon."

I told Neil about my car trouble and my husband being away on a trip. After unsuccessfully trying to start the Buick himself, Neil said, "I'll drive you home." I thought, "His beat up Chevy looks like it was put together from a collection of junkyard parts, but it does run."

Accepting Neil's offer, I got in the car. I soon complained, "It's hot in here, even with the windows down." Neil said, "It's summer, Lila Mae." I fussed, "The Georgia sun is doing its thing. I feel like I'm wilting." I was out of sorts with JJ going out of town and the Buick breaking down all of a sudden. Neil stopped at Cobb's Gas Station for sodas. My mood lifted and we talked about work and the weather on the way home.

As we approached my house, Neil said, "I don't think I can make it home without using the bathroom. Do you mind?" I hadn't figured on him going inside the house, but under the circumstances, I couldn't refuse. "Of course not. Come on in. I'll show you where it is." While he used the facilities, I walked outside to take care of the chickens.

All we had on our little fifty acre farm were some chickens, a cow, a vegetable garden, two fig trees and a grove of peach trees. I scattered handfuls of chicken feed on the ground and watched the rooster and hens run around gobbling it up. Afterwards, I chased them into the henhouse for the night. I turned to find that Neil had stepped out of the house and was quietly observing the scene.

"How long have you been standing there?"

"Not long. Do you do this every night?"

"Usually JJ does it, but he's not here so I'm doing it tonight."

"How will you get around this weekend?"

"I'll call my sister, Gwen. She went to Alabama with Aunt Minnie yesterday to visit Cousin Glena at Talladega College. She's coming home tomorrow. And Rev. Griffin's wife will probably pick me up in the morning to rehearse the children for their play on Sunday. I'll be fine."

"What about your car?"

"My brother-in-law, Clarence, is a back yard mechanic. He'll fix it if I can catch him before he starts his weekend drinking."

"So you've got an answer for everything. You always were good at problem solving and getting things done."

I rolled my eyes. "Always were?"

"Oh, I'm thinking way back. In your soul's last life, they tried to disqualify you from a car race on a technicality. There was a large prize at stake and somebody else wanted to win badly. I wish they had succeeded in disqualifying you, crooked though it was. But Dave Jackson, your former personality, was stubborn as a mule and twice as determined. He proved the promoters wrong. They had to let him race. As the lead cars sped toward the start of the third lap, Dave's jealous competitor ran him out of his lane in an illegal maneuver. Dave's car

16

slammed into a cement wall. That's how he died."

I trembled with fear and anger. "I wish you would stop talking about that race car driver. He's not me! I am living right here and now. I'm standing in front of you, plain as day. I'm Lila Mae Jenkins and my life is just fine. I don't have time to think about any Dave Jackson." As I spoke that name, the sound of an engine roared in my head. I looked down and tried to ignore it.

"Sorry." I didn't mean to upset you, Lila Mae."

I looked at his repentant face. "I'm sorry I yelled at you. It's been a long day and I'm tired. Thanks for the ride. Just don't mention this past life thing to me anymore."

"Not if you don't want me to," he said, moving toward his car. He waved goodbye and drove away.

After a supper of leftover catfish, collard greens, sliced tomatoes and my special cornbread, I tried to read the Bible for a while. The Good Book fell open at the 11th chapter of Matthew. I started reading where my index finger fell, at the eighth verse. When I got to the 14th verse, my eyes widened. I spoke aloud, "Elijah's soul was reborn as John the Baptist?" In the next verse, Jesus said, "He that hath ears to hear, let him hear." I knew I was getting into deep territory. My drooping eyelids let me know it was time to go to sleep. I said a prayer for Jimmy, his mother and step-father. Then, I fell into bed, emotionally exhausted.

About midnight, I sat straight up in the bed. The race car dream had returned. This time, after the crash occurred, a red flag stopped the race. Immediately, I saw a pretty redhead running out of the crowd of spectators. She rushed toward the crumpled car, her face clearly distressed. Then, I saw blood gushing from Dave Jackson's head injury. As I observed the scene from above the crash, I heard myself call to the woman, "Rebecca! Rebecca!" She did not hear me as her hazel eyes filled with tears.

"How can this be?" I wondered. "This must be my overactive imagination. It's like Neil supplied parts of a story and my brain filled in the rest. The dream was so vivid. It looked like I was watching a 3-D movie!

"Please, God," I prayed, "Don't let me see any more. I don't want to know."

Somehow, I got through the weekend. Inside, I felt like a zombie from the twilight zone, but I managed to mask it. The church members enjoyed the children's play about the Sermon on the Mount and the children themselves squealed with delight at their own performances. Rev. Griffin's son, Paul, played the part of Jesus. His proud mother took pictures, almost to the point of distracting the children. I had to signal her to stop. My mother did a great job making the costumes, for which I was grateful.

My car got fixed, the chickens were fed, the eggs collected and the cow milked. JJ called to say that his father was in intensive care. I agreed with his decision to stay in North Carolina a few more days. Somehow, I was relieved at this news. I did not want him to see my disturbance over the race car dream, on top of his own troubles.

On Monday morning as I drove into town, I resolved to keep my distance from Neil. This resolution was shot down when the manager assigned Neil and me to do an inventory of toiletries together. Neil sensed that something was wrong, and I soon spilled my gut. I told him about the dream including the part about Rebecca.

He replied, "I knew my nickname in that life was Becky. I guess Dave called me by my real name."

"So now, according to your theory, we have both switched genders."

"It's not the first time. In other lives, we have been friends of the same gender, males sometimes and females sometimes. We've been close to each other for thousands of years. My offer is still open if you want to know more."

"I'm pretty devastated by what I've already learned. Dying is no fun."

"No, but it doesn't last long, and what follows can be very interesting. When you stop at dying, you can get depressed. Glimpsing the soul's time between human lives can be uplifting. You get to see what your mission is and how you arrived at it. That can give your current life more focus than you can imagine. Think of all the people who go through their whole lives without learning their purpose."

"Right now, my purpose is to be a good wife and hopefully a good mother in the near future. That and working in the church, paying the bills, and having a little fun in the process. Even if I did have other lives, I can only live one at a time. End of story."

"That certainly sounds reasonable."

The manager approached and we began working seriously on the inventory. Neil offered to treat me to lunch at Gordon's Sandwich Shop and I decided to accept. As we ate our sandwiches, we gabbed about everything from blues music to civil rights. Neil was a dyed in the wool B. B. King fan. I favored Bessie Smith. Nobody can sing "St. Louis Blues" like Bessie.

Out of curiosity, I asked Neil if one of his parents was white. From a distance, he looked like a white man. He replied, "I don't usually talk about it, but my father is white. My mother was a maid in his house and he took advantage of her. At least, he bought us a house. That's more than some guys do."

"I didn't mean to embarrass you, Neil. I'm sorry."

"People have asked me that before. Oh, look at the time." Our lunch hour was ending and we had to hurry back to the Piggly Wiggly.

After work that evening, I talked to JJ by phone. He greeted me with his usual, "Hey, Babycakes. Papa's improving and might leave the intensive care unit Tuesday, depending on his test results."

"How's Mother Wright doing?"

"Well, she's calming down a little. You know how excitable and emotional she can be." When JJ chose me, he got someone very different from his mom. I'm usually calm unless I'm having one of those unexplainable spiritual experiences. Then, I can go from being cool to being stunned.

Anyway, it looked like JJ could be home by the weekend. I danced around the kitchen at the thought of being with him again. I didn't need any external music. I thought, "Oh, I miss him. Even the negative news reports on the radio can not dampen my spirits after talking to my baby. I feel like I can handle the past life stuff and anything else that comes along. And that's what it is. Stuff."

I finished cooking dinner between my dance moves. As I was patting myself on the back for staying cool, calm and collected, the phone rang again. It was Neil. He wanted to bring over a tape. I figured it was one of the blues tapes he said he had recorded from the radio. I should have known better, but I said "O.K. Just don't plan to stay long, Neil. I have things to do."

As I finished the dishes, Neil drove up. He had a tape on his reel to reel, portable tape recorder. "Did you bring some Bessie Smith?" I asked. Neil said, "This isn't a blues tape. It's a blank tape." In response to my quizzical expression he said, "If you have an hour, I can help you put together some puzzle pieces you've been missing all your life. I'll tape the whole session, then you can review the tape whenever you like."

At that point, I saw he was not going to give up, so I decided to plunge into this little adventure and get it over with.

Neil turned on the tape recorder. He instructed me in a soft, droning voice. "Close your eyes. Slowly count backwards from twenty to one. Try to recall the earliest memory you have of this life, perhaps when you were three or four years old. Then picture your young self in a beautiful forest, walking along a trail. You are approaching a clearing where there is an amphitheater. Walk toward it. You will see a figure approaching in a long, white robe. This is your guide. Greet the person and ask him or her to reveal scenes from your last life before this one, starting when you were around eight or nine years old."

I did as I was told. The guide's face was hidden by a loose fitting hood. Sure enough, I was soon watching a young ash blond white boy playing stick ball with his friends. As Neil coached me, I was about to ask the boy his name. I didn't have to. I heard his mother calling, "Dave, come home and get ready for supper." The boy told his friends, "I have to go. I'll see you tomorrow."

We fast forwarded to Dave's teenage years, when he cut school to hang out with friends, then to age 20 when he dropped out of college against his parents' wishes. His father shook his head, "I don't know what to do with you, boy. You're just plain hardheaded. You're going to have to fall down a few times before you learn to listen."

Dave's family lived in Douglasville, Georgia, not far from a farm area. The same Douglasville I talked about as a toddler.

We jumped forward three years. I saw Dave talking to two older men one afternoon near a stand of weeping willow trees. I got a panoramic view of the rural area. It looked a lot like the farms near Macon. The men wore overalls, work shirts and dusty boots. They were peppering Dave with questions.

Billy Joe, the tall man stated, "We need a driver to deliver our, er, products. Do you have a driver's license?"

"Yes," Dave grinned. "I'm a good driver. My Dad gets after me for driving too fast, but I told him his old Chevy won't go fast enough to kick up dust."

Hal, the short one spoke. "That's why you're here. We hear you have a reputation for driving fast, and the law has stopped you at least once. This is secret work. Can we trust you? If you get caught by the law, you'll have to keep your mouth shut. We'll bail you out and pay the sheriff off, but you have to keep quiet."

"I know how to keep my mouth shut."

"Good."

Billy Joe explained, "We can show you some back roads for getting to our customers. We also have a very fast Ford for you. It's got custom overhead valve cylinder heads." Dave's eyes lit up with excitement.

Hal added, "We hired a man who revs up cars that can beat any lawman in pursuit, including the revenuers. They suspect we're making moonshine, but they haven't found our still. When you're driving for us, they won't be able to catch you. And you'll make good money, kid. Up to $400 a night."

Dave exclaimed, "Yes! That's what I want. I want enough money to buy my own car and house."

Hal replied, "That's good. When there's something a person wants, he tends to be dependable."

"You can count on me."

Billy Joe bragged, "We make the best moonshine for miles around. We don't sell it direct. That's too risky. We don't want customers lining up at our place. We use neighborhood dealers who sell to their friends in a forty mile area. People like to drink and whoop it up a little after a hard week's work. Don't know why some folks think a Prohibition law can keep their neighbors sober. Even Jesus Christ drank wine."

"He probably didn't get drunk, but I know what you mean. Let the people have fun. I'm a fun loving guy myself."

"Our customers run whiskey houses. Four of them are white men and one is a nigger. We need you to deliver their orders. You'll be a genuine moonshine hauler."

"I don't know much about niggers. I've never been around them much. Is it safe where they live? I'm pretty handy with my fists, but I want to know what I'm getting into."

Hal responded, "You won't have to fight nobody. Our client, Will Thornton, is pretty laid back and his kind seem to respect him. He don't bother nobody. He just keeps them happy with our white lightning. You take the orders to him. He pays you and you leave."

"Will anybody else be around?"

Billy Joe replied, "Naw. At the time you're going, it will just be him, his wife and kid. He has a boy around ten years old named Lucius. He should be in bed when you get there. If not, he might frown at you, but Will has him under control."

Upon hearing this, I gasped. Lucius Thornton is my father and Will Thornton was my grandfather. I always wondered how Granddaddy could afford new Buicks every couple of years when the other farmers couldn't. My parents said he was a good saver. It hit me that my Buick, inherited from Granddaddy, was bought with moonshine money. And in my previous incarnation, I had delivered the whiskey that Granddaddy sold to keep up his nice house and car.

No wonder Daddy wasn't close to Granddaddy. Lucius hated his father's side business. He was afraid to challenge his daddy, so he clung to his church going, Bible reading mother, Mabel Thornton. She was also the Mother of the Moore Avenue Church of God in Christ. I went to church with her one Sunday morning and witnessed her doing the Holy Dance, shouting and falling to the floor, slain in the Spirit. I was scared.

I asked to see more of Daddy's early life. Soon, I saw young Lucius getting ready to go to church with his mother. Lucius bravely asked, "Why don't you go with us today, Daddy? We're having a church supper afterwards." Will replied, "No, thank you. I have to tend to the hogs, chickens and cows. You all go ahead." He handed Mabel the keys to the black, shiny 1926 Buick Sedan. Mabel instructed Lucius, "Get my tambourine over there. We're going to make a joyful noise unto the Lord this morning."

I suddenly had another revelation. That's why Daddy never would allow liquor in our house. That's why he grew up to be a church deacon. Grandmamma worked at keeping him from following his father's example.

Meanwhile, Dave started hauling for the moonshiners in 1920. He drove like the wind. I saw him outrace the feds in a dangerous chase. He was fearless, a daredevil. One night, he encountered young Lucius, who was returning from the outhouse holding a lantern. In the dim light, Lucius scowled at Dave. Ever the showoff, Dave could not resist bragging. He called out, "Hey, boy, you see my Ford over there? I just won a race driving that thing through the back roads. Nobody can catch her. She's one fine machine. Think you'll have a car like that one day?" Lucius replied, "I don't think so." The boy listened without much expression as Dave spun his tale about all the people who were paying admission to watch him race.

Lucius cocked his head to one side and asked, "Can colored people come see you race?" Dave said, "Naw. Racing's just for white folks. All the drivers are men like me with souped up cars. No women allowed behind the wheel either. We're all men trying to prove our cars are the fastest. But you got to be a good driver too. I'm the best. I could beat a bat out of hell." Picturing that, Lucius turned and rushed into the house just as Will emerged onto the porch.

At that point, my thoughts tumbled like an unexpected rush of water down a mountainside. I said aloud, "I've just been shown the beginning of stock car racing. It started with illegal booze and Dave was mixed up in it."

Next, I saw Dave in a club, mesmerized by a beautiful dancer named Rebecca. She smiled at him like something was going on between them. One night after the show, she walked over to his table. "Becky, he said. I can't get you out of my mind. I just bought a house and it needs a pretty woman in it. Will you marry me?" Becky looked shocked. Her eyes widened, but she was speechless. Smiling, he reached into his pocket and presented a beautiful engagement ring. "Oh, it's gorgeous," she replied. She examined the ring from every angle, and declared, "Of course I'll marry you." Dave said, "I promise to give you a wild and exciting life with lots of pretty clothes." Becky answered, "As long as you come with the package, I'll be happy."

Then, I saw the crash that killed Dave at the age of 26, the scene I had witnessed over and over as a child. I was devastated and my head started hurting. I moaned.

When Neil saw how upset I was, he brought me out of my

hypnotized state. In response to Neil's questions, I had spoken aloud everything I saw and heard while in the trance. He taped the whole thirty minute episode. I thought, "Now, what will I do with this new knowledge?"

Neil reminded me, "Like Dave, you're pretty headstrong yourself, Lila. You dropped out of college to marry Jimmy. It's part of a pattern that you might want to think about changing." I told him, "Stay out of my business. You've done enough already." The thing is I liked school but I wanted to get on with life.

My head was still throbbing and I let out a moan. Neil offered to rub my temple and shoulders to help get rid of the tension. My head was hurting so much that I decided to let him do it. His hands felt strong and warm. He has long fingers like a piano player. After a while, I felt my shoulders relax and the pain in my head went away.

I turned around to thank Neil and I saw a strangely familiar look in his eyes. He had told me that people's eyes didn't change much from one life to the next. He put his hand on my shoulder, and then leaned forward to kiss my mouth. I pulled back in shock.

"I'm sorry, Lila. I don't know what came over me. When you were narrating that story about Dave and Rebecca, I had a flashback."

I was flustered. His kiss had started a warm feeling all through my body. I looked into his eyes. The next thing I knew, we were embracing. Yes, it was wrong, but it felt so good, so exciting. Within a few minutes, we were in bed, half-dressed and rolling around like two alley cats. Our undergarments were practically torn off. Hands and tongues were everywhere as we explored each other's bodies. Nothing was off limits and I almost fell off the bed, focused solely on driving him to ecstasy. The body heat rose and our sweat mingled, funking up the room. His ample member soon filled my hotbox, stroking until I thought I would go out of my mind.

Before tonight, Jimmy was the only man I ever slept with. I was sure I knew what good sex was, but this was far and away the most exciting adventure I ever had. Strong, pulsing patterns of rapture played my body like a xylophone, from head to toe and back again. I moaned. I shrieked. I trembled. When I thought I couldn't stand it any more, his explosion came. I actually saw stars as I experienced the longest lasting orgasm of my life. I was floating. Forty minutes later, I started drifting back to earth. Unforgettable!

As I became aware of the wetness on my thighs, reality came roaring back. I was in my marriage bed with another man, having unprotected sex. This was not me. I had too much common sense to let something like this happen. Neil had drifted off to sleep, so I patted his face to wake him. "Neil, what have we done?" I asked. "You have to get out of here and this can never happen again!" Neil apologized. "I'm sorry. I don't know what came over me. It was wonderful, but I didn't plan it. It just happened."

"I knew we never should have messed with this past life stuff," I said. "Let's get out of this bed. I have to change the sheets." Neil grabbed his clothes and headed for the bathroom as I pulled the sheets off the bed.

As I put clean linens on the old mattress, I felt an energy boring into my back. I turned and gazed at the picture of Jesus above the chest of drawers. He was looking straight at me with those kind, steady eyes. I prayed, "Oh Jesus, please forgive me. I have sinned. I don't know what came over me. Have mercy, Lord. Please help me get back on track. Help me, Lord. I'm begging for your forgiveness. Thank you, Jesus. Amen."

It was dark outside when Neil finally left, taking his tape recorder with him. He left behind the tape reel from my past life regression. I hid it in a shoebox, like I was expecting Jimmy to come through the door at any minute. Then I filled the bathtub and took a long bath. I tried to scrub Neil off of my skin. It sounds silly, but that's what I did. Then, I recalled a warning from Mama when I was thirteen. She said, "Lila Mae, a good girl waits until her wedding night to give up her virginity to her husband. After she marries him, she only gives herself to him. No one else. That way she stays honorable, and no one can call her a tramp."

I thought, "Mama, I hope you never find out about this. At least, I was a virgin bride. It wasn't easy to abide by your rule, but I did. Jimmy loved me so much he was willing to wait."

The next morning, I couldn't stop thinking about what happened. My mind raced. "There is no doubt I reached pleasures I didn't even know existed. How can I have sex with Jimmy this weekend without his suspecting something? I might have to fake a headache."

Another thought hit. "My menstrual period is due in two weeks.

This is my most fertile time of the month." Then I quickly reminded myself, "I have been married for two years without getting pregnant. What are the chances of my getting pregnant from one evening with Neil?"

Jimmy had to stay in North Carolina another week when his mother's health faltered. She fainted from the stress of worrying about her husband and was briefly hospitalized for tests. Jimmy and I made love the night he returned, and one week later there was no monthly period. I thought, "I'm pregnant for sure. My menstrual periods come like clockwork. Never late. And I know who the father is. I just know. What will I do now?"

I considered not telling Neil about my pregnancy and trying to act like the baby belonged to Jimmy. But Jimmy is a pretty cocoa brown, while Neil is very light skinned. Of course, I am light skinned too, so that might not make much difference. Still, Neil is much taller than Jimmy and his features are different. Like those hazel eyes and his light brown, wavy hair. Jimmy's hair is black and wooly. I went back and forth for a couple of weeks trying to figure out what to do.

At work, Neil and I decided to keep our distance from one another. We both felt guilty. At home, I tried to act as normal as possible. Still, I could feel Jimmy's eyes on my back, like he knew something wasn't right. Maybe it was just my imagination. One morning, I got nauseous. I told Jimmy, "I think I ate some bad barbecue pork for lunch because my stomach has been aching since yesterday." Then I thought, "Suppose it happens again? What will I say then?"

The next morning, I ran to the bathroom and threw up. "Maybe it's a virus," I told Jimmy. He replied, "Maybe you're pregnant. We've waited long enough." I looked at him wide-eyed. "Pregnant? You think so?" "Yeah," he said. Why don't you make an appointment to see the doctor? "Uh-oh," I thought. "This is it." Jimmy said, "Matter of fact, I'll make the appointment for you. I want to know as soon as possible. Our parents will be delighted if we tell them a new grandbaby is on the way." He smiled broadly, the excitement shining in his eyes. I smiled back and gave him a hug.

That day, I told Neil about the baby growing inside me. He said, "There is a chance it is Jimmy's child. Menstrual cycles aren't always on schedule." I told him, "Mine is." Then he snapped his fingers as though remembering something. "We should go back to the time just before you were born when you were making your plans for this life," he said. "That might give us some guidance on what to do."

"Oh, no," I replied. "That's how I got in trouble in the first place." Neil asked, "Do you have a better idea?" I didn't. Right after work, we met in his room in the back of his sister's house to do a quick review of the time between my last prior life and this one. Thank God his sister was out of town.

Under hypnosis, I saw myself surrounded by a group of friends who were in my soul group. I had a lot of lessons to learn in the next life and I was going to need some help. Apparently, I was very popular and more than two dozen souls lined up to assist me. Kavina, an intern guide, was in charge. My chief guide was away in another dimension attending to a crisis involving many souls.

Several advanced soul buddies coached me in deciding where to be born, which gender to choose and which parents to select. Because I needed to work on my tendency to be arrogant, impatient, and selfish we agreed that I should be a female and a mother. I had been unsympathetic to the downtrodden and to minorities in my life as a race car driver, so we decided that I would be black in the next life. I insisted that if I had to be a black woman, I must at least have a beautiful body. We picked one out from a lineup of possibilities that appeared on a large movie-like screen. We even previewed some possible scenes from the next life, all dependent on my human choices.

The time came for my soul group to decide who would incarnate with me as friends, teachers, obstacle makers, boyfriends, and relatives. When that was done, the subject of marriage was raised. No less than ten members of the group volunteered to be my husband. I eliminated four of them who really did not belong to our group although they were close associates. That left six.

I was astonished to hear my soul ask, "Are you willing to share me during the course of this lifetime? I can learn different lessons from each of you and take on more challenges." They seemed to be amenable to the idea of consecutive relationships, so I announced, "I will marry all of you, but you will have to take turns."

The souls agreed to this plan. My longtime soulmate, Jeroe, volunteered to be my first husband. Although we had shared many lives, we had never married before. I agreed to marry him first. Frator, whom I had married many lives ago, asked to be my last husband. He had other work to do in the early part of his new incarnation. He said, "You will recognize me when I appear in your human life. My body will be surrounded by a bright, white light that only you can see." I smiled and agreed to marry him last.

One of the associate souls whom I had eliminated as husband material asked to be reconsidered. "I can help you through some tough transitions," he said. My reply was firm. "You can be my friend or relative, but not my husband." I could see he needed clarity.

At this point, Kavina intervened. "I think you're trying to do too much in this one life. Remember, one of your issues is that you are overly ambitious. It's tough to fix everything in one lifetime. It's been done, but it's not easy." I said, "I believe I can do it all." Kavina advised that I wait for the counsel of my chief guide, Gayla. No one knew how long Gayla would be away.

One soul who was helping me prepare for re-entry to human life said, "I will help you to rid yourself of prejudice against those who aren't like you. You know, each soul has its own journey and it's not up to you to judge." My soul said, "I'm pretty normal. I like people who are in my groove. They're naturally easier to like."

The intern chimed in, "That's why we're having this discussion. This new life will bring some serious challenges. You'll learn to love people because of their divine spark, which is made in God's image. You'll learn to look past outward appearances, behaviors, personal habits and social status. You'll discover what really matters. But there will be pain. Part of you will want to revert back to the old way. If you fall into old habits, there's no telling how many lifetimes it will take to make the corrections."

My soul said, "Oh no, I've made up my mind. This is my last go round on Planet Earth. No matter how many bumps I hit on the road, I'm going all the way."

As I listened to this conversation, I mentally asked the assemblage how many children I would have. The intern guide said, "Just one. A girl. But your relationship with her will be strained." A young soul stepped forward and volunteered to be my daughter. He had suffered accidental death as a 17 year old boy trapped in a coal mine.

My soul asked him, "Why would you want to volunteer for the kind of life this girl will have?" He said, "I've been a super macho type for the last three lives and I need to find some balance. I need to experience the feminine side, and I need to learn about creating good relationships, even under stress. Taking the role of your daughter will help me do that."

My soul thought about this proposition for a moment, then replied, "All right. I accept you as my daughter in this coming incarnation." After I repeated this to Neil, he asked if I wanted to end the session. I said, "No. I want to hear what Gayla has to say."

Next, I saw a scene that occurred sometime later, in human terms. It's impossible to say how much later since time does not exist on the other side. Everything happens in the "eternal now." Anyway, my chosen mother for my next human life was pregnant and Gayla had not returned. Another soul was petitioning to join with the fetus and be born to my chosen mother.

My soul shifted into high gear. I concentrated on the image of Kavina and she appeared. When I shared the situation with her, she said, "This is unusual. You could wait for another opportunity." My soul emphatically said, "I want to go now."

"There may be a way to incarnate while your guide is away. We can go before the Council of Elders and request their permission. I don't know what they'll say since you have such an ambitious agenda."

"Let's go to the Council." That group consists of highly developed, wise beings. They are deeply infused and aligned with God's own spirit. The Council granted me a hearing. Kavina counseled me to be very respectful in their presence.

The hearing room was an awesome place with ornate carvings. The Council members wore purple robes. The images that appeared in my hypnotized human mind were translucent, just solid enough to make out what was going on.

Kavina introduced me, as was the custom. Then, I outlined my proposed life plan. After listening to the plan, the Council members were stern. The Council Chief said, "You are too ambitious and could end up with a fragmented, confusing life." They tried to dissuade me. In the end they agreed to let me have the experience I had planned. The Chief said, "What you really need to get in this human life is the idea of serving others. That's the big agenda. Don't just think it. Act on it.

"Here's your challenge for your human incarnation. You must overcome and rise above:

- Selfishness
- Greed
- Prejudice against those unlike yourself
- Letting ego control your life

You must acquire some habits too:

- Willingness to listen
- Openness to spiritual growth
- Courage to take risks for the sake of others
- Viewing events from the perspective of eternity
- Unconditional love for all of God's creatures
- Service, service, service

If you intend for this to be your last human incarnation, you must meet all of these conditions."

Suddenly, a massive light being from a higher *mansion* or level of God's *house* of infinite dimensions appeared in the Council room. Awareness flashed as my human mind remembered, "In my Father's house are many mansions. If it were not so, I would have told you."

The light being spoke. "I am Barama. As an emissary from the heart of God, I will incarnate on Earth during your sojourn there. It is unusual for one of us to take a human incarnation, but the situation is critical. In that world's leading country, the United States of America, the leadership will lose its way and the people will suffer grievously. They will be gripped by feelings of fear, anger and betrayal. I will come as a beacon of hope to show them how to move from the darkness to the light. My words will inspire and unite millions of people. When you hear me speak truth with quiet strength, you will remember who I am."

My soul asked, "How will I know?" Barama replied, "You will be overcome by a deep feeling of peaceful energy. Every cell in your body will feel it. This is a gift intended to uplift you in the difficult life you have chosen."

Then, the Council member seated to the right of the Chief Elder spoke. "I will incarnate on the other side of Planet Earth during the same time period. As the leader of a nation there, I will support Barama's mission. From both sides of the earth, we will have one message. We will help people find the courage to choose *intentional peace* and to reclaim their connected humanity. You and many others will benefit."

Barama's concentrated light presence expanded, filling the room, and then vanished. Everyone sat in silent reflection, watching the afterglow from his essence.

The Chief broke the silence. "God knows your possibilities and has offered you a measure of grace as you pursue your proposed life plan. Be warned. You must be willing to accept the consequences of your choices, which will include much suffering." My headstrong soul said, "I understand. I am ready to go."

After hearing this, my human face was crestfallen. Neil brought me out of the light trance. He tried to explain to me why I had to experience life as a black woman.

"Some people who are born white have a special problem. They must be reincarnated again and again into different races and cultures, then into the white race again. This is to help them erase the ego notion of superiority. All of God's children have gifts and each gift is special. The main problem among some in the white race is an erroneous belief that their gifts are better than other people's gifts. It is a very difficult concept to eradicate, even after hundreds of lives.

At the same time, some minority group members believe that their gifts are less valuable than other people's gifts. This leads to low self esteem and sometimes to feelings of hopelessness, helplessness and frustration. Again, this is a learned human error. The two errors reinforce one another.

These misunderstandings cause people to stay in the birth-death cycle, just as you have, until they learn the lesson that we are all made in God's image. We are different versions of *one connected humanity* created by one God. Now you are moving toward a deep understanding of your relationship to the family of man."

"That scenario sounds somewhat plausible," I said, "if you let yourself believe in reincarnation. But why did I choose such a hard life?"

"Because you're stubborn," Neil answered.

I related to him that my early memories of this life included my parents' repeated efforts to break my pattern of willfulness. Neil listened quietly.

"My parents tried to beat the fire out of me. They were afraid that I could mouth off and be in real danger in the Deep South. I worked hard at being good, but I was naturally stubborn. I refused to cry when I got whipped. My sister and brother would let out a yelp with the first swing of Daddy's strap or Mama's switches, but I locked my mouth shut. As the blows fell, my constant thought was, 'This is not right. When I grow up, I'm never going to whip my children like this.'

"Once when Daddy was particularly frustrated from a day of Southern humiliation to his Black manhood, Mama confronted him as soon as he came home. She was exhausted from another hot, muggy day with excitable children and their playmates, and she unloaded her misery on Daddy. She recounted her three children's misdeeds, having told us beforehand, 'Wait till your Daddy gets home. Just wait.' The quiet tension among us children had been growing for a couple of hours, granting Mama some relief from the chaos.

"As promised, Daddy did his duty. That day, he had again been denied a promotion on his job at the post office, even though he had trained the young white man who got the promotion and became Daddy's new boss. He got out his strap to whip all of us, starting with Gwendolyn, the oldest. She screamed up a storm and pleaded, 'I'm sorry, Daddy. I'm so sorry. Please, Daddy. I'm sorry.' After the strap connected with her backside for the fourth time, Daddy stopped. Her remorse had worked. He instructed her, 'Now, don't do that again. You mind your mother from now on.'

"I was next. I assertively protested, 'Daddy, I didn't do anything.' My little brother, Terrell, had reported a false accusation to Mama so that I wouldn't be left out of the punishment. Daddy glared. 'Your Mama said you've been bad and you're going to get a whipping.' The tension in the room was thick as sorghum syrup, but there was nothing sweet about it. I grimaced with each blow and looked at Daddy with defiant eyes. I was thinking, 'How could you do this?'

"From the first blow, my vow of silence activated. My sister and brother became coaches, yelling 'Cry Lila. Cry!' I refused to play that game. Daddy paused after the strap slapped my back the third time, asking 'What did you do that for?' I answered in a trembling, but determined voice. 'I didn't do anything.' That only enraged him, and one blow after another rained down. Then, my mother joined in the chant, 'Cry, Lila. Just cry and you won't get a bad whipping.' I looked at her with a mixture of bewilderment and anger. How could she have believed Terrell?

"Finally, Mama saw that the whipping wasn't doing any good. She yelled, 'Stop, Daddy. Don't kill her.' But he was thinking about his damaged spirit from the day's reminder of his second class status. He kept going. It felt like knives were sticking in me all over. When the pain was too much to bear, I fainted. That was my last whipping. My little brother got off scot-free that day as my parents concentrated on bringing me back to consciousness."

Neil said softly, "That's the suffering the Council was talking about. Even though you were falsely accused, you had to endure suffering. That's because you did not, as a child, understand the law of cause and effect and how to lessen its impact. You needed a savior." I said, "I finally got one, my Aunt Minnie. She kept me for three summers, the best childhood summers I ever had. I'm still trying to mend fences with my parents. They did the best they could, but my ideas were very different from theirs."

The subject turned back to the life plans I had made on the other side. I knew I could modify the details, but was the plan pretty much in place? Was I was going to have one daughter and six husbands? And why wouldn't I have a close relationship with my daughter? Since Neil had seen his own life plan, he knew that he would not be one of my husbands. He said, "I will remain a bachelor and die fairly young."

I spun out of control, railing against Neil for getting me pregnant and changing my life so drastically. He told me he had not intended to do that, but apparently the plan was going forward. I told him, "I know about free will and I believe in it. God lets us make choices as human beings. I don't have to follow a plan that was concocted before I was born. That's just a guideline."

Neil looked me straight in the eye and asked, "And what is growing in your belly? A guideline or a baby?" I slapped him and walked out. I thought, "Neil used his past life knowledge to seduce me. If the stuff he told me is true about having to make up for this life's wrongdoing in the next life, his next life will be rough."

Driving home, I took deep breaths and tried to calm down. The only positive thing I learned from all this is that some guys are attracted to me because they have been my soul buddies in previous lives. I guess that takes care of the last thirty percent of my attraction factor. If you are one of my old soul friends, don't tell me. Just be there for me.

Disturbing thoughts raced through my mind. "This baby's birth could be the beginning of the end of my marriage. On the other hand, depending on how the child looks, things could go normally. I just need somebody to talk to so that I can make it through this pregnancy.

I reflected, "My brother has turned out to be a pretty good friend, but his mouth is too big. Terrell might tell our parents. My Aunt Minnie? No. I'm choosing my sister, Gwen. My blood oath best friend forever. I won't tell her everything. I will tell her I got caught up in the moment and the baby's father could be someone other than Jimmy. She will understand. Gwen has shared lots of intimate stuff with me about her less than ideal marriage. It's been our secret. We'll walk through this experience together. I will follow my daily routine the same as always, and work through the eighth month."

During the next few months, I often found myself staring off into space. Luckily, JJ thought that was one of those quirks pregnant women have. He pampered me and made me as comfortable as he could.

One evening, I decided to risk introducing the subject of reincarnation to see if there was any way JJ could understand what happened to me. "JJ, one of my co-workers was saying we have more than one human life. He said your body dies and your soul is reborn to live in another human body."

"That guy is crazy. There are a lot of people running around making stuff up, Lila. I know you. You hear about something and believe maybe it's possible. Don't let anybody fool you. There's such a thing as being too open minded. You have only one life. Our job is to do the best we can with the life we have. That's why I decided very early that I would not waste my life or leave it to chance."

"And you haven't. You've come a long way since those early days when your family was poor."

"Yeah. I know what poverty looks like and I don't intend to be there. I'm not waiting for another life. I'm planning and working on improving the life I have."

"So you don't think we could have made some plans before we were born?"

"You mean in your mother's belly? Come on, now. Be realistic, Lila. And stop listening to people who talk crazy."

"I guess you're right." That was the end of that conversation.

At work, Neil decided to ask for a transfer to a Piggly Wiggly in Atlanta. Seeing my growing belly was more than he could take. He left when I was in my seventh month. He did call me at work to give me his new phone number. I suppose that was the best thing for both of us.

Of course, both sets of potential grandparents were thrilled at the thought of their first grandchild. Papa Wright was recovering nicely and looking forward to his new grandson. He insisted it would be a boy, although I knew better. My parents, whom JJ and I visited once a week on Sundays, offered to buy the crib. Right after I took maternity leave from work, the ladies at Mt. Carmel planned a baby shower, though I wasn't supposed to know about it.

At the shower I said, "I think the baby is a girl." Cousin Mary agreed. She said, "I can tell by the way you are carrying the child high in your belly." For once, I let my hair down and had a great time at the shower. The church ladies were generous, and I returned home with presents galore. This baby will have everything she needs and more.

On the morning of March 4, 1964 about 3:00 AM, my water broke. At first I thought that I had peed in the bed. Once I became coherent, I realized what had happened. I woke up my groggy husband. "JJ, we need to call Dr. Potter." JJ always had been slow to wake up. He muttered, "Huh?" I said, "It's time. My water broke." He gasped and threw back the covers. "Call Dr. Potter," I repeated. I had written the doctor's number on a pad right by the phone. JJ stumbled to the phone and dialed the number.

Dr. Potter told him he would meet us at the hospital. I struggled out of bed and threw on a maternity dress. My pains had been coming off and on all day, but they had not been regular. In my visit to the doctor two days ago, he said I was already dilated two centimeters, but that first pregnancies were tricky. Labor could be slow.

At the hospital, I was disappointed to learn that I had only dilated four centimeters. Since my water had broken, however, they decided not to send me back home. Over the next few hours, the labor pains became stronger and more regular. I was in agony. "So this is what women have to go through," I thought. "Thank God I'll only have to do it once."

We called my parents and my sister about 6:00 AM, but told them they didn't have to rush over. We apparently had a long wait. My mother and Gwen arrived at 9:00 AM to lend moral support. Daddy and Terrell would come later. At 4:30 PM, I felt what had to be the mother of all pains. I yelled for medication. Mama told me to breathe, but I was already nervous about how my daughter would look. I didn't need pain on top of worry. "Just give me something!" I screamed to the nurse as she entered the room. JJ was a nervous wreck. Daddy steered him into the hallway.

Soon afterward, I was given an epidural and wheeled into the operating room to give birth. Doctors didn't let family members in the room during childbirth. Before long, my daughter was emerging headfirst to meet the world. I tried to stay coherent and watch the birth via a strategically placed mirror. When the doctor held my daughter upside down, she let out a loud cry. "Well, she's got a good set of lungs," Dr. Potter said. He laid her gently on my belly. I could not believe I had actually given birth to this little reddish ball with limbs flailing everywhere. Unlike most babies in my family, she was almost completely baldheaded. That was unusual.

Soon, the nurse had swaddled the child and put a solution in her eyes to ward off infections. My afterbirth was expelled and I quickly found myself in the recovery room, exhausted and sleepy. Two hours later, the nurse awakened me and I was taken to my room in the maternity ward. Within minutes, JJ, Mama, Daddy and Terrell were by my side.

JJ asked, "How are you feeling, Babycakes?" I replied, "Pretty tired, but otherwise fine." Mama commented, "You'll forget all about that pain soon. You two have a beautiful little girl." Daddy chimed in, "Yeah, she's a pretty little thing. We can't tell who she looks like yet." Mama said, "She doesn't have a head full of curly hair like all my babies did,

36

but she'll get some eventually." JJ said, "Well, she's got a couple of little wispy strands. She'll probably end up with a whole lot of hair, like her Mama." When I didn't respond, Mama said, "We're tiring you out. You need to rest."

I said, "I am still kind of out of it." Mama said, "Come on, Daddy. Let's give Lila Mae a chance to rest so she can get ready to hold and feed the baby. By the way, did you two pick a name yet?" Simultaneously, JJ and I replied, "Bessie Ella." I said, "We named her after two of my favorite singers, Bessie Smith and Ella Fitzgerald." Daddy shook his head. "You always did like music," he said. Then he, Terrell and Mama disappeared through the door. Soon after, JJ kissed me, his eyes shining with joy. Then, he was off to call everybody he knew to announce the birth of our 21 inch long daughter.

The first three months were a real adjustment. Babies really do change your life forever, but I didn't mind. Even with feedings every four hours, spit-up and messy diapers, I fell in love with my child. All was not smooth sailing, though. I had seen my parents and the church folks looking at the baby's light eyes. After her christening, one woman made a comment in the bathroom about the baby's blue-gray eyes. I told her we had some white ancestors. I knew that wouldn't stop the talk. I was just buying time.

When Bessie was almost four months old, I returned to work at the Piggly Wiggly and my mother agreed to babysit her grandchild. One night after picking our daughter up from Mama's house, JJ asked, "When do you think Bessie is going to get her real eye color? I thought it would come in after the first couple of weeks. That's what my mother said. But her eyes are hazel." Gwen and I had prepared for that question and his observation. I swallowed hard and gave the ancestor line. JJ frowned like he wanted to believe it very much, but there was some doubt. Like the doubt I had seen in my mother's eyes.

One morning when I took the baby to Mama, she said, "My friends are gossiping about this baby. They keep talking about her hair and her eyes. If they say anything to me, I tell them to mind their business. Lila Mae, just between you and me, I don't know why she looks like she does."

"You said your grandmother was half Cherokee Indian and half white."

"Yes, but her eyes were brown. Her hair was almost straight, but dark brown. None of us inherited her hair texture."

"Aunt Minnie's hair is wavy."

"The waves are much tighter than Bessie's hair."

"Well, she got it from somewhere. Mama, can't you just enjoy your granddaughter?"

"She's a sweet child. I just don't know where she came from."

"From my womb, that's where. I have to go to work now." I kissed Bessie as she lay in Mama's arms. "See you, Mama."

Mama shook her head as I headed out the door. My angel sent a warning thought, "This arena is too small." I shuddered to think about what that might mean.

By the sixth month, when Bessie's head was fully covered with loose, light brown waves, JJ confronted me. "Look, Lila Mae. I know you are light skinned, but both of us have wooly hair. So do my parents and yours. Bessie's hair is different. Not tight curls or thick, tight waves like some Black babies have, but loose waves. And it's light brown. Do you have something you need to tell me?" I stared blankly. "What do you mean?" He said, "You know what I mean. One of the guys at the barber shop made the comment, 'Mama's baby, Daddy's maybe.' The guy was looking straight at me. I said, 'Sounds like somebody's jealous.' But he just expressed what I've been thinking. I don't want to think it. I need to hear something from you."

I said, "I don't know what to say. I love you, JJ. I wanted more than anything to give you a child. She belongs to both of us." He held my shoulders and looked me in the eye. "Tell me the truth," he demanded. I dropped my head, breathed a deep sigh and admitted, "In a crazy, lonely moment when you were in North Carolina with your parents, I got swept away. Just one stupid mistake. I was praying all along that the child was yours. I still want to think that she is."

"Who is he? Is he white? Is it your boss?"

"No. He's mixed. A mulatto, I guess. He was just a friend, really. He caught me at an emotional moment."

"Is he somebody I know?"

"No. You don't know him."

"Where is he?"

"He moved away from Macon. He used to work near me. As a

matter of fact, I recently learned that he had an aneurysm last month that traveled to his brain. He died within hours."

"You're lying."

"No. It's true. Gwen was the only person I told. She was hoping the baby would be yours too. We still don't know for sure."

"How did you find out he died? Have you been in contact with him?"

"No. His insurance company called me at work. He knew I was pregnant and he made the baby the beneficiary on his life insurance policy. He left her $50,000 in my care. The check came yesterday. I didn't know how to tell you."

JJ dropped his hands from my shoulders and punched a hole in the wall. Then he walked out of the door, slamming it behind him. I knew this was the end of the line.

Yes, there could be other scenarios. He could forgive me and ignore the pointing and gossip wherever we went in our small community. We could use the money to make a better life for ourselves and Bessie. He could forget that he had been trying to get me pregnant for two years and another man accomplished the feat in a one night fling. But what were the chances of that?

I picked up the phone and called Gwen. Between sobs, I told her, "Gwen, it's all over. I have to leave Macon and start over. JJ knows Bessie's not his child." Gwen asked, "Is he there now?" I replied, "No. He got really emotional and walked out. I don't know what he might do."

"Lila, you know that man loves you. He always has. He's just upset. Give him some time." I said, "You didn't see the look in his eyes. He feels like he has been betrayed. Something precious has gone out of our relationship. Trust. I don't know if he can ever trust me again."

Gwen paused for a few seconds, collecting herself. Then she said in a quiet, determined tone, "I'll be right over."

I stood dazed for a moment. I said aloud, "My soul chose a hard life and I have to live it." The tears started as I looked around the bedroom I would probably never see again. A guidance thought entered my head from somewhere deep inside. "Look for the bright spots. Treasure them when they come." Mechanically, I reached for the old brown suitcase in the back of the closet. Throwing a bunch of dresses on the bed, I started packing then and there.

That's how I ended up on this barstool in Atlanta. Thanks for listening. I'm going up to check on my sister and my daughter.

Section Two

Jimmy Lee Jenkins

Life may not always be the party we hoped for,
But while we are here we might as well dance.

- Unknown

Hello, my friend. I'm glad you're here to help me pick the peaches. These Elberta peaches are the best you can find in Georgia. Sweet and juicy. Let's have one before we get started. Mmmm. Good! I have an idea to make the time go faster. I hear that in the bush in Africa, history passes down by word of mouth. You know, we all have a history. Mine stretches back thirty-two years. Please listen to my story while we work.

On October 23, 1939, I arrive, a helpless baby whose parents are sharecroppers in Tallapoosa, Georgia. My parents are Fanny and Charlie Jenkins. Both of them are graduates of Brenner Elementary, in a county where eighth grade ends a colored person's schooling.

Where do we live? In a shotgun house with newspaper covered walls and sagging floors. I have an older sister named Carla. Although she is only five years old, she watches me while my parents work in the fields, taking turns to check on us now and then. Carla starts school the next year. Then, Mama carries me to the field wrapped and tied on her back. I feel the steady rhythm of Mama's strong muscles. My parched lips brush across the salty wetness on her back.

In the summertime, Carla babysits me again. Her new friend, Sassie moves with her parents to a nearby cabin. They are sharecroppers too.

Sassie comes to play with Carla now and then. They play house, but they include me too.

When I get old enough, we make up games all day. We take the homemade broom outside and sweep the dirt into patterns. We draw pictures in the dirt with sticks, decorated with rocks. Carla makes mud pies and invites me to taste them. A couple of times I do. Ugh! We have rock throwing contests. Carla always wins. Her long arms can throw rocks further and faster than my little arms can. I keep trying though.

Our only real toys are a Raggedy Ann and Raggedy Andy no longer favored by the boss's children. I wonder why the dolls' hair is bright red. Carla tells me she once saw a doll with brown skin and black hair. I don't believe her.

By the time I am three, I fully understand the meaning of the sweat that is pouring down my parents' faces and matting their clothes when they walk through the door. Daddy drops into a chair all worn out. Mama lets out a sigh and heads for the kitchen. She knows we kids have mostly been eating cornbread and gravy all day.

Our little plot of land provides vegetables for dinner. That land is borrowed from the man Mama and Daddy work for, just like the house. We don't own anything. Not even the cows that Mama milks. She is allowed to keep a portion of the milk for our family. We eat little meat. When we do, it's usually some wild animal that Daddy has killed, like possum or rabbit. Now and then, we have fish from the brook on the owner's property. Daddy gets to keep one out of every three fish he catches, usually the smallest one. Mama boils the fish heads for soup, adding onions and rice. We waste nothing.

When Carla and I walk barefoot at home, we watch out for splinters. We have no bedroom slippers. Never heard of them. My Mama cradles an injured little foot in her hand and takes out the splinter by applying kerosene, letting it set till the splinter peeks out, then pulling out the little sliver.

As a toddler, I look through the holes in the bedroom/living room floor and see the ground. Carla, says, "Monsters live down there. They're going to slip through the crack while you're sleeping and take you away."

"There are no monsters under the floor. You're just trying to scare me."

"Want me to call them?"

I try to be brave, but I end up yelling, "Mama, Carla's trying to scare me." Mama says, "Stop, Carla. Leave that boy alone." I finally get over her teasing as I grow older.

Then, a terrible tragedy strikes. Carla gets real sick. Mama sends Daddy to get Miss Precious, a colored, practical nurse who works private duty up the hill. Miss Precious says it looks like scarlet fever. Daddy doesn't have money for the hospital. In those days, they don't do much for Black people anyway. By the next evening, Mama's home remedies to keep the fever down are not working. Carla gets hotter and hotter.

In the middle of that pitch black night, stars and moon hiding, Daddy runs two miles through stubby fields and briered woods to Dr. Howzer's back door. Daddy begs him to come see about Carla. The doctor says, "I'm not leaving my house this time of the night for no colored girl. I'll see her sometime tomorrow." Daddy pleads, but the white doctor slams the door in his face.

Meanwhile, Mama and Miss Precious, who usually takes care of an old white woman, keep doing the best they can to get the fever down. They take ice from the icebox, chip it up with the ice pick and put it in our round tin bathing tub. Then, they light a lamp, walk outside and draw up buckets of well water, carry the water to the tub and pour it in. They pick up Carla and sit her in the frigid water. She cools down some and starts shivering. Miss Precious says, "Let's put her back in the bed." Carla's temperature starts heating up again.

Daddy comes through the door sweating and exhausted, with a look on his face that I will never forget. Daddy has always been the one who said, "Never give up. You never know what God has in store for you." Now, it is like God Himself shut the door in Daddy's face, like all hope is swept away. I have never seen his shoulders droop like that. I am scared. Miss Precious has to leave when her boss comes for her. Daddy and Mama keep a vigil at Carla's side all night.

I sleep in my parents' room that night. A moaning sound awakens me at sunrise. When I creep into the bedroom my sister and I share, I see a sheet covering her face. My parents are holding each other in a tearful embrace. At the age of nine, Carla is gone. I fall into Mama's lap, but she can't console me. I suddenly realize that I will never see

Carla's beautiful smile or hear her unforgettable laugh again. My tears start flowing.

My daddy is a rugged mountain of a man and my mama is little like a bird. She looks fragile, even though she isn't. She is kind of high strung, but Daddy can usually calm her down. Ordinarily, his big bass voice softens as he touches her shoulder and says, "Now, Sugar, everything's gonna work out." You can see her shoulders relax when he says that. This time, no words can soothe her, so Daddy gives Mama her space. His own heart is breaking. Only time can heal this tragedy.

After the funeral, my parents don't talk to me about Carla, except to say, "Your sister's in heaven." I pray that she makes it there after telling me all those stories about monsters. It is so hard, staying in that room by myself. I miss Carla, even the teasing. Many a night, I cry myself to sleep.

I wonder, "Why won't Mama and Daddy let me talk about Carla? She didn't just disappear. Sometimes I can feel her in the room. It's like she's watching over me." I want to tell Mama, but she just says, "Carla is gone." She lives in my heart and I guess she lives in theirs, but the subject is closed off.

Several nights, when I close my eyes to sleep, I get a picture in my mind of Carla waving. When that happens I promise her, "The next time a special girl comes into my life, I'm going to give her all the good things you never had. I'll do it for you. I love you, Carla." Then, she smiles and fades away. I never tell anyone.

It's clear from their conversations that Mama and Daddy have a vision. Their eyes are fixed on something better for our family. They pray, wait and watch for their chance. Almost two years later, when I am finishing first grade, God smiles on them.

My Uncle Raymond needs somebody to run his 150 acre farm. He writes to my father, "I have been by myself since my wife ran off to Chicago two years ago to live with her sister. She divorced me up there. She got tired of the farm. Now, a stroke has crippled me. My right side is weak. Please come and run this place for me. There is plenty of room for your family. I have no children. A couple of farm hands have been trying to keep things going, but I can't get around to supervise them."

Daddy folds the letter and hugs Mama. "We're going," he says.

"What about the money we owe the boss? He's not going to let us leave until we square that debt."

"Follow me." Daddy leads us to my parents' bedroom, gets down on the floor, and pulls out a locked box from under the bed. My eyes widen as Daddy opens it with a key that has been hanging on a chain around his neck forever. He takes a wrapped object out of the box. Gently removing the blanket around it he explains, "This is a solid gold candelabrum. See the custom made design of roses climbing up the stem? It was given to my great grandmother by a Quaker woman. We vowed to keep this in the family, no matter how poor we were. Now, I'm going to leave it here to pay the boss what he says we owe him. Sharecropping draws you deeper and deeper in debt, but this candelabrum will buy our freedom from this place. It's our way out."

Mama shouts, "Praise God!" and the whole family starts dancing around the room. Daddy chants, "Thank you Jesus! Thank you, Jesus! Thank you, Jesus!"

We move to Uncle Raymond's farm. It's about two miles from where we are standing now. When we arrive, we discover that Uncle Raymond has cows, horses, hogs, chickens, sweet potatoes, turnip greens, collards, squash, corn, watermelons, cantaloupes and peach trees. The farm is not in good shape, so Mama and Daddy set to work. Daddy says, "This is the break we've been waiting for. Finally, we're living in a nice house. Jimmy has his own room. Together, we can make this farm produce!"

The house has four large bedrooms, and the living room is just a living room like it is supposed to be. Uncle Raymond has built the place himself, with the help of friends and neighbors. His house is about half a mile from the Thorntons, though I don't know it that first summer.

In the fall, I start second grade at the Bibb County School for Colored. Every morning before school, I help Mama gather the eggs. After school, there are more chores. I understand why I have to work hard. I am on the team with my parents, making a new life.

My new school with its peeling paint isn't much to look at. Still the two story structure is an improvement over my old one room school with only a wood burning pot bellied stove for heat. This plain wooden building has radiator heat and good, strong floors. The first and second grades are combined in a large room with one teacher, Miss Burrows.

A first grade girl named Lila Mae catches my eye on day one. She is pretty and scrappy at the same time. She doesn't act like most girls. At recess, she challenges the other kids, "I'll race you across the playground. First one to the cherry tree wins." She runs like the wind and often wins. She isn't afraid to race bigger kids either. If she falls and scrapes her knee, she blows on the knee to soothe it. Then, she hops over to the outdoor water fountain, fills her tiny, cupped hands with water and rinses off the broken skin. Before long, she is ready to race again.

More than once, Miss Burrows scolds her, "Remember, you're a girl, Lila Mae. Act like it. Stop competing with these boys." Lila Mae's mama dresses her in frilly dresses, but she might as well be wearing pants. She is a tomboy for sure. But she is a quick-witted tomboy, the smartest girl I know. And she's strong too, to be so skinny.

While I'm looking at Lila Mae, another girl is looking at me. Her name is Lessie Ann Miller and she is in the second grade like me. She is short, a little plump, and sweet as an angel. She always gives me desserts from her lunchbox. Since her mother is a great cook, I appreciate her kindness. I look forward to those oatmeal raisin cookies, sweet potato pie, fresh apple cake and gingerbread. I can taste that gingerbread now.

Sweet as Lessie Ann is, there was no way that she can compete with the spirited Lila Mae for my affections. By third grade, I work up the courage to ask Miss Thornton, Lila Mae's mama, if I can walk her daughter to the crossing where we meet the school truck. Some of us ride up front in the cab and some of us ride in the bumpy truck bed. Miss Thornton laughs at me, but decides that I am harmless. At any rate, she knows Lila Mae can defend herself, so she consents. I am the happiest boy around.

On the way to the crossing, Lila Mae's big sister walks ahead of us. Gwen is in fifth grade and considers herself too grown-up to walk with the little kids. Lila Mae plays games during the half-mile walk down the dirt road. Sometimes, she pretends she is driving a Cadillac. Other times, she looks up at the cloud shapes and pretends that they are animals or creatures who live among the stars. Then again, she tries to call the birds to her, and gets frustrated when they fly away. Sometimes we skip or run down the road. Often, Lila spots a patch of daisies and runs off the road to pick one. She sticks it in her hair and grins like she has just discovered gold. The daisies and Lila Mae have two things in common. They are both wild and pretty.

One morning she lingers too long picking flowers. I shout, "Lila Mae, get out of those daises!" She gives me an impish look. I say, "If you don't come on, we're going to miss the school truck." Just then, Gwen looks back and calls, "Come on, Lila Mae! Right now, or I'm telling Daddy."

Lila Mae plucks one more daisy for her little bouquet, and then takes off running, passing me. I shout, "Hey, girl. I waited for you. Now you're trying to leave me." She runs like the wind, but I am right behind her. We make it to the school truck on time.

Near the end of my third grade year, Uncle Raymond takes a turn for the worse. He has been growing more and more frail and dependent since we arrived. His high blood pressure finally gets the best of him. He dies, leaving his property to my parents for their lifetimes. After their deaths, the will says, the farm will go to his younger brother. I know right then that I will have to get my own land and make my own way.

For the next three years, our family does well. We are part of the middle class. Then, my daddy dies of a stroke the summer after I finish sixth grade. I am devastated because Daddy has definitely been the head of the family. He set goals and kept us moving toward them. He worked hard, but I believe he never really stopped grieving over Carla.

With Daddy gone, I don't know what will happen next. Mama and I can't handle the farm alone. I can tell she is worried. I am worried about her deep sadness.

To my surprise, a skinny, balding widower at our church starts courting my mother about six weeks after Daddy dies. He has a teenaged daughter named Doris. I don't know whether Mama loves Mr. Wright or not, but she is a practical woman. She is used to having a partner to lean on. For his part, Mr. Wright needs a mother for 16 year old Doris. He starts coming over to help Mama with the farm. In less than four months after Daddy's death, Mr. Wright marries Mama, and Doris becomes my big sister. Her personality is different from Carla's, but they have one thing in common – teasing me.

The Wrights move in with us and life goes on. He is a decent man. I call him Papa, but I still don't like the idea of him replacing my real Daddy. I obey him, but I don't feel close to him. Not at first. After he comes, though, I see Mama smile again. I pray that she stays healthy because if she dies, we lose the farm to Uncle Raymond's brother.

My step-sister's favorite pastime is razzing me about Lila Mae. Lila and I are inseparable in grade school. When I reach eighth grade, I realize that the next year will be different. I will attend the high school where Doris graduated and wait a whole year for Lila to join me.

That eighth grade year is special. Even though it feels like I have known Lila Mae forever, it is that year that her parents let me take her on our first real date. We go to the movies. When my mom drives me to pick her up, Lila comes to the door grinning from ear to ear. She is wearing a fresh daisy in her hair. After that day, every time I see a daisy, I think of Lila Mae. When I want to do something special for Lila, I bring her a bouquet of daisies. Let the other guys do the usual rose thing. Matter of fact, I persuade my mother to grow daisies in her flower garden.

We have several movie dates over the following months. We fall into a pattern. Mama drives me to Lila's house in Uncle Raymond's big old Packard. Mama needs a cushion to see above the dashboard. Lila and I sit in the wide back seat, holding hands down low where Mama can't see us. We smile at each other, but we don't dare sneak a kiss. Mama has eyes in the back of her head. The first couple of times, Mama goes into the theater with us and sits three or four rows behind us. Then, she starts dropping us off while she visits her cousin in Macon. That's when I begin putting my arm around Lila's shoulder while she watches the movie. When I kiss her on the mouth one afternoon, she warns me, "Don't try anything else. My mama will be mad. Mama says the girl has to set the limits."

"Okay," I say, thinking "At least I get to kiss her on the mouth once in a while and not just on the cheek."

Following my mother's instructions, we leave right after the movie ends. She waits for us out front. She is always prompt, and so are we. We don't want to mess up this arrangement.

That fall, I go to Connor High, where I hit my stride in sports. I win medallions and trophies every year running track and playing basketball. I am a very effective shooting guard on the basketball team.

More than once I shoot the tie-breaker from twenty feet back. Lila's mother brings her to some of the away games to cheer for me. My grades are average. I don't spend a lot of time studying.

When Lila Mae joins me at Connor, she excels academically, always making the honor roll. By eleventh grade, she is president of the student council. She has given up some of her tomboy ways and finally has some meat on her bones, in all the right places. I really love her. She fascinates me. Doris says I'm too young to be in love. I don't think she knows what she's talking about.

Every now and then when Lila Mae and I have a spat, Lessie tries to make a play for me. I talk to her a little to make Lila Mae jealous, but I always go back to Lila. I ask for her forgiveness even when I think the spat is her fault. I can't bear to think of losing her.

Lila and I both run track at Connor. I am a sprinter and she is a distance runner. In the spring of my junior year, we both win medallions at a track meet in Macon. On the way home my mama says, "Jimmy, you've been sweet on Lila for a long time. She is the kind of woman a farmer needs. A strong woman. Strong legs, lots of energy. Not somebody who gives out after an hour's work under the summer sun."

"I know, Mama."

"I'm serious, Jimmy. You don't want a fussy little flower that will wither when the first strong wind comes along. That's how Uncle Raymond's wife was. When Lila grows up, she'll make you a fine wife."

"I agree. When the time comes, I'm going to marry her."

I remember watching Mama work side by side with Daddy all day long. I can see her wiping off the sweat and keeping up her pace. That's what it takes to have a successful farm. I mean to be a first rate farmer like my parents. Looking to the sky I say, "Daddy, I'm going to prove that I remember what you taught me. You patiently showed me everything you knew."

Life gets bumpy sometimes. Near the end of my eleventh grade year, Lila really upsets me. She gets so involved in her school activities that she starts ignoring me. I complain to her, and she tells me she is busy with various student council projects. I discuss my frustration with my buddy, Tyree. He says I need to get her attention.

"Lila takes you for granted. Why don't you really spend some time with Lessie Ann? The word is she went all the way with Ralph Calhoun and then he started seeing her friend, Mamie. She could use some comfort and you could use some experience. I know Lila Mae isn't giving it up."

"I can't do that. Lila would drop me for good."

"Man, you don't know how girls think. Lila will chase after you to prove she can get you back."

I think about Tyree's advice. The next day at lunch, Lila sits with the officers of the Student Council. There are no vacant seats at their table. I spot Lessie Ann sitting alone and decide to join her. She beams when I sit down. By the end of lunch, I have a date to take her to the movies. I have a brand new driver's license, so everything is set. That Friday, we drive into Macon and go to the movies. The first couple we see going up to the colored section in the balcony are Mason and Trina from Connor High School. We know right away that everyone will hear about our date by Monday morning.

We sit in the back row and neck. I even caress Lessie's soft thigh. She puts her hand over mine and moves it in a circular motion. I think, "So this is what girls like." I feel my dick stretching out. After the movie, Lessie directs me to drive to a spot up on a hill underneath the stars. She suggests that we get in the back seat. I tell her, "I've never had sex."

"It's easy. I'll show you." Those words cause an immediate reaction in my anatomy. I am excited and grateful. Following her instructions, I unfasten her brassiere and feel her full, soft breasts. She pushes my head down between them and says, "Kiss me." I kiss her over and over with great energy. Then, she unzips my pants. Before I know it, I am inside her. She is gently moving. Her hands push my butt down and I instinctively start to pump up and down. In a few minutes, I feel an unstoppable force moving in my loins. It floods inside Lessie.

Fortunately, Lessie has come prepared with tissues in her purse to clean up the wetness. There is a lot of fluid. I guess it has been building up for a long time. Afterward, I remember our one lesson in health education about condoms.

"God, don't let her be pregnant. I'm buying some condoms

tomorrow. I'll hide them away for times like this." The next day, I buy a box of rubbers and practice putting one on, but I never use them. Two years later, I take them out of their hiding place and they are old and fragile.

On Monday, all the kids in the "in crowd" are talking about Lessie and me. I don't betray Lessie by bragging about having sex. All they know is we went to the movies together. I make a point of thanking Lessie for a good time. Lila passes me in the hallway and turns her head. My advisor, Tyree, says "Don't worry. She's already thinking about how to get you back."

He is right. On Wednesday, Lila invites me to dinner at her house the following Saturday afternoon. She cooks the meal herself. We are an item again. Meanwhile, Ralph Calhoun rediscovers Lessie after he hears about her date with me.

In April 1958, a month before graduation, I win a basketball scholarship to Clark College in Atlanta. Still, there isn't enough money and I don't see myself making good grades in college. I do the practical thing and get a job at the feed store to save up for my own little farm. I have plans for Lila and me.

The next year, Lila graduates and gets an academic scholarship to Spelman, one of the best women's colleges in the South. Her parents are excited and supportive. They have always wanted her to go to a good school and have saved up some money. I am devastated. I figure she will meet some smooth talker at Morehouse, the men's college next door to Spelman in Atlanta. Lila Mae might take on sophisticated city ways and forget about me. She swears she loves me and will never stop, no matter who she meets. I want to believe that.

I call Lila at her dorm twice a week. We don't talk long because long distance is expensive. Also, the girls are lined up at the pay phone to talk to their sweethearts and their families.

I have my eye on the goal of buying us a farm. When Lila comes home for Christmas, I plan to ask her to marry me. I have put a downpayment on an engagement ring. It has a small diamond, but it comes from the heart.

On Christmas Eve, I go to the Thorntons' house and ring the doorbell. Lila Mae meets me at the door with the brightest smile I could ever hope for. Her parents are there and we exchange greetings. When

Mr. and Mrs. Thornton leave the room, I kiss Lila and get down on one knee. "Lila Mae, will you marry me?" I ask. I already know her answer because of the love shining in her face when she sees me down on one knee looking into her eyes. She says "Yes. Yes. Yes!" I get up and hug her so hard that she gasps, "I can't breathe." At that moment, I do not know my own strength. I just know she has made me the happiest man in the world. We are officially engaged.

When her Daddy comes back in the room, Lila rushes to show him the ring. His face turns ashen. I say, "Mr. Thornton, I want to marry your daughter. I guess you've known that for a while." He replies, "Well, you know we like you a lot, JJ. I just hope you aren't planning to talk Lila Mae out of finishing school. She's just a freshman and she's got three more years after this."

I explain, "Sir, I'd like to marry her next summer. I've been in love with her since the day I first met her." Mr. Thornton says, "If you love her, you'll wait for her to finish school. She's smart and she has a bright future." Lila Mae's mother feels the same way, even though she likes me. Lila looks shocked and disappointed. As for me, I can't see waiting three years to make Lila my wife.

Lila and I hatch a plan. In May, I will drive to Atlanta in my old truck and pick her up on campus. Then, we will go to the courthouse in Atlanta and get a marriage license. If her parents still feel the same way, we will get married secretly with Lila's roommate and my best friend as witnesses. We won't tell either set of parents until it is all over. I know my parents won't object to our getting married, but we don't want the Thorntons to think we are playing favorites, inviting one set of parents and not the other. Anyway, they might change their minds by spring.

It's funny how things don't work out the way you expect. The next March, Mr. Thornton's diabetes gets out of control. His legs develop sores that won't heal. Finally, the doctor amputates them both above the knee. Since Mr. Thornton's job requires him to be mobile, he has to retire on disability. That changes everything. He doesn't really have enough money to keep Lila Mae in college, even with the scholarship. She could work while going to school, but she is longing to marry me just like I want to marry her. Finally, Lila's parents relent and we begin planning a July wedding.

Lila Mae's granddaddy died just after Thanksgiving in 1959, leaving Lila his 1956 Buick Roadmaster. We are starting out with that car, my Ford truck, and the fifty acre farm I bought at a tax sale. Papa gives me a cow and a few chickens to get started. The farmhouse is in bad shape, but I have the skills to fix it up and Lila can decorate it.

Lila Mae grows irritable as our wedding day gets closer. She complains, "Every Negro in the county is trying to decide how this wedding should be organized. I want to keep it simple."

"Now, Lila Mae, you know they mean well. These folks have watched us grow up together. They are excited that we're actually getting married.

"I heard two ushers debating about which song Gwen should sing just before we take our vows. Everybody has opinions."

"Yes, they do. Look, Lila, they're treating this like it's their own wedding. Maybe it's because they never had a nice wedding ceremony. They're living their dreams through us."

"They're making me nervous."

"Baby, at a time like this, when your whole life's about to change, you can get the jitters. Just calm down. It's one day out of our lives. I've made up my mind to enjoy it no matter what."

Lila's eyes dart from side to side like they do when she's thinking about a problem. "J.J., you're right. All the ladies have gone out of their way to make our wedding special. Mama has sat up night after night sewing the sequins on my gown. I'm sorry to complain so much."

"It's all right, Babycakes. This is a big step. I've been looking forward to it since we were kids."

"I've dreamed about it."

Lila grins and the sparkle comes back to her eyes. We hold each other tight, and then kiss passionately, shutting out everything except our love.

Even though Lila has been saying she doesn't want a fancy wedding, you wouldn't know it on the big day, July 23, 1960. She is glowing. She seems to float down the aisle, with her dad holding her arm to keep her off the ceiling. The church is crowded and the funeral home fans are keeping the guests' hands busy.

There must be 200 people in the pews. About half are invited and the others have crashed the party. Some of them I have never seen before. I think, "These folks must be from out of town. Maybe they came with the volunteer wedding planners Lila was complaining about. But it's all fun!"

A few of the guests bring food to the reception downstairs and plop it on the tables so carefully laid out by the church ladies. Lila frowns at this, but I say, "Let's just roll with it, Babycakes." She smiles and I see the tension melting.

The DJ is playing Mashed Potatoes by James Brown and the Famous Flames. I tell Lila, "Let's dance." I don't like to brag, but I can get down on the dance floor. Lila unbuttons the train from her gown, throws it over the chair and we are off. She moves her feet energetically, following my lead. Soon everybody is jamming on the floor. We have a natural party, a few feet below the church pews. Of course, no liquor is served.

On our wedding day, Lila Mae is still a virgin. She has always demanded that I respect her. I know she is worth waiting for.

My dalliance with Lessie in high school is a distant memory. We say our vows, realizing we are really both rookies at lovemaking. Still, we recall all kinds of stories from our friends. Guys brag a lot in the locker room. Plus Lila used to read those romance magazines growing up.

That evening, I take Lila to the Paradise Motel about thirty miles away. It is black owned, neat and comfortable. We aren't welcome in white hotels in Georgia in 1960. When we walk into our room, I think, "At last, this woman is all mine. I've waited a long time for this moment." Lila willingly, joyfully gives up her virginity that night. Sure enough, she spots the sheets when I push through.

My wife is affectionate and submissive in bed. It is the one place where she really lets me take the lead. I am in heaven.

After coffee the next morning, we drive home to our farm. Lila asks me to get in the bed so she can serve me breakfast in bed. It is a dream of hers. I laugh, "There's not much food here. I didn't have a chance to buy groceries. You may have to serve cereal."

Her body droops, arms dangling, mouth turned down. A few seconds later, she perks up like some coach just gave her a pep talk. "It will be the best cereal you ever ate, served with love." Next comes the surprise. When my wife opens the cabinets, there is food galore. The refrigerator is stocked too. I say, "Somebody's mama has been here."

"Maybe two mamas. It's too early for Santa Claus."

Lila starts cooking. I lie under the covers, completely at peace as I watch my wife doing her best to please me. After we eat, she lies down beside me and cuddles. Soon, we are making love. From that day forward, she never denies me.

I hear other fellows talk about how their wives pretend to have headaches, but Lila seems to enjoy being intimate with me as much as I do with her. She has lots of sexual energy, which makes us very compatible. In other areas of our lives, we are equal partners. I respect her brain power and she listens to my ideas. She is a good cook and I faithfully wash the dishes. We work together.

We are a good match moneywise, too. Lila knows how to live on a budget. I don't have to worry about her spending every dime we earn. We both believe in putting away a little money every payday, even when times are tight. That allows us to plan for our future and the children we will have. Lila even fixes her own hair and sews some of her own clothes. Thank God she took home economics in high school. We are grateful that my mother gave Lila her old sewing machine. Both sets of parents look out for us.

Lila and I are active at Mt. Carmel Baptist Church and have a prayer life at home. She teaches the primary class of Sunday School and I am an usher at church. Every other Sunday afternoon, we have dinner with her family or mine that first year except for the times we have church fellowship dinners. We settle into a regular routine.

We have our own separate activities too. On Friday nights, I go to the pool hall to have fun with my friends. I often beat my buddies because I am a natural when it came to the cue stick. Lila and her girlfriends play bid whist every other week. Their whist club meets in the members' homes on a rotating basis. She gets a kick out of those games. There is a lot of preparation because the ladies try to outdo each other with their refreshments.

The only thing missing in our lives is having children. After spending the first year of marriage getting established as husband and wife, I am ready for fatherhood. Lila is willing, but not as excited about the idea as I am. We don't use birth control and we make love frequently, but month after month nothing happens. Finally, we go to see Dr. Roper. He says we might be trying too hard and just need to relax and let things take their course. He also raises the issue of adoption, but I really want my own child. I decide to stop obsessing over it and trust that it will happen in due time.

Life goes on pretty smoothly until the morning my mother calls from Dallas, North Carolina. She and Papa moved there seven months earlier and built a house on the 350 acres of land his family owns. Mama says, "I had to rush Papa to the hospital in Gastonia. He had a pretty serious heart attack. I'm so scared for him."

"I'll be right there, Mama, as soon as I can get up there. Don't worry."

I take off right away and end up staying in Dallas over two weeks. The doctors move Papa to a bigger hospital in Charlotte and Mama and I commute back and forth every day. Then, she has to be hospitalized because all the stress and worry breaks her body down. I am up there supporting my parents, but missing my wife. I can smell Lila's warm, sensuous body scent and I desperately yearn to be with her.

When I get back home, Lila Mae greets me with so much affection. I am a happy man, thrilled to be in the saddle again. She has a special kind of energy that first night I'm back. Life falls into a routine until a month later when Lila starts throwing up. She says she thinks it is a virus, but I think it might be the baby we want so badly.

Lila thinks the baby is a girl. For some reason, I start thinking about the first born of Fanny and Charlie Jenkins. Carla's life ended way too soon. I vow to protect this little girl, starting in her mama's belly. At night, I gently rub Lila's belly and talk baby talk to our child. About midway into the pregnancy, I am thrilled to feel the baby kicking. I think, "She has strong legs! Maybe she'll run track like me and Lila." I joke with Lila about our future track star. Some evenings I ask if our daughter has been practicing. I make sure Lila is eating right and getting her rest. When we have sex, I am careful not to go in too deep. My world revolves around my wife and my baby.

Somehow, though, Lila isn't very excited about this baby. She looks sad sometimes. I think, "Maybe the baby is draining her energy. I have no idea how it feels to be pregnant." I decide to call my mother in North Carolina. Mama explains, "When a woman is pregnant, all her hormones go crazy. That can make her moody. It can make her have cravings for certain foods. Lila has no control over those feelings. Just be patient, JJ. And let her know you love her as her body is changing."

Meanwhile, my wife has me completely in the dark. She's keeping a secret about fooling around while I'm out of town, thinking about her. She goes all the way through the pregnancy letting me think the baby is mine. She later says she thought maybe it was. I wonder if she was hoping for a miracle or just trying to fool me.

Nothing has ever hurt me as much as that betrayal. My heart aches and I feel so ashamed in front of our friends and neighbors. I'm thinking, "I don't know how much they know, but they must have figured out that I have been played for a fool. How can I live in our little community and see these people every day? What are they saying behind my back? Little Bessie doesn't look anything like me. Those bluish gray eyes stand out like a neon sign announcing that she isn't mine. If she just looked a little like me, I might have been able to swallow my pride and save my marriage."

I have loved Lila almost my whole life. She's like another part of me. From day one, her energy and my energy have blended together to form a powerful bond. All this time, I've been thinking, "Lila and I have a love that will last forever. I would do anything for her and I trust her completely. I know her almost as well as I know myself."

Then, she shocks me with this betrayal. I know she's only human, but she knows how much she means to me. In my mind, I see us living out our lives together. I tell her, "Lila, I'm going to protect you and love you until the end of our days." After I find out about her affair or "foolish mistake" as she calls it, I know things can never be the same. Not with that light brown haired, hazel eyed baby.

After Lila Mae admits what she has done, she tells me Bessie's father has died and left the child fifty thousand dollars in Lila's care. That's like pouring salt in the wound. I'm working hard to give my family a good life and he leaves her fifty thousand dollars. I can't believe that Lila and that guy have not been in touch with each other. If he hadn't died, she might have run off with him. She swears she wouldn't have, but who knows? I am confused and dazed. I can't even punch the guy in the face because he is dead. Maybe God knows best.

Right in the middle of my shock and confusion, Lila Mae packs up and leaves with Bessie. I have no idea where they are and her family doesn't tell me. Her mama says she doesn't know either. Lila might have been trying to spare me more pain, but I feel worse being all alone. I feel like there is really no way out.

I hate that Bessie has to start off her life like that. I love kids. At times, I think about her and Lila and wish I could see them again. I wonder how they are doing. Lila's sister, Gwen, knows where they are but she just says they went up north.

"I don't mean them any harm, Gwen."

"You hardened your heart and didn't give Lila Mae a chance. Your wife really does love you."

"I'd like to believe that." I know I need to give up the resentment and forgive her after all this time. Staying mad doesn't help her or me.

At this point, six weeks have passed since Lila ran away with Bessie. I have been going to work like a robot and walking around with my head hanging down. I am lost in a dark, deep hole and everybody can see that. Fortunately, people have sense enough not to ask me about my wife and child. They know. One funny guy tries to crack a joke, but my friends shut him up. Nobody seems to know what to say to me, so they say nothing. One of the church ladies pats me on the back on Sunday, and I look at her blankly. I feel half angry and half guilty, disconnected from everything and everybody.

On Thursday my best friend, Tyree, calls to say "Man, the guys at the pool hall are bragging that they believe they can beat you since you haven't played for a while. You need to come back and whip their sorry behinds. I know you can do it. Why don't I pick you up Friday evening?" He must have called at just the right moment because I say, "Yes. I'll show them a thing or two. Come pick me up around seven."

I open up to Tyree as we drive to the pool hall. After listening to my complaints for a while, he turns philosophical on me. He says, "I've heard that whatever happens to a person, happens for a reason. There's a lesson you are supposed to learn." I ask, "What kind of lesson am I supposed to learn from my wife having another man's baby and leaving me? I loved that girl and she played me."

Tyree is through coddling me. He replies, "Maybe you loved the ideal Lila Mae, the one you created in your imagination over the years. The one you chased after and talked about constantly. As long as she fit your mental picture, you were content. You gave her some leeway, but

58

basically you were in control. When the weaknesses of the real person showed up, you lost control. You were thinking, 'This can't be my Lila Mae. She doesn't act like this.' You had the girl on a pedestal, JJ. You couldn't let her reveal her whole self. You just saw part of her. When she fell off the pedestal, you couldn't pick her up. You went into shock. Not saying I blame you. It was a tough situation. But Lila Mae saw no way out except to leave. Maybe that was for the best. If God gives you another chance, you can learn to accept that person, warts and all."

I just stare at Tyree, but I hear what he's saying. Something in me shifts. That evening, I am unstoppable at the pool table. I win game after game.

The following Monday, the preacher comes by and tells me that God is still watching over me. Rev. Griffin tells me to lay my burdens at the feet of the Lord and He will give me peace. That night, I pray and I cry for hours. I ask God to stay with me and help me to heal. I feel like He hears me. The next morning, I find myself smiling for the first time in weeks.

One Saturday morning about eight-thirty, I hear a knock on the door. I open it and I'm surprised to see Lessie Ann Miller standing there with a foil covered tray in her hands. I say, "Good morning. What brings you over here?" She replies, "Oh, I've been thinking about you and decided to bring you some of my banana-walnut pancakes, sorghum syrup, fried apples and sausages. Are you hungry?" I rub my hand across the stubble on my face and answer, "I guess I am. Come on in."

She sits down at the kitchen table and watches me devour that tasty breakfast. We talk casually about the weather, church, and such. We avoid entirely any discussion of Lila Mae and Bessie Ella. When she leaves, I realize that the visit has lifted my spirits.

The next day, we have a church dinner after the service. Lessie is on the food and hospitality committee and has baked three of her memorable sweet potato pies for dessert. I pick up a slice of pie when I get my dinner, to make sure all of it doesn't get away before I can taste it. After that, we have a joint service with two other churches featuring all of our choirs. I sit with Lessie at that service and we keep sitting together in church from that day forward, except for the days I usher. I know people will talk, but it comforts me to sit next to somebody who really cares for me. I become aware that she has loved me for years.

With Lila Mae around, I couldn't really appreciate Lessie. I was blinded by the energy and glow surrounding Lila Mae. To this day, there is a special place in my heart where my first love lives. That place stores memories of intense joy and pain, the highest and the lowest of emotions. With Lessie, my feelings are more in the middle range. With her, I am comfortable but not ecstatic. Her quiet, steady manner calms me down and sustains me. I love her in a completely different way.

After Lila Mae has been gone about a year, I receive a certified letter from a lawyer in Washington, D. C. The letter says my wife has filed for divorce on the grounds of separation for one year. There are papers for me to sign. I haven't really thought much about a divorce, but deep down in my soul I have known it was a possibility. Lila asks for full custody of Bessie and there is no request for child support. At that point, Lessie has been hinting about my getting a divorce. I haven't been ready to do that because even the thought of going to court in Macon is so upsetting to me.

Even as I re-read the papers from Washington, I am surprised by the surge of conflicting emotions that I feel. Growing up, I never expected to be divorced. And now, even if I sign the papers, I don't know if I want to marry again. My thoughts run in all directions. "I love Lessie, but what if she betrays me too? I can't go through that again. Lessie has never done anything to make me doubt her. Except she did date Ralph Calhoun in high school and he still lives in Macon. I know I'm being suspicious and jealous, but it's hard for me to trust anybody now. Maybe Lessie and I can live together for a while. Nah. That won't sit too well with Rev. Gibson. He thinks the world of Lessie. Her parents won't like it either." I decide not to do anything until I give myself more time to think about it.

After about two weeks, I call my mother and tell her about the situation. She listens patiently as I describe my dilemma. Then she advises me, "Let go and let God handle things. Ask Him to guide you, and we will be praying for His guidance too. He'll show you what to do."

That night, I pray in earnest and turn my problem over to the Lord. Nothing happens at first. Ten days later, I receive a second notice from the lawyer in Washington. As soon as I open it, something inside me says, "It's time." I realize that this is God's answer to my prayers. I sign the papers and mail them the next day. All of a sudden I feel lighter, like a big load has been lifted from my shoulders. I still don't tell Lessie. I want to wait until the divorce is final.

Two and a half months later, I receive a copy of court papers from Lila Mae's lawyer stating that the divorce has been granted. That evening, I go to Lessie's house for dinner. The tablecloth features a daisy print. My heart skips a beat. As we sit on the porch swing afterwards, I tell her that Lila Mae and I are divorced. She is shocked but clearly delighted and relieved. She asks, "Why didn't you tell me this was going on?" I reply, "Lila Mae filed papers up North and I signed them. She handled everything, so I decided to wait until it was all over. I got the court decree today."

I tell Lessie I have been on an emotional roller coaster and I need some time before marrying again. Seeing the distress and disappointment in her face, I say "It's better for me to come into the marriage with stable emotions so that we can have a stronger relationship. I'm still healing."

Lessie's eyes silently ask if I still love Lila Mae. I give her a reassuring hug, look into those questioning eyes and I say, "I love you, Lessie." This is the first time I have uttered these three words since we have been seeing each other. She kisses me passionately.

Five months later, I give Lessie an engagement ring. We don't immediately set a wedding date. In about six months, when Lessie tells me she is pregnant, we decide on a small church wedding the following month. In fact, we get married right after the 11 o'clock service and all the members, our parents and our closest friends are there. These are people who watched us grow up and who care about us.

Now, six years later, we have three children. They all look like their daddy, although they have some of Lessie's sweet features too. I have regained my respect. I feel like God has given me the woman who is best for me. She even works by my side as we build an addition to the house. She's a patient and kind mother, too. My parents adore Lessie and they're crazy about their grandchildren. Yes sir, Lessie takes good care of me, and I love her cooking! I've put on a few pounds. She's gained some weight and she snores pretty loud, but nobody's perfect. Life is good.

Section Three

Henry Ray Lofton

All the world's a stage and all the men
And women merely players.

- William Shakespeare

Hello. I'm Henry Ray Lofton. Got a moment? I see by your badge that you're visiting with the Patient Outreach group. While everybody else is in the social room listening to the singing, I'd like to tell you a very interesting story. My story. Come over here and have a seat. Make yourself comfortable. I won't take too much of your time.

I am like James Weldon Johnson's poem, "blacker than a hundred midnights down in a cypress swamp." That line is from his poem, "The Creation," that my class memorized in the ninth grade. That's when the lighter skinned kids nicknamed me Midnight, and they did not mean it as a compliment. They had learned from some of the white folks that if you were very dark, you were nothing. At the bottom of the barrel. At first I was hurt by my classmates' teasing, but my mama told me they were ignorant. After that, I refused to believe what they were saying because they didn't know any better. Now, I'm very comfortable in my black skin.

Look, my skin is still smooth and velvety, and hear my voice -- deep like a well in dry country. Sometimes, when I am talking, people will turn their heads to see where that deep bass voice is coming from. I get a kick out of that.

Several years ago, I started exercising three days a week to make the most of my five foot nine inch frame. I was born with a little limp, but that adds to my charm. Too much perfection can be boring. Heh, heh, heh.

I always did like to study people, especially those who boarded The Southern Express somewhere along the route from New Orleans to New York City. One such passenger on my train was Lila Mae Jenkins. At the time I met Lila Mae, I was thirty-eight years old and working as a Pullman porter on the train. In those days, that was a good paying job because we had a union, thanks to A. Phillip Randolph. The tips were nice too. Pullman porters were a step above redcaps who helped people with their luggage. We also provided service to our guests throughout their stay on the train. All of us were Afro-American men and proud to wear the uniform. We served with dignity and good humor.

The train stopped in Atlanta on the afternoon of September 18, 1964 as usual. As I jumped down from the car and placed a step stool on the platform, I spotted this tall, shapely girl. She was carrying a baby and a small bag, rushing to board the train. Another woman, more stacked, lumbered along beside her, half dragging a large suitcase.

When they got near the entrance of my car, I could see that they were both fine, but the girl with the baby had the saddest face I had ever seen. She looked like somebody had just put her through a wringer and hung her out to dry. She clutched the child as her companion struggled to lift the brown, battered suitcase onto the car. I immediately reached out to help them.

The two women hugged as the younger lady and child boarded. There was a crowd leaving Atlanta that afternoon, so I temporarily lost track of the distressed mother. Apparently some gentleman helped her put the suitcase away in her car.

Around dusk, I left my passengers in the Pullman sleeping car to look for the unhappy young mother. I walked through the cars and found her staring out of the window as her baby girl lay sleeping on the adjacent seat wrapped in a blanket. The train could get pretty cool at night. It was hard to regulate the temperature. The woman shivered. I spoke up. "Are you cold? I can get you a blanket from the Pullman car." She looked up gratefully and replied, "Yes, please bring me a blanket. I didn't realize it would be this cold in here."

A few minutes later, I returned with the navy blue blanket plus a cup of hot coffee. Smiling, I said, "This should do the trick. I can't have a pretty lady like you uncomfortable on the train." She reached for her purse to give me a tip, but I said, "Don't worry about the tip. You can pay me with a smile. There's nothing so bad that you've got to look that serious."

She sighed, "You just don't know." Wrapping herself in the blanket, she stared into the shadows of the passing landscape. The seat across from her was vacant and things were quiet on the train, so I decided to break the rules and sit down. "It might help to talk about it," I said. She looked at me, but said nothing. It wasn't like a mean look. It was a helpless look, like she didn't know where to start. She turned toward the window again, slowly sipping the coffee and fingering the blanket. I just sat there and let her take her time.

Finally, she looked straight at me and blurted out, "I'm going to New York to start a new life." I said, "That's pretty heavy. I gather the old one was not very satisfactory."

"Nope," she said, taking another sip of coffee and nervously fingering her daisy necklace.

"Have you ever been to New York?"

"No."

"You know somebody in New York?"

"My cousin. I wrote to him four days ago. I don't have his phone number, but I can find him."

"New York is a big place. And you have a baby. You can get lost running all over the city trying to find your cousin. How do you know your cousin wants to be found? And when was the last time you heard from him?"

"It's been a while. But I heard that he was doing well up there."

I was getting concerned about this young lady. "Have you thought about what you will do if you can't find him?" I asked.

"I don't know." Tears were forming in those beautiful brown eyes.

"Look, you don't need to go to New York chasing a shadow," I said. "I'm getting off this train in Washington. I have a room there and my landlady has a vacant room to rent. It's in a big row house in a nice neighborhood."

"What's a row house?"

"Row houses are joined together. There is no space between them, but they are spacious and attractive. Why don't you rent the vacant room there? At least you and the baby will have a roof over your head until you figure out your next move."

Her strained face relaxed. "Maybe that would be a good idea," she said.

"I will call my landlady so that everything will be ready when we arrive."

A big grin lit up her face. "Thank you," she gushed.

"A smile at last!" I got up and hurried toward the dining car where I could make a call.

From Union Station in Washington, we took a cab to Ontario Road in the Adams Morgan area. I paid the driver and we managed to get the bags and the baby up the steps and inside the door of the house. Mrs. Mitchell, the landlady, was waiting to greet us. I introduced Lila Mae and Bessie to Mrs. Mitchell. She liked them right away. Lila moved into a spacious room on the second floor around the corner from Mrs. Mitchell's bedroom. My landlady was a widow. Her house was paid off by insurance at her husband's death. With two rooms rented, she was doing pretty well financially.

After Lila Mae was settled in her room, I got my rolling cart and we walked to the Safeway grocery store on Columbia Road. Mrs. Mitchell was kind enough to babysit Bessie. I showed Lila Mae some neighborhood markers, like the bus stop and the dry cleaners. I bought a few things and Lila bought supplies for herself and Bessie. When we got back home, Mrs. Mitchell had prepared lunch for all of us.

"Now, don't expect this every day," she said. "This is a welcome to Washington lunch." The sadness in Lila's face had given way to a warm smile as she realized she had found a temporary haven. Between Mrs. Mitchell and me, we told Lila how to get downtown, to the National Zoo, and to a couple of local churches.

When Lila mentioned that she'd like to buy a good used car and had the money saved to pay for it, Mrs. Mitchell had a solution. Her sister, Helen, bought a new car every two years and was about to do so that very week. Helen kept her cars in excellent condition, but always wanted the latest model. With Lila's consent, Mrs. Mitchell called Helen at work. That evening, Helen drove up to the curb in her

Volkswagen Beetle and a deal was struck. Lila knew how to negotiate and she got a good price. The women agreed to close the deal in two days.

I was amazed that Lila Mae had that much money saved up. That was unusual for a woman her age. I thought, "There is more to this young woman than meets the eye." She had revealed almost nothing about her life, only that she was from Macon, Georgia and had just left her husband. I could tell that she had class, though. Her posture was perfect and she had good manners. Still, there was a mysterious edginess about her, like a not quite housebroken tigress.

My own life was somewhat muddled at that point. Back in New Orleans, I was staying in a kind of temporary situation, trying to figure out my next move. I guess you could say I was in a rut.

Everything changed when I met Lila. When I first saw her, my heart thumped. It was like I knew her from somewhere. She said I seemed familiar too. I felt like I couldn't lose track of her. I wanted her to be a significant part of my life. Still, I needed to find out where she was coming from before I made my move.

When I left D. C. for the run to New York, I couldn't get Lila Mae out of my mind. When I met her, she looked so lost. I mean, she was in a daze on the train. I felt like she needed me to help her through whatever was making her life miserable. Be her protector. She was sincerely grateful to me. Still, I had my own problems.

On the trip to New York, I found time to talk to my old friend and fellow porter, Ben. I told him I felt I was at a crossroads in my life. I reminded him that I had a messy situation in New Orleans, a sick wife in a marriage that died long ago but was not legally terminated.

"Ben, I went to the courthouse and filed for divorce three months ago. We're already legally separated and have been for five years. Still, Bettina refuses to sign the divorce papers. She's basing it on the technicality that I moved back into the house, but that was only to help her with expenses. We have absolutely no romantic relationship. It's a practical matter. She's retired on disability. Even though the mortgage is paid off, she can't afford to pay the utility bills, the real estate taxes and her medical expenses. Otherwise, I could put the house in her name only and be through with it. She refuses to sell the house, which has both our names on it, and she won't go to an apartment or a nursing home. She's stubborn as a mule."

"Why did you move back in, Henry?"

"If I am going to be paying real estate taxes and utilities on the house, why should I also be paying rent on an apartment? I'm only there about two days a week, as you know. We have separate bedrooms. I have my life and she has hers. It just seems practical. Still, I'm tired of it. I'd like to end this arrangement and end the marriage."

"You say she's sick. Does she have enough insurance?"

"That's the other problem. I'm carrying her on my insurance. She lost hers when she retired. If we divorce, the health insurance company won't let her continue on my policy. She could qualify for some kind of welfare if she sold the house, but she won't do it."

"Man, I'm not a lawyer, but it looks like she's got you in a bind."

"Yeah. Now I've met someone that I find fascinating. I don't know if anything will develop or not, but the New Orleans situation is like a noose around my neck. I don't know what to do. I don't hate Bettina. She's the one that got me this job. Her cousin was a porter. As you know, you have to be "sponsored" by someone to get in the union. You can't just walk in off the street. She persuaded her cousin to speak up for me and open some doors. I did owe her for that, but I have paid in full by now.

"I bought one of the nicer houses in the lower Ninth Ward, a large frame house. Then, I had it brick veneered. When I got an inheritance, I paid it off. She's been enjoying it for fourteen years. I just want to be free. She can have the house."

"There must be something she wants. Ask her what she wants out of this. Why is she holding on to this marriage when she knows you want out? See if she'll tell you. Don't go down there and threaten her with divorce again. Just ask what she wants."

"I guess it's worth a try. But suppose she says she wants me to be her loving husband?"

"Let her know she can't have you. That's over. Unless you can think back over the good times and find a reason to stay."

"I did that reflecting thing years ago. It was like jumping into the middle of a brier patch trying to find a speck of gold dust. Our marriage failed early on. There's no reason to stay."

"Man, you've really made up your mind."

"I'll let you know how the conversation turns out."

As the train rumbled into New Orleans, I braced for the challenge that I knew was coming. I took a cab to my home near the mighty Mississippi River. Bettina was on the front porch watering the hanging plants. She loved flowers, but they were much fewer in number now that she lacked the strength to care for them properly. I walked through the scrolled iron gate and up the walk carrying my travel bag.

"Hello, Henry. How was your trip this time?"

"A little tiring. How are you doing?"

"Not too good. My emphysema is acting up. I have to use a breathing machine more often. They gave me a unit to keep at home so I wouldn't have to keep running to the hospital."

"That sounds serious. Be sure to follow the doctor's orders." Bettina had been a chain smoker since her early teenage years and her addiction finally caught up with her. She had a hard time quitting even after she found out she had emphysema. Doctors had to remove one lung. Now, even moderate exertion caused labored breathing and coughing.

I walked into my room and closed the door. Sitting in the old rocking chair, I pondered my strategy. With her worsening condition, it seemed to me she needed a companion or caregiver around. Better still, she could go to a nursing home where people were always on duty. She shouldn't stay by herself. Her mother and sister live in Texas. Maybe she could move in with them. I'll just lay out some choices and see how she responds. But first, I'll ask what she wants.

I walked into the living room where Bet was hooked up to the portable respirator, watching TV. Her lack of physical activity had added at least fifty pounds to her already full figure. That couldn't be good.

"Bet, I'm concerned about you being on that respirator and living here alone. You know my job keeps me gone all the time. Have you thought about what you want to do about this situation?"

"You could change jobs and spend more time at home."

"No, I'm not going to change jobs. I like what I'm doing. It's your life we're talking about. You do have options. What about moving to Texas where your mother and sister can help you?"

"I see you're still trying to get rid of me. I told you I don't believe in divorce."

"Do you believe in a loveless marriage? There's nothing between us and you know it."

"You're trying to upset me!" she cried, reaching for a box of tissues. Then she began to cough. She spit into a container on the table beside her recliner, then coughed several more times. Finally, the coughing subsided.

"I think you should talk to a counselor or your minister or somebody. You're sick and you need to be near your relatives or in a nursing home where people can attend to you. I'll help you financially. I don't have a problem with that."

"Why can't I be with you?"

"Bettina, that's over. I need to move on and so do you."

"I'm not going to Texas and I'm not going into a nursing home."

"You're not taking good care of yourself. The last time I was here, I looked in the cupboard. It was full of junk food. You're not eating healthy food. You're just letting yourself go downhill. Are you depressed?"

"I want my husband back."

"Even before we separated, we argued all the time. We're not right for each other."

"But we're not separated now. You're here."

"If that's the way you're looking at it, I will make plans to move out. This time, I won't be back. Maybe that will stimulate you to do something positive for yourself. Please get some counseling. I'll pay for it. Just get some help."

Bet slumped down in her chair and began to cry. I had to get out of there and just walk around to clear my head. I thought, "This relationship is dragging me down. Talking with Bet is like being sucked into a dark hole. I can't reason with her, and she won't get help."

I checked out the want ads, but did not find a room right away. I decided to concentrate on finding a place on my next trip down. Meanwhile, I packed up the items I wanted to take with me. The next day, I went back to work on the Southern Express.

This time, I went all the way to New York. Ben lived there, and I visited with his family for a couple of days. When I told him what happened in New Orleans, he agreed that I had to move out of the house there. He suggested that I move my home base to Washington, so that most of my time off would be in that city. I liked the idea.

I returned to Ontario Road five days after I left there. Lila Mae had her Beetle and was studying to get a D. C. driver's license. In talking with Helen, she had learned the process for applying for a government job. This girl was on the ball. When I found out she had a year of college behind her, I advised her to go back to school so she could earn more money. She listened. Mrs. Mitchell offered to babysit Bessie.

Lila had some experience working in a grocery store, so she took a temporary job at the Safeway up the street. Then, she applied to enroll at Howard University on Georgia Avenue. Apparently she had good grades from Spelman because she was accepted at Howard and her freshman year credits were accepted. In January, Lila began taking sophomore classes. Later, she received a scholarship for full time study at Howard. She decided on a major in economics and a minor in social studies.

I thought I was just helping Lila Mae through a phase as I rolled toward D. C. on the Southern Express the day we met, but over the next few months I fell in love. Later on, I convinced myself that she loved me like I loved her. If she didn't, I would win her over and make her love me. I was frankly concerned about the young dudes she was meeting at Howard. They would certainly be more educated than me. I figured experience was my strong suit. I was kind of a loving father figure. And I was making good money. I tried to demonstrate that she could depend on me financially and every other way.

For job purposes, I changed my home base to D. C. instead of New Orleans, as Ben advised. I spent most of my days off with Lila and Bessie. Lila made friends at the college, but I guess they mostly had lunch or study sessions together on campus. She kept her school life and home life separate. Once in a while, she would mention a project she was doing in a class.

When Lila came home, she had to cook, do laundry and housework and take care of Bessie. I shared some of her precious free time when I was in town. The Smiths, who lived down the street, had a young son named Colin. They offered to babysit some evenings and I offered to foot the bill. With this arrangement, I took Lila out to dinner at some of the ethnic restaurants in Adams Morgan. We also enjoyed the jazz and blues clubs in both Georgetown and Adams Morgan. We dropped in to the Bohemian Caverns on U Street once to hear Lionel Hampton. The sad young lady I first met was happy and spirited at this point, quite a transformation.

Lila seemed to view me as a good friend for a long time, but I noticed that her feelings were starting to change. Her eyes sparkled when I arrived at the house. Bessie always ran to greet me and I would toss her in the air and play with her. Then I'd give Lila a quick hug and a kiss on the cheek. I was willing to wait and take things slowly. I didn't want to risk running her away. Mrs. Mitchell thankfully stayed out of our business.

Before I realized it, a year had passed. It was the happiest year of my life. Lila had taught Bessie to call me Uncle Ray. I spoiled the child with little gifts and played with her like a father. I believed the look in Lila's eyes was more than gratitude. After all, she had not brought home any of the young college men. She respected me.

Back in New Orleans, I was renting a room for my overnight stays. I still checked on Bettina and sometimes took her some groceries. She had not changed her mind about the divorce. Ben had done some research on my options. He said I could file for divorce in D. C. and say that I did not know Bettina's current address. That way, I could advertise in any New Orleans newspaper that I had filed for divorce. The ad would have to run for five days. The key would be putting the ad in a Jewish newspaper with a small circulation. She would never see it. I liked the idea. All other options seemed to be closed. I launched the process.

On one of my days off, I suggested to Lila that we take Bessie to the zoo, as we had done several times before. Lila told Bessie the name of each animal as we moved along. After stopping for a snack, we visited Bessie's favorite creatures, the monkeys and apes. She reached up to be taken out of the stroller so that she could walk around like the older children. While the child gazed at the monkeys, I slipped my arm around Lila's waist. I said, "You are a dedicated mother. In fact, you are a very special lady. I have enjoyed every minute that we have spent together over the last year."

She looked puzzled. "Is this a farewell speech? I have enjoyed being with you too and I hope we can continue to have fun together."

I looked her in the eye. "Lila, I really like you, and I want you to consider moving beyond friendship and having fun. I want you to be my lady."

She smiled. "In a way, I guess I already am. I don't have another boyfriend. The guys at school seem so immature compared to you. They're interested but I'm not. Then there's the fact that I'm still married and I haven't taken any steps toward getting a legal separation or a divorce. I have settled into a routine of going to school, working, taking care of Bessie and going out with you. You've never pressured me and I've appreciated that. I have needed this time to heal."

"Want to talk about it? The wound you are healing?" I asked. She shook her head from side to side. "No. I just need to take action," she said. "And I will. I know I can get a no fault divorce here based on one year of separation if my husband signs the papers."

By this time, Bessie had grown tired of the monkeys and was getting restless. Lila placed her in the stroller and gave her a bottle filled with apple juice. We walked in silence for a while, lost in our thoughts. Bessie soon fell asleep. I said, "Let's go home." Lila nodded agreement. We reached the parking lot and placed the sleeping toddler in the car.

I started the ignition, and then turned to face Lila. I asked, "Since you have decided to start legal proceedings with your husband, are you willing to let me get closer to you? I've wanted to for a long time." She answered by touching my cheeks with both hands and gently guiding my mouth toward hers. Her tongue played across my lips and soon we were engaged in a long, passionate kiss. I explored her mouth with my tongue, and then she deeply inserted hers. I hadn't expected such a dramatic response. The normally cautious tigress had emerged from her cage.

Fortunately, Mrs. Mitchell had gone away for the weekend. When we returned home, we fed Bessie and put her to bed. Then, I invited Lila to my room. As she entered the door and dropped her robe, I gasped. Lila's body was even more beautiful than I had imagined. Her breasts were full and perky, her nipples prominent with desire. She had smooth skin, a tiny waist and the cutest belly button. Her round butt was firm and sexy. There was no flabbiness anywhere.

I sat in bed with a sheet covering me, and there was a large protrusion lifting it up. I could not mask my desire for her, nor did I try. We embraced and explored each other's bodies. I hoped the Listerine I had just gargled was not too overpowering for her. Lila's mouth tasted fresh like Mother Nature in spring. When I pushed into her garden, her hot moist flower closed tightly around me. I yielded completely to my pent up passion. Thus began a new phase in our relationship.

Lila, Bessie and I were truly like a family, with me coming and going because of the job. Whenever we went out, people stared. I didn't know if it was because of the age difference between me and Lila or because Bessie's appearance was so different from mine. I had wondered if her father was white, but I never asked. Lila was completely closed on the few occasions that I brought up the subject of her life in Georgia. I knew that she talked with her sister regularly. Apparently, she also communicated with her parents now and then. Something didn't seem right, but I didn't probe. She respected my privacy and I respected hers. I never talked with her family and she never talked with mine.

Both my parents were dead anyway, and my step-brother lived somewhere in Illinois. I wasn't sure where. Daddy died soon after selling his riverfront farm acreage to some developers. He made a killing and left me half a million dollars in his will. I'm a good money manager. I paid off my mortgage in New Orleans and invested in stocks and treasury notes. I did not share any of this information with Lila Mae. Bettina didn't know about it either because Daddy died while Bet and I were separated.

By the time Bessie was two years old, she was running all over the house, getting into things, opening drawers and spilling stuff as toddlers will. Mrs. Mitchell was a meticulous housekeeper and I could tell that Bessie was tiring her out. Still she loved the little girl.

I suggested that Lila and I move out of our rooms at Mrs. Mitchell's house and buy our own place. Lila was uncomfortable with the idea of buying a house together without marriage. She suggested getting her own apartment, but I said that would be throwing money down the toilet. She was still married to that farmer down in Georgia. She had had divorce papers drawn up and mailed to him, but he had not responded. Common sense told me that I shouldn't marry her until I got my own affairs in order, but I didn't know if my solution to that problem would work. The divorce ad would run in New Orleans under Legal Notices in about ten days.

Lila contacted her lawyer and asked him to send a follow-up letter to her husband in Georgia. The letter stated that she would not require child support. She didn't tell me anything else. For some reason, she wanted to close off this part of her life by herself. All I knew about her husband was that his name was Jimmy. Lila said he didn't understand her and the marriage was frustrating. After receiving the follow-up letter, Jimmy decided to sign the divorce papers. In a few weeks, the decree was granted and Lila was free.

Before the divorce, Lila's light was shrouded by some darkness from the past. After she got the divorce, she was like an unshaded 1,000 watt light bulb. You couldn't miss that radiance. Even people passing her on the street could see it.

I got scared. This fine woman was single and could get just about any man she wanted. She flashed that radiant smile at everybody. I knew I couldn't be around all the time and I wondered what she was doing while I was aboard the train. I have to admit that I was jealous. I knew she had to go to school, study, work and take care of Bessie, but my imagination wouldn't let me rest. I could just see some other man trying to date her. Especially those young college men.

My situation did not go as smoothly as Lila's. By some freakish coincidence, Bettina had a Jewish doctor. He saw my ad about the divorce and asked her about it when she came in for an exam. She went off. I knew I'd have to start over.

One Friday afternoon, Lila and I were playing with Bessie in the parlor. Mrs. Mitchell was visiting her sister. Someone knocked on the door. I got up to answer it.

"Just a minute." Swinging open the door, I faced a clean cut young man wearing jeans and a Howard University sweatshirt. "May I help you?"

"Yes. I'm looking for Lila Mae Jenkins."

"She's here. Come in."

Lila heard our voices and came to the door, holding Bessie. "Hi, Carl. I was expecting you tomorrow."

"Yeah, well it turned out I didn't have to work today. I would have called, but I didn't have your number." Standing in the foyer, he grinned at her like she was made of gold.

Lila said, "Oh, let me introduce you. Carl, this is my daughter, Bessie."

"Hello cutie." Bessie eyed him warily.

"And this is my friend, Henry. Henry, this is Carl. We're working on a project together."

"Hello, Henry. I thought you were her father."

I said, "No. It's nice to meet you, Carl. Come have a seat."

Lila spoke. "Did you bring your ideas for the Economics Model we have to create?"

"Yes. I wanted to get some feedback from you."

I said, "Bessie and I will go to the kitchen for ice cream."

He didn't stay more than half an hour, but the incident stimulated me to action. Lila's divorce had been granted and this young man was obviously interested. Yes, they were working on a class project together, but his eyes spoke of other things.

My feelings were churning, echoing the social unrest in America. Malcolm X had been assassinated in February 1965. The Muslims were in an uproar, and many people of color were concerned about the direction of the country and their own prospects for full human rights. As an individual, I was seeking the best direction for my life.

Finally, my emotions overcame reason. The weekend after Carl stopped by, I proposed marriage and several days later, Lila accepted. I placed a dazzling, two carat rock on her finger. Her divorce was not supposed to become final for one year. I networked through friends to reach a judge who was willing to waive the one year wait. A few weeks later, we got married at the courthouse with Mrs. Mitchell and one of Lila's Safeway co-workers as witnesses. It was a quiet afternoon ceremony on June 15, 1965. Lila and I had dinner that evening at Trader Vic's with its warm Polynesian ambiance.

Lila contacted a real estate agent to search for a house on Capitol Hill. That area was full of once grand homes that had been allowed to deteriorate. Many had been sub-divided into apartments or rooms for rent. Absentee landlords pocketed the money and looked the other way. Then someone pointed out that these homes were a stone's throw from the Capitol Building where the nation's laws were enacted. The neighborhood deserved better.

Soon, savvy, adventurous people were buying Capitol Hill addresses at rock bottom prices and fixing the properties up. They called it urban renewal. Some blocks had several renovated houses, while other blocks still looked like the ghetto. We found a spacious home on a block where three other homes were being fixed up. Two of the houses on the block were being completely gutted, but we purchased one that didn't require such drastic measures. We repaired the roof, added insulation, had the kitchen and two bathrooms updated and installed heating and air conditioning systems before moving in. I felt that the house would be worth big money down the line. During the time we were waiting to move in to our new home, Mrs. Mitchell was able to find new tenants. The timing worked out fine for everybody.

Our marriage was off to a good start. Lila and I had a strong emotional bond. I was happier than I had been in years. That summer, I asked Lila to quit her job, since she would be responsible for maintaining our home as well as being a mother to Bessie. Whenever my train approached Union Station in D.C., I knew that I was only six blocks from a loving home. By then, I had pushed Bettina completely out of my mind.

My new wife had a good handle on interior design. She discussed her ideas with me and I discovered that she knew how to find good bargains. I gave her a fairly generous allowance for furniture and accessories. Each week, I saw progress as she put our beautiful home together.

More than anything, I wanted to help Lila achieve her dreams. She was such an exciting, vibrant woman and a very satisfying bed partner. She didn't hesitate to initiate a romantic encounter when the vibrations were right.

Every now and then, she had a faraway look in her eyes. I figured that was from something in her past that she wasn't ready to share. After all, I had my own secrets. I thought it would all work out in the end.

We soon met our new neighbors, the Moores. Eddie was an army doctor at Walter Reed. He looked like a soldier, tall with perfect posture. He and his jovial wife, Janice, had been married ten years but had no children. Janice was a secretary who lost her job when her company folded. It was a hassle for Lila to take Bessie to Mrs.

Mitchell's house through morning traffic before going to class, so Janice offered to baby-sit. She and Eddie both loved children and still hoped to have their own. Soon, Janice was taking care of Bessie on weekdays. Our lives flowed in a comfortable rhythm.

Lila took summer school classes in 1965 and 1966 to make up for the time she had not been in school back in Georgia. She was focused on graduating. Focusing wasn't easy because the whole country was in an uproar. Martin Luther King and Malcolm X had stirred up the social system of the country by demanding full rights for Negroes.

By Lila Mae's senior year, 1968, college campuses were incubators for civil rights protestors, and Howard University was no exception. That year, the spirited Lila Mae jumped in with both feet. She and a few friends focused on Moodies, formally known as Moodard and Lanthrop, a local, somewhat upscale department store. It had an old style, tony Southern tea room.

The only blacks the store employed were janitors, cooks and tea room waitresses. The waitresses' uniforms were black dresses with white starched aprons featuring wide bows that had to be tied just so. Their uniforms were inspected before the women's shifts began. Their hair had to be neatly curled, or straightened and brushed back with a bun at the nape of the neck. In most cases, the bun was store bought, but that was the expected look for a Moodies waitress. The women conducted themselves like servants in a wealthy household. This made well to do people feel at home and gave other customers a chance to pretend. Just a game people play, as far as I'm concerned.

Many of these women took pride in their appearance and their work. Not just anybody off the street could be a Moodies waitress. I could identify with that because that's the way it was with porters. You had to know somebody or jump through a few hoops to become one. You were proud to wear that uniform. There was a certain status involved, and I mean that in a positive way.

The problem was that Lila Mae had grown up in a middle class family. I thought that she unconsciously looked down on blue collar people who wore uniforms. She denied this, saying that her husband was a farmer. Yet there was something in her attitude about getting "decent" jobs for black people at Moodies that bothered me. She spent long hours planning protest strategies and picketing the store with her ragtag friends. Their hippie, "anything goes" look was in sharp contrast to the attractive appearance of the waitresses they were trying to liberate. These protestors were middle class young people rebelling against their parents' ideas on neatness and decorum, while raging against the "plantation outfits" of the waitresses. Their posters showed drawings of waitresses in uniform with a big red "X" across their bodies. This was not a positive campaign. The protestors never bothered to get to know a single one of the waitresses. They were disconnected and misguided if you ask me.

I decided to give my wife a reality check. I did some networking and located a Moodies waitress, Edna Mathis, who was married to Doug Mathis, the cousin of a Pullman porter. I arranged for us to have lunch at the couple's home. I told Lila I was going to take her out to lunch. She didn't know where we were going. When we pulled up in front of the Mathis home in Northeast Washington, Lila asked, "Why are we stopping here?

"This is where we're having lunch."

"Okay, Henry. What's going on?"

"Remember what I was saying about getting to know the people you are trying to liberate? Edna Mathis, who is a Moodies waitress, lives here with her husband and son. We're having lunch with them so you'll know who you're representing with those picket signs."

"Oh, brother. Is this really necessary?"

"I think so. I think you'll learn something and so will the rest of us."

Lila sighed. She was less than enthusiastic about this little experiment. Doug saw us coming up the walk and opened the door to greet us.

"Welcome."

"Thank you. I'm Henry Lofton and this is my wife, Lila." We shook hands.

"It's good to meet you. Come in and have a seat."

The living room and dining area were contained in one large room separated by a carved mahogany buffet. I said, "That buffet is a beautiful piece of furniture."

"Edna inherited it from her grandmother, who received it in a bequest from the white woman she served as a personal maid."

"It looks very valuable. I've never seen one like it."

Yeah, I think it's worth something all right. My wife is in the kitchen. She'll be out shortly."

I asked, "Where's your son? Will he be joining us?"

"No. He's out with the Boy Scouts today, Henry. They're planning for a camping trip."

Lila smiled, "That sounds like fun."

"They are excited. Speaking of excitement, Lila, I understand that you are one of the protesters who have been picketing outside of Moodies."

"Yes. We're trying to get Moodies to open up better paying jobs to Afro-Americans."

"Edna enjoys working there. She's been there six years. Some of the women have been there twelve and fifteen years."

Just then, Edna emerged from the kitchen rolling a cart containing a vegetable casserole, baked chicken, and spoon bread. Edna was an attractive and vibrant woman. She had sparkling brown eyes, even white teeth and a smooth caramel complexion.

"Hello, I'm Edna. Welcome to our home."

"Hi. I'm Lila. Let me help you with that. It looks and smells delicious."

The women placed the food on the table, which had already been set with dishes and flatware and a lovely floral centerpiece.

"Dinner is served," Edna announced. As we took our seats, Doug and Edna held hands and reached for our hands. With the circle formed, Doug said the grace. This was different for Lila and me, although Lila had begun singing the grace with Bessie at mealtimes.

There were compliments to the cook all around as everyone enjoyed the delicious meal. Then, we got into the discussion on protesters at Moodies.

Edna asked, "How did your group of students pick Moodies as the place to protest?"

Lila said, "We had to start somewhere. Somebody mentioned that they made the waitresses dress up like maids, so we decided to picket. We want them to open up other kinds of jobs for Afro-Americans."

"Did it ever occur to you that there are people who would love to have our jobs? We always look attractive. They train us to have perfect posture and to use a warm, pleasant tone of voice. We don't just throw on an old wrinkled, greasy uniform. We must look perfect, including our hair and make-up. Not everybody can make it into our ranks. It is a privilege to be a Moodies waitress."

Lila's mouth opened in shock. When she could find her voice, she said, "We thought you were being forced to bow and scrape."

"There is no disgrace in a gracious bow. It just means that you honor the other person as a fellow human being. At least, that's what it means to me. If I thought less of myself, it might have a negative meaning. Some of the customers might think my slight bow means I see them as better than me, but they would be wrong. I like dressing in my crisp uniform and serving my customers."

"We thought we were opening up opportunities for you."

"I don't mind your trying to get better job opportunities for Afro-Americans. Just don't do it by saying there is something wrong with our job. We like what we're doing. Open up the other jobs for people who want them. I wouldn't want to be in sales or management. Please don't give the impression that a Moodies waitress is someone to be pitied."

"I…I really have to apologize. We were looking at the big picture. We never thought about how it would affect you and the other individual waitresses."

"Well, I'm glad you're here so that we can reach an understanding."

Doug added, "What Edna hasn't told you is that the waitresses are being grilled by their supervisor. The boss thinks that one of them might have contacted the student protesters and asked them to come."

"Oh, no one from Moodies called us. We were just tossing around ideas and someone thought we could get Moodies' management to change its hiring policies."

"The waitresses have been told that they will be fired if they were involved in starting the picketing. These are women with families, some of them single mothers. They need their jobs."

Edna said, "We really took a chance by having you come to our home, but after Doug talked to Henry, we thought it might do some good."

"I have a much better understanding now. We can go after better jobs without demeaning waitresses or anybody else. We can change our strategy. This has been very educational and the food is good too."

I said, "I tried to share some of these ideas with you, Lila. I thought it best to let you hear if from someone who is being potentially hurt by the protests. You don't mean to hurt anybody. Your heart is in the right place. It's just that the details and the individual people are just as important as the big picture. I wouldn't want anybody liberating me from being a porter. It's a job I love."

"I understand, Henry. I know you and your buddies are close. You have a real support network going. When you're on the outside of a situation, you don't always see the impact of your actions on other people. I've learned something today. I want to expand opportunities without hurting people. Change is hard."

"Time to switch to a sweeter subject," Edna said. "How about some key lime pie?"

Doug and I simultaneously shouted, "Yes!" We enjoyed pie and coffee, then Lila and I thanked our hosts for inviting us. On the way home, Lila was quiet. I could almost hear her mind's engine running as she processed the revelations of this day.

The protesters did change their strategy. They did not slow down, though. Civil rights activities were taking more and more of Lila's time in her senior year at Howard.

Meanwhile, Bessie was spending more and more time with the Moores. The child started calling Janice "Mama." Then, Lila's grades started to slip. She was skipping assignments and going on weekend bus trips to protest discrimination in Virginia and Maryland. She started skimping on the housework, and she had always been a neat housekeeper. She had quit her part-time job the year before at my request. I had wanted her to spend more time with me during the brief periods that I could be in Washington. Instead, she was frequently on the phone with her protest friends.

I worried about Lila's new passion. Talking to her about it only created tension and resistance. I admit I was old fashioned about some things.

"Lila, you're not keeping the house like you used to. What's going on? You were always neat before."

"Nobody's perfect, Henry. I'm spending time trying to make life better for Afro-Americans. We've been discriminated against long enough. Our Action Committee at Howard is determined to change things."

"Just make sure you remember home. Your family comes first. We need you too. The kitchen floor is a mess."

"I'm doing the best I can. I can't do everything. You know you could help out sometimes. This is important work I'm doing!"

"I'm not saying you should quit what you're doing. Just slow down some. You've changed your appearance so much, you look like a different person."

"This is the natural look. My Afro and African clothes and earrings show who I really am."

"You're mixed, and so is Bessie."

"I'm politically Afro-American."

We had variations of this heated discussion several times. I had to admit, though, Lila still kept herself neat. Her Afro was shaped beautifully, unlike some of her friends' hairdos. Still, she stopped wearing the pretty dresses I had bought for her. I wanted Negroes to prosper just like the next person, but I thought my wife was going about it the wrong way.

The last straw was when she started having strategy sessions in our home. When I arrived at Union Station following my New Orleans to Washington shift one Saturday morning, she wasn't there to pick me up. I was exhausted from a really busy night and more than the usual number of obnoxious travelers. When I called her, she said she was tied up and asked if I could take a cab. I was pissed. I decided to take the six block walk to our home, giving myself a chance to cool off.

I opened the door to find five young people sitting cross-legged on the living room floor planning a sit-in. They had beards, scruffy hair and rough dried clothes. No iron had been anywhere near their garments. There was a faint odor of pot in the air. Then I noticed sleeping bags against the wall, indicating that these protestors had spent the night in our home. I walked into the dining room where Lila Mae and another girl with a shaved head and big earrings were bent over the table making protest signs. Bessie was nowhere in sight.

I was furious. I grabbed Lila Mae by the shoulders and told her, "We need to talk right now in the bedroom." She said, "We're almost finished. I'll just be a few minutes."

At that, I bellowed, "Everybody out! Right now! Get your stuff and get out of here." The group picked up their belongings and hightailed it out of the house.

"Those are my friends. You have no right to treat them that way."

As we walked into the bedroom I asked, "Where is the baby?"

"Bessie spent the night with Janice and Eddie. They are taking her to the zoo today. She's fine."

"Lila," I said as calmly as I could, "a man has a right to be welcomed when he comes home from work. You are so involved with your friends that you have lost all sense of family responsibilities. You are disrespecting me and neglecting Bessie. I bought her a little pop-up story book and she isn't even here. Have you forgotten about your husband and child? And I smell marijuana in the house. Were you smoking?"

"No." "That was Bruce. I was in the kitchen making sandwiches when he lit the joint and started passing it around. I made him put it out."

I was stupefied. "You're feeding these people our groceries? They'll set up permanent camp here."

"They were hungry."

"You're not making any sense to me. Just get out of here. I need to sleep."

When I woke up five hours later, Lila was not at home. I showered, got dressed and walked next door. Janice Moore greeted me. "Hi, Henry. Come on in." Eddie was playing with Bessie. They were rolling a ball to each other on the living room floor. I asked them if Lila had called or come over. Janice said, "We haven't seen her since last night."

I sat down and had a heart to heart talk with the Moores. I said, "Thank you for taking care of Bessie. Her mother is going overboard with this protest phase. I don't understand it. I think Lila is neglecting the child, although she doesn't seem to realize it."

Eddie said, "We have noticed a change in Lila Mae over the last few months. We have been concerned about Bessie and we're happy to spend time with her. The only problem is I'm about to be transferred to California. I just gave a notice to our landlord that we'll be moving next month. To be honest, we hate to leave Bessie behind. We have grown so attached to her."

I jumped into the opening. "Maybe Lila had this baby too young.

She is so mesmerized by the civil rights movement that she has forgotten about being a proper mother. She's not on good terms with her parents or I would ask them to keep Bessie for a while."

Janice said, "I know that Lila loves Bessie. Otherwise, I would love to adopt her."

"She's not available for adoption," I replied, "but we may be able to work out something on a temporary basis. Just until Lila gets herself together." I took off some time from work and secretly hired a lawyer to look into temporary custody procedures. He said that getting the Moores named as guardians would be the best option. That could be handled easily and quickly, he reported. Of course, Lila Mae would have to sign the papers. I told him to prepare the paperwork and get a court date.

As it happened, Lila's father fell ill two weeks later. She decided to take time off from school and her civil rights activities to travel to Georgia and visit him in the hospital. I arranged for her to travel in a Pullman car to make the long train trip more comfortable. Then, I persuaded her easily to leave the baby with the Moores. I had the feeling she didn't really want to take Bessie to Macon. Maybe it was because she thought her ex-husband would take the child. It was the first time she had been to Macon since she boarded that train in Atlanta over three years ago.

In Lila's absence, I received the guardianship papers and signed her name on the designated line. I had not yet adopted Bessie so I did not have to sign my name. I gave the paper to the Moores, telling them that Lila had signed her name before she left on her trip. They excitedly signed the papers, went to court and got guardianship. Four days later, they left for California with Bessie.

Meanwhile, Lila Mae's father died of diabetes. They cremated him and had a memorial service. I asked her if she wanted me to come, but she said I didn't have to. I never got the chance to meet her parents. I didn't think she would take her father's death too hard, but I knew she would be upset about Bessie. I was prepared to console her.

I believed the baby would be better off at that time with two loving, stable parents. I thought, "The Moores will be good to Bessie. They will give her lots of love and probably spoil her. Lila needs time to get herself focused. All she can think about is civil rights. She will get over this. In my heart, I believe I did the right thing. Lila is messing up in her classes and just getting off course. Not having the responsibility of caring for Bessie will take some pressure off of Lila."

I suddenly realized I was going to miss the child myself. At that moment, I was overcome with emotion and I cried like a baby. It was going to be a challenge to repair my relationship with Lila. I wanted us to understand each other and be happy. We had been arguing so much lately over the changes she was going through.

When I picked up Lila Mae from the train station, I tried to prepare her for what I had done. I told her the Moores were out of town and Bessie was with them. She nodded, "Oh. Okay." I wanted to see what her mood was, following her father's death.

She said it was strange going back home after being away for more than three years. "Some things have changed. My ex-husband has remarried and his wife is pregnant with their second child. She's fat as a pig, but she is a nice person. My mother is frailer. She had been taking care of Daddy and she looks worn out. Maybe it was best that he died when he did. My sister, Gwen, says she will spend more time with Mama while she is recovering from her grief. Gwen looks good. She has lost some weight. For one thing, her husband has quit drinking after a scare over liver trouble. Things seem to be going better for them."

I asked, "Did your ex-husband ask about Bessie?" She replied, "He asked in passing, but he's really into his new family. I did the right thing to leave him when I did. And I have been thinking about what you said before I left. I really should spend more time with my daughter and with you. It's hard to focus on personal things like home and family when there is so much injustice in the world. That's my dilemma."

At that point I said, "Sit down, Lila Mae." We both sat down and I continued. "The Moores are in California. Eddie's transfer came through and I let them take the baby with them for a while. You seemed so confused that I thought you needed time to get yourself together."

She pounced. "Where in California? Why didn't you call me? How long did you say Bessie could stay?"

"I kind of left it open. You know, I had to work. I couldn't be here to keep her until you got back. You were gone for two weeks."

"Where is she? What city?"

"I don't know yet. They'll contact us when they get settled. Don't worry."

"I can't believe you let my child go without calling me."

"You know Bessie loves the Moores and they love her. They'll take good care of her."

"That's not the point." Just then, I was saved by the ringing telephone. One of Lila Mae's protest friends was calling. When she hung up, she said, "I'm going on campus to find out about the class work I missed. I'll be back later." Out the door she went. I knew this conversation would be continued, but I had to leave for New Orleans the next day.

Two weeks later, the fat hit the fire. Lila Mae had a dream that her daughter was looking for her and couldn't find her. In the dream, Bessie was standing in a desert and calling, "Mama, Mama, where are you?" Then she looked up and cried out, "God, help me find my Mama. My Mama's lost." I guess Bessie called on God because the Moores had taken her to Sunday School more than a few times and they were Christian people.

When I got to D. C., Lila Mae peppered me with questions. I told her the dream was all in her imagination. I said she was just stressed out. My wife was looking at me all wild-eyed, and I don't think she heard a word I said. After a deep sigh, I finally admitted that for Lila Mae's own good, I had signed her name to guardianship papers to let the Moores keep Bessie for a while. Lila's stunned expression was more than I could take. I looked away.

"You bastard," she shrieked. "You gave my baby away." She started screaming, crying and shivering uncontrollably. She yanked her hair as if trying to tear it out. I grabbed her and she began kicking like a wild animal, still screaming at the top of her lungs. She broke away and started throwing lamps, the telephone and anything she could get her hands on. A neighbor knocked on the door. I managed to open it and begged, "Call an ambulance. I think my wife is having a nervous breakdown."

At the Howard University Hospital, they sedated Lila and ran tests. After several days, they concluded that she would need extended care in an institution. She was reduced to sitting with arms folded, rocking back and forth, holding a doll someone had given her. She had not spoken a word, nor did she acknowledge anyone's presence. I notified Gwen of Lila's condition. Gwen said she had been comforting her mother, but would ask the church ladies to take over so that she could come to Washington. I did not share with Gwen the source of Lila's pain.

The next day, Lila was transferred to St. Elizabeth's Hospital, a mental institution located in Southeast Washington between Alabama Avenue and Nichols Avenue. They changed Nichols Avenue to Martin Luther King, Jr. Avenue later on. Anyway, the locals called the hospital "St. E's" or more graphically, "the crazy house." It was located in an undesirable part of town, along with smokestacks belching pollution, a high crime rate, low voter turnout, fried chicken take-outs and illegal drugs. There were more liquor stores on the corners than one would call normal. The large hospital campus was surrounded by tall, stone walls with black metal gates. A guardhouse stood near the entrance. It was an imposing place. In spite of the manicured grounds and well meaning staff, the hospital was frightening to me.

When I went to visit Lila, I approached her room with dread. I didn't know if she was still quietly rocking or if she would attack me. I felt so guilty. She was sitting in a straight chair, unresponsive to my knock. I thought Lila Mae might never be in her right mind again. She stared at the flowered wallpaper like she was looking at a ghost. Her normally neat appearance had given way to a slovenly look with uncombed hair, ragged fingernails with peeling polish, and a frozen expression of bewilderment on her face. All her joy had evaporated. A dryness had settled into her spirit. She sighed, moaned and hummed "I'll Fly Away" like she was ready to die. She never looked at me.

I thought, "'I've messed up big time. If she could just snap out of this, she has a chance for a good life. I sent the baby away to relieve Lila of a burden she didn't seem to want. She's been living in a fantasy world that really didn't include Bessie or me." Yet, looking at her staring at the wall, I knew she was worse off after Bessie left. Maybe she was going to be miserable and mixed up no matter what.

Gwen kept her promise and showed up on the doorstep of our home. I had taken vacation leave to stay close to Lila. Soon after Gwen arrived, I drove her to the hospital. The conversation in the car was strained, as I left out key points in the story of Lila's breakdown. Gwen was guarded in what she told me too.

At the hospital, Lila Mae glanced blankly at her sister and looked down at the floor. Gwen instinctively embraced Lila and stroked her back. Pulling up a chair and rocking Lila like a baby, Gwen softly sang an old church song, "Rock of Ages." As she went through all the verses, I saw Lila's eyes come to life. It seemed like she was remembering something comforting from her childhood. Lila and I didn't go to church, but she had told me her daddy was a deacon.

When the song was over, Lila softly said, "Gwen?" Gwen replied, "This is your sister, honey, and everything is gonna be all right." I saw Lila Mae smile for the first time since her breakdown. Gwen started another song, "What a Friend We Have in Jesus," and Lila joined in. Those two had a songfest, singing in harmony, and two nurses stopped in to listen for a while. The nurses and an orderly joined in, blending their harmonies on "Standin' in the Need of Prayer." I thought I was in church. I tried to join in the singing, but my throat was empty. I felt a strong spiritual presence in that room. It pierced my heart and I had to turn away to hide my tears. When I finally looked at Lila again, I could see she was healing right before my eyes.

A few days later, Lila told Gwen I had sent Bessie away. When Gwen asked me about it, I said that it was temporary and that I thought it was the best thing to do. Lila had told Gwen about her protest activities when she went to Georgia for her father's funeral. Gwen was an easygoing person and had been worried about her sister's activities. She seemed to comprehend on some level what I was saying. Still, our relationship was strained.

When Gwen left ten days later, Lila was almost her old self again. The doctor said he thought she could go home with medication and be an outpatient for the next few months. On the day I brought her home, she seemed nervous, but the medication calmed her down. I had put Bessie's things away in her closet so that they would not get Lila upset. I pampered her and got a home companion to stay with her when I went back to work. I had hoped that our lives could return to normal. A new normal.

In April 1968, frustrated hopes and pent up energy reached a fever pitch in America. Just as Malcolm X had been assassinated in February 1965, Martin Luther King was killed in April 1968. People exploded with rage. When King died, there were riots in Washington and in other major cities across the country. I worried about Lila's welfare while I was on the train. I was very protective of her. Thank goodness the rioters did not hurt her or damage our home or neighborhood. Still, I worried that this national unrest would make Lila more upset and slow down the healing process

One evening near the end of April, I brought Lila Mae a bouquet of daisies, her favorite flower. She gave me one of her rare smiles and a quick hug. I was hoping for closer contact later that evening. It had been a long time since I made love to my beautiful wife. I had been having trouble with my prostate, but I was feeling better that evening. At least I wanted to hold her close and know that we could be lovers again someday. I missed her warm energy.

While she was putting the flowers in a vase, I told her, "Lila, I have been thinking. I don't know why the Moores have not written or called us, but I believe we can contact all the army bases in California and find Eddie Moore. I have a list of the bases. I can call them tomorrow. When we locate the Moores, I will get airline tickets and we'll fly out there to get Bessie. I can't stand to see you so sad."

"Maybe they don't want to be found, like you told me about my cousin that day on the train. Maybe they intend to keep Bessie."

"It's worth a try. I feel so guilty about this situation. I'm going to make every effort to locate her. Then, maybe you'll find it in your heart to forgive me."

"Thank you, Henry. I can't imagine going the rest of my life without my daughter."

"You won't have to. We'll find her."

Every night since returning from the hospital, Lila had slept on the very edge of our queen sized bed, as far away from me as she could get. On this night, she moved closer and touched my arm. I held my breath, afraid to move too fast. Then, she caressed my face. That was all the encouragement I needed. I put my arms around her and held her tightly. Her muscles relaxed in my arms. That was a good sign. I did not want to move too fast. I kissed her on the cheek and released her. She stayed close to me as she drifted off to sleep. In time, I could envision a long, slow buildup to glorious lovemaking.

The next morning, I began calling the three California army bases. At first, I did not know how to get to the people who could give out information. I soon learned the routine. I had to talk to someone in the

Protocol or Post Locater Office. They could tell me if Colonel Moore was assigned to that base.

On my third and last Army base, I reached the Fort Irvin Training Center near Barstow, California. I learned that this center was located in the Mojave Desert, one of the hottest and driest places in the world. Eddie Moore was assigned to this southeastern California base. They transferred me to the staff duty desk for contact information. For some reason, no one answered the phone initially. I called back and was able to get an address for Colonel Moore.

Lila suggested that we write to the Moores to let them know we planned to come and get Bessie. She said we should thank them for their willingness to care for her. Lila composed the letter and we both signed it. Four days later, we tried to call the Moores, but their number was unlisted.

On Saturday, we boarded a plane headed for California. Landing in Los Angeles, we drove to Fort Irvin. We found the subdivision near the base where the Moores lived. As we approached their house, the tension mounted. There was no car in the driveway. We knocked on the door, but got no answer. The next door neighbor came out of his home and walked toward us.

"Are you looking for the Moores?"

"Yes. Do you know where they are?"

"They moved two days ago. Eddie was a short timer when he arrived here. He reached the twenty year mark in the military and decided to retire. They were renting that house on a short term lease."

"We're friends from the east coast. Do you know where they moved?"

"They said they were initially moving in with family in Arizona, but they weren't sure where they would settle."

Lila was getting pale. I said, "Let's get out of here." I thanked the neighbor and we hurried back to the car. I had only driven a short, silent distance before Lila began to cry. I spotted a quiet area near a Joshua tree and parked the car. She was devastated.

"Lila, I'm so sorry. This is not the end of our search. We'll find Bessie Ella."

She did not answer me. She just stared into space. I thought, "Lord, don't let her have a setback."

90

By the time we pulled into a motel parking lot, Lila was calmer. She said, "At least you tried." The desert is not the ideal place to be if you are depressed. There are few signs of vibrant life. I was very uncomfortable that evening and anxious to board the flight back to Washington the next day.

Back in D.C., I encouraged Lila to return to her classes. Although she had missed several weeks, there was a chance that she could pass most of her subjects. I suggested that she request make-up work. Concentrating on her studies could help her to focus on something positive. She agreed to go back. I pledged to support her in every way.

When the school year ended, Lila did not qualify for graduation. She had to drop two classes because she had lost so much time, but she successfully completed the others. I praised her for her accomplishments and urged her to go to summer school. Meanwhile, I returned to work.

When I saw my wife looking sad one Saturday afternoon, I knew we needed to talk again about Bessie. I began, "Lila, I know I messed up. What I did was to try to find solutions to some really tough problems. I went about it the wrong way. I just couldn't figure out any good answers. You don't know how I worried about you and Bessie when I was on that train. To me, you seemed to be swallowed up in the protest movement, and you were just going through the motions with Bessie. Half the time, when she was trying to get your attention, you didn't even look at her. You were busy talking on the phone with your friends. I thought you just needed some time off. I wasn't trying to send her away forever."

"Well, that's just what you did. Dr. Moore is retired from the army. The army can't tell me where he is. Janice and Eddie have no intention of giving Bessie back to us. Janice told me once that she wished she had a daughter like Bessie. She wants to keep her."

"We'll find the child before long. Maybe we can hire a private detective."

"Where would he start looking? They might have changed Bessie's name."

"Lila, I want to make things right. Somehow, we'll get her back. I've already spread the word among the Brotherhood of Sleeping Car Porters to be on the lookout for a couple matching Janice and Eddie's descriptions with a fair skinned little girl. They have shared this with their network of family and friends. Somebody is bound to send us some information.

"That's a good idea. Thank you, Henry. I hope you're right."

There was something else I needed to tell Lila. I had made no progress on completing my divorce. I couldn't hide it forever, but I was afraid Lila would leave me. She noticed that I was worried about something, but I said, "It's an old problem I've been trying to work out. I won't bother you with it. I'll figure it out."

"It might help to talk about it."

"I'm not ready to share it yet."

"Is it a health problem? Are you okay?"

"An old friend of mine is sick in New Orleans. I've been helping out. I need to get out of that obligation."

"Sometimes people will take advantage of you."

"Well, don't you worry about it. I'll take care of it."

Lila began an intensive summer school session. She had six weeks of classes. During that time, I made another frustrating appeal to Bettina, offering her the house in New Orleans plus a cash settlement in exchange for a divorce. I suggested that she could advertise for a roomer so that the rent could help her to meet her expenses. When she rejected that idea, I even offered to pay a part-time caregiver for one year. She did not budge, literally. When I left the house, she was leaned back in her recliner munching on a large bag of corn chips and flipping channels with the remote control. All the while, she was inhaling oxygen from a machine.

I decided that the New Orleans blister had to come to a head. My friend, Ben, had relatives in El Paso, Texas. In Juarez, just across the border from El Paso, Mexican officials were granting divorces to people from the U. S. in one day. I could fly to El Paso, take a cab across the border and get the divorce for $500. With the help of Ben and his relatives, I made the arrangements. There was one hitch. I needed Bettina's signature saying she consented to the process.

I had dangled the carrot without success. Now, it was time for the stick. In one last visit to the house, I told Bettina "I have arranged to have the utilities, which are in my name, shut off tomorrow. There is no court order making me pay those bills. I also will not pay the taxes on the house. Let the city take it. The taxes are due now.

"You have rejected my generous offers. Now, either you will sign the divorce papers, or you will go without water, sewer, gas and electricity. You will also lose the house. Somebody will buy it for the amount of the taxes owed. At this point, it's a loss I'm willing to take."

She cried, coughed and pleaded, but I did not budge. Finally, she saw the light and signed the papers. True to my earlier promise, I signed over the house to her and gave her a cashier's check for $30,000. I did not tell her the divorce would be granted in the next two days. As I left the house, she said, "We'll see what the divorce judge has to say about this."

Back in Washington, I told Lila that Ben had invited me to visit and take in a Yankees ball game over the weekend. I knew she had to study for her summer school classes. She was okay with the idea. Early Thursday morning, I boarded a flight headed for El Paso. Upon arrival, I took a cab to Juarez, signed a "residency" form, paid my money and filed for divorce. The next afternoon, I returned to pick up the divorce papers. Ben's cousin and I had a Margarita to celebrate. I spent the night at his house and flew out on Saturday morning headed back to Washington. Now, I needed to find the right moment to tell Lila what happened. I had jumped through a major hurdle, but there was one more to go. I did not know how she would react.

I returned to our home and was relaxing on the sofa when Lila came in from school. I greeted her with a hug. She asked, "How was the game?"

"Oh, exciting. It was a nice change of pace. The Yankees won." I had gotten this information from Ben.

"Good. I'm glad you had fun."

"How's school?"

"I'm almost finished. Just two more weeks and I'll be certified for graduation."

"Wonderful. Then we'll celebrate by going to New York to see a Broadway play. Your choice. I'm in New York every week, but I've never been to the theater there."

"I've always wanted to go to Broadway! You choose the play and surprise me."

In two weeks, Lila completed her requirements for a Bachelor of

Arts degree. I was very proud of her. She had kept going against some tough odds. That Saturday, she and I boarded the train headed for New York City to celebrate. I told Lila, "This is where you were going the day we met. Now you'll get to see the big city, Miss College Graduate."

"Yes. Without my daughter." There was no smile. Her face turned ashen.

"Lila, I'm so sorry. We'll find Bessie, I promise. I won't rest until we find her. Just take a deep breath. It's going to be okay."

Lila was pensive during the train ride. There was very little conversation. As the train neared New York City, however, her face lit up. This was a place she had dreamed of visiting as a child. This was her dream come true. I was determined to make the trip one of the great joys of her life. I had purchased tickets to the musical, *Hair*, at the Biltmore Theater. It was Broadway's first experiment that included a brief scene with the whole cast in the nude. The play had little plot but lots of energy. It reflected other surprising developments of the 1960's. I thought my creative wife would enjoy the experience. She did.

As we ate a late dinner at a four star restaurant following the play, the tension I had observed in Lila earlier in the day had disappeared. She was relaxed and quite excited about being in this beautiful, fairytale setting.

We spent the night in New York. For the first time in many months, Lila cuddled with me in bed and did not resist my foreplay. We made love. She brought me out of the desert and into a lush, fabulous garden.

Back in Washington, Lila began to think about her next steps. She talked about getting a job with the federal government. I told her to take her time. She needed a break. She decided to start researching the job market without putting a lot of pressure on herself. I thought that was a good idea.

One Saturday afternoon, I finally worked up the courage to talk with Lila about my situation in New Orleans. I started from the beginning.

"Lila, when I met you, you were married and so was I. My wife was in New Orleans and your husband was in Macon."

"You were married?"

"Yes. Both of us were secretive about our past. When you filed for divorce, I went to a lawyer to start divorce proceedings too. I never told you because my situation was so complicated. I had been legally separated from my wife for several years. The problem was, she was sick and I was carrying her on my health insurance."

Lila looked shocked. "Henry, are you telling me that you are still married to a woman in New Orleans?"

"No. We are divorced now, but for a long time she refused to agree to a divorce every time I asked her. She was living on a disability check and depending on me to pay the utilities and taxes on the house. I had paid off the house with an inheritance after my father died. I offered to sign that house over to her and give her a cash settlement, but she refused.

"After you and I became close, I knew I needed to get out of that marriage. You got your divorce. You were free, but I wasn't. I was afraid of losing you."

Here I took a deep breath. I heard my voice crack when I said, "Lila, the day we got married, I had not gotten my divorce from Bettina."

"What are you saying? We're not legally married."

"That can be corrected."

"You're a bigamist."

"I was, but I'm not anymore. I had to threaten to shut off the house utilities and stop paying the real estate taxes to get her to sign the papers."

"So how will she live? You said she's sick."

"She gets her disability check and I gave her a cash settlement. It was the only way to get out of the marriage."

"So you gave her the house plus a cash settlement. Where did you get the money?"

"My father left me a large inheritance. He owned valuable land on the river, and he sold it to a developer. I invested the money and kept my job. My wife didn't know how much money I had because Daddy died while she and I were separated."

"So our so called marriage is based on a lie. This is a pattern, Henry. You lied to the Moores and forged my name to the guardianship papers."

"I couldn't bear to lose you, Lila. Looking back, I know I should have told you before we married. I suggested that we move in together, but you didn't want to do it without marriage. You were talking about getting an apartment. I thought I might lose you. I know what I did was wrong. Haven't you ever made a mistake?"

She turned and stared straight ahead at the wall. It was her turn to take a deep breath. "Yes, Henry. I have. When my husband was out of town, a man I trusted took advantage of me. He is Bessie's father."

"So that's why you ran away from Jimmy. Was the baby's father white?"

"No. He was mixed race. Jimmy is brown skinned."

"Does Bessie's father know where you are?"

"He died a few months after she was born."

"Of natural causes?"

"Yes. Why did you ask that?"

"I was wondering if Jimmy did him in."

"No. Jimmy was upset when he realized what had happened, but he never knew Bessie's father."

"Okay, so we both had secrets. Mine may have been more complicated than yours, but I was doing the best I could."

"So was I. The evening you rescued me on that train, I was in need of help. I had no clear plan except getting away from rural Georgia."

The point is we are both legally single now. I love you more than I have ever loved anyone. I want to marry you the right way."

"Why should I marry you now? Maybe this is a good time to make a clean break. I've graduated from college and can start out on my own. I appreciate all you've done to get your divorce, but after you sent Bessie away I don't know if I can trust you."

"I know it will take a while for me to earn your trust again. Just don't turn away. Let me earn it. I promise there won't be any more secrets. And I hope you won't keep any secrets from me. I want us to talk to each other openly." Her brow lifted like she didn't know whether to believe me or not. I was grateful that she was still there with me at that moment.

Lila caught me off guard by asking, "What was your marriage to Bettina like?"

"We were not really compatible. She was a chain smoker and a big time shopper. She refused to live within a budget. When Bet and I were legally separated years ago, I moved out and stayed away for three

96

years. We had separated emotionally years before that. God knew best. We didn't have any kids. She had three miscarriages before we stopped trying. I think it was related to her cigarette habit, which couldn't be good for a developing baby.

"I'm not saying I was perfect either. I was knocking back quite a few beers back then. Anyway, I rented an apartment, got myself in shape and had a series of girlfriends. None of them meant a whole lot to me. They were temporary tenants in my life, just time fillers.

"Bettina got emphysema and retired on disability. I moved back in to help her out. It was a practical arrangement. Not only did I finish paying off the house, but I also paid half of the utilities each month. It was better to invest my money in something I owned than to throw it away on rent. There was nothing romantic about it. I went my way and she went hers. To my way of thinking, that was almost a divorce, even though she wouldn't sign any papers. I planned to leave again when she got better. Only she didn't get better. Her condition worsened. I stayed there and helped her financially even though I was gone most of the time on my job.

"Then I met you and my whole world changed. Looking back, I know I made a huge mistake. I kept trying to divorce Bettina, especially after you got your divorce. It's not an excuse, but things moved so fast so deeply with my feelings for you that my head was spinning. And I was afraid to lose you."

"I have to think about this Henry. It's a lot for me to absorb."

"I understand, Lila. Take your time."

Lila and I decided not to take any quick actions that we might regret later. We agreed to maintain the status quo. I went out of my way to be considerate of Lila, trying to heal our relationship. Even so, I felt a definite chill when I got close to her.

Lila remarked that on her job applications there was an item called "marital status." She said, "I guess I'll have to check single."

"It's up to you. You have the power to change that. Just say the word."

She studied my face as though trying to tell whether or not I was sincere. Things were dicey where our romantic life was concerned. I tried to be patient, but I missed kissing and holding her. She wasn't mean, just distant.

One afternoon in early September, we were relaxing and watching television when the doorbell rang. I asked, "Who could that be? We're not expecting anybody, are we?" Lila said, "Not that I know of." As she walked toward the door, the bell rang twice. Somebody was impatient. Maybe a kid playing, I thought.

When Lila opened the door, there stood Mama Bates in her size fifty-four print dress, her black straw hat slightly lopsided. She looked Lila straight in the eye and asked "Who are you?" Lila calmly answered, "I'm Lila Mae Lofton. Who are you looking for?" Mama Bates glowered, put her hands on her commodious hips and snarled, "I'm looking for my two-timing, no good son-in-law, Henry Lofton." Lila's face turned pale. I had been standing behind a tall dieffenbachia plant observing the scene. Mama Bates spotted me and almost knocked Lila out of the way as she strode toward me.

At first, I thought she was going to hit me with her pocketbook, but she merely adjusted it on her arm and spat out, "What's the meaning of this, Henry?" I sputtered, "Didn't Bettina tell you? She signed the divorce papers."

"You're Bettina's mother?" Lila asked.

Mama Bates answered, "Yes, I'm his wife's mother. And how do you happen to have the same last name, young lady? Are you a long lost sister?"

Lila almost whispered, "We're married." She looked at me dumbfounded.

"Unless he married you more than fifteen years ago, you're not his legal wife. He's been married to my daughter for fifteen years." Lila groped for something to hold onto. She grabbed the edge of the table to steady herself.

I said, "Bettina and I are divorced."

"She told me she signed some papers, but you two haven't gone to court yet.

If there is no court decree saying you're divorced, Bet is your wife. Period. She told me you all had broken up and were getting back together."

"No, we're not. I don't know what she told you, but Bettina and I were legally separated years ago. I had been helping her out because of her illness. She signed papers for the divorce. I put the house in her

98

name and gave her a cash settlement. We're not getting back together."

"She intends to stay married to you. Why? I don't know. You have tricked Bet and you've tricked this young girl. Made a fool out of her. You ought to be run out of town on a rail. You are low, LOW, **LOW!** If I wasn't a Christian lady, I'd tell you what I really think of you. Are there any other wives?"

"No," I replied. "You've upset Lila. You need to leave and let me straighten this out."

"How can you straighten anything out? You think you're entitled to two wives."

"Bettina and I are divorced. She didn't have to appear in court. I'll send her a copy of the papers. I thought the court was sending them."

"You're lying. You just want that young lady to think she's really married to you."

"You're in my house. You can't talk to me like that."

Just then, Mama Bates spied the broom. She walked over and grabbed it. As she lifted it in the air, I knew she intended to run me out of my own house.

Lila shouted, "Stop!" Mama Bates held the broom in mid-air. Lila continued, "Henry told me all about this situation. He got the divorce. He's no longer married to Bettina."

Mama Bates dropped the broom, looking stunned. "How could you do this to my daughter?" Turning to Lila she said, "Just remember, he might turn on you when your youth and good looks are gone. He is a scoundrel!" She marched out the door, slamming it behind her.

I said, "I'm so sorry, Lila."

"I want to see the divorce papers."

"I'll show them to you right now." I retrieved the papers from my dresser and handed them to Lila."

"This is in Spanish? I took two years of it, so I can read it." She paused and studied the decree. "Why Mexico?"

"Quick and easy. I had waited for what seemed an eternity to get Bettina's signature on the dotted line. I didn't want to wait any longer. You heard her mother say Bet was planning to tell the judge she didn't want the divorce. This was the best way out. I've been through the mill."

"If Bettina is anything like her mother, I can see that." Lila hugged me, stroking my back. "How about some tea and soup? We have vegetable soup left over from yesterday, and there's French bread."

"I'd love some. Then, if you don't mind, I'd like us to go for a walk. I need to breathe fresh air."

"That sounds like a good idea."

We ate in silence, but our eyes spoke of love. I felt a warmth flowing from Lila that had been absent for a long time. I felt completely at peace. On our walk together, we acted like kids. She jumped over cracks and I clowned around.

"I've never seen you act so silly, Henry."

"I've laid down a burden. And I don't want to act like I'm your father anymore. You're grown up, graduated from college, and about to start working full time. I want us to be full partners to each other, open and supportive."

"Will you commit to helping me find my daughter?"

"I am absolutely committed to finding Bessie. When we do, I want to adopt her, if you are willing."

"You'll have to ask Bessie."

"Fair enough."

The next time my train arrived in Washington, my wife had another question. "How did Mrs. Bates find our house?"

"As well as I can piece it together, Bettina had been having one of her bad spells and her mother had come from Texas to help out. Bet's mom was aware that the marriage wasn't ideal, but she didn't know the details at that time. That was when Bet called me and left a message on our new answering machine. I don't know how she got the telephone number. The only number she was supposed to have for me in Washington was at my job. Well, our number is listed, so maybe she got it from directory assistance.

"I thought the standard greeting from the factory was still on the answering machine. Without my knowledge, you had changed the greeting. It said in your sweet voice, 'Hello. You have reached the Lofton residence. Henry and Lila are not available at this time, but if you leave a brief message, we will call you back. Have a good day.' The first time, Bet hung up. Then, she called back with the message, 'Call me, Henry. You know who this is.'

"You asked me about that message. You heard it before I did. I told you I thought it was somebody from the job. I didn't know what to say. I was still figuring out how to tell you about Bettina. I decided I would call Bet back the next day and let her know the divorce had been granted. I also decided to get an unlisted number because I know how emotional she can be. I thought she might harass us.

"The next day, Mama Bates showed up at our door. I guess she got the address from the phone company. You know the rest."

"I see."

"Let's take our time, Lila. I want us to start over."

"Speaking of starting, I took the Federal Service Entrance Exam and got a high score. I expect to get some job offers soon. I want to start working for the U. S. Department of Justice."

"That sounds about right. You're very interested in human rights and civil rights."

"Yes. It should be a stimulating work environment."

"What last name are you using on your applications? Lofton or Jenkins?"

"I decided to go back to my maiden name, Lila Mae Thornton. That way, even if we remarry I can keep my maiden name."

"That doesn't sound very promising. At least you're still here. I'm not giving up on you."

"Henry, I need time to process everything that has happened. I can't be rushed, okay? I'm about to launch my real full time career and that's what I'm concentrating on."

"Just don't push your personal life too far in the background."

"Henry, while you were on the train this week, I had a dream. I had been wondering what to do about our relationship. This is going to sound a little strange, but I have a guardian angel. When I'm worried about something, she shows up in my dreams and gives me advice. She told me that before I was born, another soul agreed to help me through some of the transitions in my life. It wasn't clear, but I believe that soul was you. I wasn't supposed to marry you. We were supposed to be friends. Maybe that's why things happened the way that they did."

"You're right. That does sound strange. I have tried to be your friend, but that does not mean I can't also be your husband. We lived as husband and wife for three years. We're supposed to be together. I love you, Lila Mae."

"You've helped me a lot and you've hurt me a lot. I'm not ready to marry you right now. While I'm trying to get a foothold in a new job, I would like to have your support. I promise to support you in your work and your life. We've both had some rough spots in our journey. Let's just hold hands and coast for a while."

"Just hold hands?"

"I mean let's just be together without talking about marriage right now. I'm not excluding intimacy."

"Whew!"

"Ha-ha. You're so funny sometimes.

"Miles Davis is in town. I'm inviting you on a date."

"I accept."

Lila and I started dating in much the same way we began our relationship. The only difference was the steamy finale to many of our dates once we returned home. It wasn't marriage, but it was good.

Once Lila started working, she immersed herself in her job. I reminded her now and then about balancing work life and personal life. She listened. She began talking about her friends at work. It seems she had made lots of friends. They sometimes had lunch together. One evening, she suggested that it would be fun to have a Christmas party for her new friends at our home. I remembered her protest buddies from college and reminded myself not to make the mistake of being judgmental or jealous this time. I would show her that I respected her choice of friends. I agreed to the party and helped her to prepare for it. Meanwhile, Lila was invited to three other parties. She bought me a new suit and told me to get ready for fun.

I don't know when I have had as much fun as I did at the parties we attended and the one we gave. Through her actions, Lila let me know that she wanted me to be her partner, married or not. I had a chance to tell a few jokes, which everybody enjoyed. I put aside my usually reserved manner and let myself relax. Everybody at these functions was more educated than I was, but it didn't seem to matter. These were genuinely nice people. My self-esteem got a big boost.

On Christmas day, I went overboard with gifts for Lila. My investments had done well and I decided to buy her a mink coat and matching hat, among other gifts. She couldn't believe I had spent so much money.

I told her, "For years I have pinched pennies hoping to become a millionaire. I'm not there yet, but my investments have done well. At this point, becoming a millionaire isn't so important anymore. I just want to enjoy you."

"Henry. I'm so glad we decided to stay together. When I was a little girl, I dreamed of giving grand parties and wearing furs. You have helped to make that possible. You also listen patiently while I chatter on about things that happened at work. You're a great listener. I need to learn from your example."

"That could take years. Can you spare the time?"

"Henry, will you marry me?"

My expression froze with open mouth and widened eyes. Then I burst out laughing. I was in shock. I danced around the room with her, still laughing.

"Does this mean 'Yes'?"

"Yes, my darling Lila. Yes, yes, yes!"

We decided to marry in April, but that was not to be. In February, I felt a piercing pain in my left leg, which turned out to be bone cancer. The leg was already an inch shorter than the right leg. Now I had to have the shorter leg amputated and retire on disability. No way could I walk through train cars on one leg.

I could not believe what was happening to me. What should have been the most joyous time of my life was marred by pain. I did not want to be a burden on my beautiful Lila, but I was not so unselfish that I could let her go. I worked hard on my recovery, following the doctor's orders.

Lila was now taking care of me as I had taken care of her at the beginning of our relationship. She dutifully prepared my meals and attended to my needs. She encouraged me. When I got the blues, she cheered me up. Lila was so creative. One evening, she closed the drapes and did a strip tease routine for me in the living room. This period turned out to be one of the happiest times of my life. I knew that Lila loved me, and I found out how strong and determined she was.

I decided I would not give in to my changed circumstances. I would get a wheelchair and do as much as possible for myself. Finally, I hired a part-time nurse to take some pressure off of Lila. She deserved to get on with her life and with her career.

Our plans for an April wedding had to be postponed, but by July there was no sign of the cancer. I suggested targeting an October wedding date. Lila favored a private ceremony at home. We had not attended church, so we were not familiar with the ministers in the area. One of Lila's co-workers recommended a Unity minister whose church was only a few blocks from our home. That was fine with us.

Time passed quickly. On Friday, October 3, 1969, Lila and I went to City Hall to get a marriage license. The clerk found a record of our previous marriage. We explained that my divorce was not final at that time and we needed to remarry. The clerk gave me a funny look, but I was calm and collected. Lila was cool too.

We proceeded to a clinic to be tested for tuberculosis. The next order of business was to plan the wedding. We decided to invite a maximum of six people, including the two witnesses. We wanted to do this quietly.

The following Thursday, October 8th, Lila took the morning off from work and walked over to the Unity Church. She asked the minister if he would marry us. She told him we had been living together for a while and we wanted to be married. He stopped by to talk with the two of us the next day, and then agreed to conduct the ceremony in our home on Friday, October 15th. After the wedding, I made out a will leaving everything to Lila Mae. She was the only family I had, except for my brother.

The cancer stayed in remission, and we had a very good year together. We investigated two false leads about Bessie's whereabouts. We were deeply disappointed, sick at heart, but we kept hoping. Then, the dreaded disease returned. When I got really sick, I checked myself into this hospice. The care I needed was too much for Lila and the half-time caregiver, and I could see the strain on my wife's face.

The disease quickly spread all over my body and I lost weight, but not too much. Because this happened so fast, my body still looks pretty good on the outside. I have my pride. I don't want to look like a skeleton in the casket. Anyway, that's that.

I am so glad you came to visit today. And I'm especially glad you stopped by my bedside. I needed to tell my story. Thank you for listening. My time is short now. I probably won't be here the next time you come.

Section Four

Rev. Ezra Randolph Padgett

Now there are varieties of gifts, but the same Spirit;
and there are varieties of services, but the same Lord;
and there are varieties of activities, but it is the same God
who activates all of them in everyone.

1 Corinthians 12: 4-6

J arrett, my friend, thank you for inviting me on this fishing trip. I needed to get away and relive some of our boyhood escapes to the lake. Let me check. Yep, I've got the sun tan lotion. You know, it's a shame we haven't seen each other since you moved from Wisconsin to Baltimore. You said we have about fifty miles to go, so let me tell you a story. It will make the trip more interesting. It's about my life since I saw you last. Actually, the story starts with my college days in Washington.

I left my home in Wisconsin to attend George Washington University in September 1935. Soon after arriving on campus, I noticed that there were a number of international students. Coming from the pale, homogeneous sea of humanity in Wisconsin, I was fascinated by the varied landscape of colors and features among students from Africa, Asia and South America. I thought, "God is an artist. He didn't just paint the trees and flowers in vivid colors. He painted people too. How awesome!"

I started attending gatherings of the foreign students. One student stood out. She was a smart, energetic, pretty girl from Ghana named Weijah Mensah. She had dark, velvety skin and a beautifully expressive face. Her smile was dazzling, her eyes magnetic. Although her waist was small, she had a full round butt that mesmerized me. I loved to see her walking across campus in her native dress. She displayed a beautiful spirit that uplifted everyone around her. I had never experienced anything like it.

I didn't know what I was going to choose for my major when I arrived at G. W. I was considering pre-law. When I discovered that Weijah was going to major in business, I decided to do likewise. Ever since I was a child, my father had wanted me to be a lawyer. That was an old, unfulfilled dream he had for his life. I had to make my own choices.

I unconsciously created a situation where Weijah and I would be together as much as possible. We became good friends in my freshman year. I joined every organization that she joined – the choir, the campus newspaper staff and the intramural volleyball team. Although the boys and girls teams were separate, we cheered for each other. Weijah and I began dating exclusively as sophomores. Since my parents were Quakers, I knew they wouldn't have a problem with interracial dating.

During Christmas break of my junior year, I took Weijah home. I wanted Jasper and Elizabeth Padgett to meet the woman I had been gushing about since my freshman year. Ironically, Weijah and my parents found many commonalities in their lives. The Padgetts were farmers, and Weijah had grown up on a large farm in Ghana. My parents and Weijah compared farming techniques. Some were similar and others were quite different. Our American farm was more mechanized. When gold was found on the Mensah's farm, the family prospered. This gave Weijah the resources to come to America.

During the second semester of our junior year, Weijah and I were eligible to spend a semester abroad. We were both honor students. We applied early and made England our first choice destination. With limited slots available, that was a long shot. I know now that God blessed us to be accepted and to go to the same place, the University of Cambridge. That semester, we took advantage of an opportunity to take horseback riding lessons English style. I had never felt so free and so exhilarated!

106

Weijah and I married in Washington, D. C. in May 1939, two days after graduation. Her parents, Kwami and Abina Mensah, and mine flew in for the graduation ceremony and the wedding. My oldest brother, Peter, was best man. Weijah's best friend, Indira, was maid of honor. We were married for nineteen years.

We decided to start our married life in St. Louis, Missouri where Peter was living. After checking out the city, we identified a need for a hardware store. We researched the industry and Weijah wrote a great business plan. I presented it to a local bank. On the first try, we got the money we needed to open the store.

A year later, we had a thriving, successful business, Padgett's Hardware and Lumber. My wife and I enthusiastically worked long hours. Our zeal paid off. We bought a beautiful home, traveled abroad, enjoyed the arts and made many friends. We did not have children, but we were very much in love. It was enough.

After sixteen happy years, Weijah was diagnosed with diabetes. Two years later, her kidney function began deteriorating. In those days, there were no effective treatments available for failing kidneys. It was rough on her. Rough on both of us. In 1958, she died of kidney disease.

My world fell apart. I couldn't adjust to being a widower. That's when I turned to God. A friend sent me a subscription to the *Daily Word*. I started reading it every day and I found myself being lifted out of the doldrums. I noticed that the publication was associated with Silent Unity. I found a Unity Church about a mile and a half from my home and started attending the services.

I began the journey toward understanding that I was a spiritual being having a human experience. I learned that my spiritual self was eternal, but my physical self had a limited life span. I recalled hearing this before, but somehow it passed over me like so many garbled, nonsense words. My materially based life had not allowed room for such ideas. Grief cut through my resistance and doubt, opening the way to healing. I knew on a deeply conscious level that Weijah's bright spirit was still alive.

Later, I became interested in the classes offered at the Unity church. I wanted to know what New Thought was all about. Was it true that habitual thoughts become beliefs? Have my beliefs shaped my reality? If I changed those beliefs, would my personal world change?

While pondering these questions, I had to continue the routine of operating the store. There were employees to be supervised and vendors to be paid. I needed to fire the janitor. He'd been warned several times, and the floor still looked smudged. I wondered, "Can't he see the grime on the shelves? Does he need new glasses or what?"

That evening, I realized that my dissatisfaction with the man's work was trumped by my distressing sense of loss. I didn't have the energy to fire him and start with someone new. I felt drained. Somehow, running the store wasn't satisfying anymore. When Weijah was my partner, I greeted every morning enthusiastically. Not any more.

I decided to sell the business, not knowing what would come next. I stepped out on faith. While I was looking for a buyer, I had a spiritual dream. I heard an insistent voice calling me to the ministry. This had not even entered my mind. I had gotten involved with the church to heal my grief.

Within nine months, the call came two more times. I had not yet sold the business and was getting frustrated. I talked to my pastor. He suggested that my refusal to answer the call to the ministry might be blocking the sale of the hardware business. I did not understand how the two things could be connected, but my prayers to sell the store quickly had gone unanswered.

Finally I asked, "God, what do you want me to do?" Within seconds, I got a mental picture of myself standing in the chancel of a church, facing a congregation. I surrendered to my calling. The next day, an eager buyer showed up, ready to take over the hardware store.

In the fall of 1961, I entered the Unity School of Christianity at Unity Village and began my ministerial studies. Three years of questioning, praying and growing in faith followed. I had vigorous discussions and debates with my fellow ministerial students. In the summer of 1964, I was ordained as a minister. I returned to my church in St. Louis as an assistant pastor. After a year, I was called back to Unity Village to assist with updating the business end of the operation there. After two years, I felt ready to lead my own church.

In 1967, there was an opening at a mid-size parish in Washington, D.C. I had fond memories of the city from my undergraduate days and decided to apply. God was with me. I was called to be the senior pastor. I said goodbye to my friends and prepared to move east.

I was forty-nine when I began serving as pastor of the Unity Church Center on Capitol Hill. My years there have been challenging and rewarding. With my business background, I have tried to schedule my responsibilities so that everything runs smoothly and activities are spread out fairly evenly. Christmas and Easter are, of course, exceptions.

Still, Thursdays are my busy days year round. For some reason, people like to come and talk to me on Thursdays. I don't know whether it's because Thursday is so close to the weekend and they need to unload before their weekend activities or what.

Fortunately, people of all ages feel comfortable talking to me. Maybe it's because I seem like such a regular guy. I think you'll agree I'm ordinary looking, five feet eight inches tall with a round belly and thinning auburn hair. I'm not fat. I just picked up some padding in the middle over the years, unlike you. Don't laugh. I think my face is unremarkable, a healthy pink complexion and a gap between my two front teeth. I'm your average middle-aged white guy.

But I have a gift. It is the gift of listening and acceptance. That gift draws people to me. I pass no judgments on race, color, creed, gender, sexual preference, national origin, handicapping conditions, past mistakes, personality or anything else. I just accept everybody as they are because I know we're brothers and sisters created by the same loving God. In fact, I am fascinated by the variety of ways God has expressed Himself in His human creations. I'm still learning new variations of the human story.

I can thank my Quaker parents for raising me to accept all people as they are and to pray for them. I wish more people had had that experience growing up. The world would be a lot different. My Quaker heritage goes back four generations.

I see myself ultimately as an awakening agent, waking people up to their spiritual nature. Listening attentively and asking a few non-threatening questions can bring up all kinds of repressed fear and guilt from people's past. Sometimes, I believe, I succeed in helping them accept themselves. Then, they can purposefully choose the changes they will make and the pathways they will take. Thank God for that.

From the beginning, the women in Washington were very aggressive in trying to pair with me, but I politely turned them aside.

Weijah set such a high standard with her brilliance and her loving, unselfish support that I didn't know if I would ever be satisfied with another wife. I chose to devote myself to my work and my riding.

Outside of my ministry, my big passion is horseback riding. I have a horse named Flame, and when I am astride him, I am one with the wind. He is boarded at Rock Creek Park in the upper northwest section of Washington. Flame is an appendix quarter-horse, half thoroughbred, half quarter-horse. He is a large, strong animal, seventeen hands tall. That means the distance from the ground to his withers, the top of his back, is about five feet eight inches. Flame's coloring is gorgeous, chestnut with a distinctive white star on his head and white stockings on his legs. Flame and I do trail riding in the park. When I want to run him full out, I load him onto my horse trailer and head for the track in Upper Marlboro, Maryland. Running with Flame absorbs my full attention, and all the burdens of life slip away. I ride year round.

Fall is my favorite season. Some people say spring is full of possibilities, but I have observed that fall ushers in many blessings in my life. In early October 1969 on a relatively cool Thursday morning, I met Lila Mae Jenkins. I had been sitting on the window seat in the living room, having a cup of cappuccino. Gazing out of the picture window, I noticed that the leaves on the maple tree were still green, except for two burnished gold trailblazers. It would not be long before I would have to haul out the rake in response to the Divine order of the seasons. My other tree, a magnificent magnolia, dropped its leaves indiscriminately throughout the year. At Christmas, the magnolia leaves decorated both the sanctuary and the mantel of my living room fireplace, flanking the candelabrum.

My musing was interrupted when I spotted a young lady knocking on the door of my church across the street. It was eight o'clock in the morning. "Why on earth is she knocking on the church door at this hour?" I wondered. She walked down the steps, hesitated, then walked back up and knocked again. In my jogging clothes, I bounded out the door and called to her.

"Miss, no one is there yet. I am the pastor, Rev. Padgett. May I help you?" She turned and looked at me with what I can only describe as a jumble of emotions. She tried to smile, but the mask was thin. Underneath was a well of sorrow, reflected in the worry lines in her forehead. I darted across the street, ducking rush hour traffic. As I approached her, I was struck by her incredible beauty. She looked straight into my eyes for a moment, touching something deep inside, then dropped her gaze and almost whispered, "I need help."

"All right," I replied, digging into my pockets for the keys to the church. I had rushed out without them. "I don't have the keys with me. I live across the street. Would you wait for me here? Or you could come over for a few minutes. I was having coffee. I could make you a cup. You look like you could use one."

Why I offered to take her to my home I do not know. It violated all my rules for counseling women. I was clearly flustered. It was as though I was absorbing her energy of frustration and confusion. This was all wrong.

"Okay," she said. "I could use some coffee." As we crossed the street together, I experienced a rush, as though something momentous was about to happen in my life. I was scared. Not easy for a minister to admit.

Over coffee, Lila Mae introduced herself. She said she and her boyfriend had been unofficially living as husband and wife. They were ready to make it legal. I knew lots of couples in the area who were living together, so I wasn't surprised. Still, the way she explained the situation was a little different from the norm. She was somewhat guarded in what she said. In response to my question, she said she and Henry were both single and eligible to marry. They wanted a quick wedding. I wondered if she was pregnant, but did not ask.

Looking toward the mantle above my fireplace, Lila suddenly perked up. She said, "What a beautiful candelabrum! Usually you see them in silver, but that one is gold colored and beautifully carved."

"It's not just gold colored. It's solid gold." I took the candelabrum from its resting place and brought it to Lila for closer inspection.

"This looks like a museum piece. These roses carved into the stem are gorgeous."

"It's a family heirloom. My parents gave it to me two years ago. It is one of a pair. The family legend is that my great-grandmother gave the other half of the pair to a newly emancipated slave woman who saved my grandfather's life. As a young boy, he had some mysterious ailment and she cured him with herbal medicines."

"Rev. Padgett, I've heard this story before! I heard it from a descendent of that healer. The other candelabrum was used to buy the family's freedom from a landowner who held them hostage to a sharecropping debt. It was the only valuable thing they owned, and it bought their freedom."

"Lila, it was no accident that you knocked on the door of my church. Now, I know the whole story of the candelabra and so do you. What a fantastic story it is."

Replacing the candelabrum on the mantel, I arranged to visit the couple at home the next evening. I told Lila the three of us would talk together about marriage. I wanted to hear any concerns they might have.

Friday evening, I drove my Volvo to the address Lila gave me. Their home was four blocks from the church, located on a street in the midst of gentrification. The small front yard was well maintained, dotted with pansies and bordered by a decorative iron fence. I rang the bell. Lila smilingly greeted me at the door and ushered me into the parlor. I noted that the large room was tastefully decorated. A vase filled with daisies adorned the coffee table. A dark and handsome gentleman sat on the long, tan sofa, with a colorful throw covering his lap. He was an amputee. My mind quickly sifted through possible causes: cancer, diabetes, war injury. We both smiled as Lila introduced us.

Henry appeared to be much older than Lila. I got the feeling that he genuinely loved her and that she was willing to care for him. I learned that both of them had been married previously and they appeared capable of making a mature decision. They had applied for a marriage license the previous week.

As I looked around the room, I spied a picture of Lila wearing a big Afro. It reminded me of Weijah. Now, Lila wore her abundant hair in flowing curls around her shoulders. She was attractive either way.

When I asked the couple about having children, their eyes met. Lila, lowering her head, said "No children." I felt the energy shift in the room, but I couldn't read exactly what that was about. I assumed it was a compromise agreement. I agreed to marry them the following Friday morning in a private ceremony at their home.

I arrived at the Lofton household Friday at 9:45 A.M. ready to perform the ceremony at 10:00 o'clock. Friday was normally my day off, but I didn't mind helping this couple. I had my riding gear in the car, ready to head for the stables immediately after the wedding. There were four guests to witness the ceremony, and they were in good spirits. The groom was joyous, but his bride appeared nervous at first. Her eyes were downcast through most of the short ceremony.

By the end, I saw her tense shoulders drop as her gaze met that of her new husband. The anxiety was replaced by an amazing, radiant smile. I was relieved to think that this marriage might be off to a good start after all. I signed the license, received a generous check and invited Lila and Henry to attend Unity whenever they could. Then, I left the couple with their guests.

Flame was waiting and I was eager to ride him. I had not seen my buddy since Tuesday. Flame had been my closest earthly ally since Weijah died. In the saddle, my cares drifted into the crisp air and I was absorbed into the trees, grass, blue sky and the powerful animal beneath me. One with nature. One with Spirit. Flame's steady trot felt reliable and responsive to my body's direction.

I ride English style. This lets me feel the muscular movements of the animal beneath me so that I can guide him more readily by shifting my body and varying the pressure of my legs. Western riders sit in a saddle that feels like a chair. They miss the intimate sensation and interaction you get with English riding. Also, riding is my main exercise, and English riding gives my muscles the workout they need.

On this day, the trail was clear of other riders. Sensing my readiness, Flame picked up the pace to a brisk canter and we silently bonded. Our merged energies took me to another reality where peacefulness reigned. I rode for a couple of hours until I felt raindrops on my head. Then we headed for the stables where I brushed Flame's glistening coat and inspected his hooves. He was in good shape.

Having a horse can be expensive, but everyone deserves at least one luxury. My salary is modest by Washington standards. Because I live in a parsonage maintained by the church and I have some savings from my former career, I can afford the special pleasure of having Flame in my life.

That evening, I fell into a reflective mood. I joined ten couples in matrimony in the past year. Some were already members of the church and others joined after they married. The rest I never saw after the ceremony. I wondered what this couple would do. I was jarred from my reverie by a phone call from one of my very active members, Rob Hadly. He invited me to Sunday dinner, and having tasted Sandra Hadly's delicious cooking, I accepted.

When I arrived for dinner on Sunday afternoon, the smell of lasagna was in the air. Sandra emerged from the kitchen, followed by an attractive 40ish brunette. "Uh-oh," I thought. "They're playing Cupid. I wish people wouldn't do this."

"Rev. Padgett," Rob began, "this is Deanna Gibson, one of Sandra's co-workers."

I shook her hand and smiled, "Hello, Deanna. It's a pleasure meeting you." She beamed at me, displaying perfect white teeth. For some reason, my thoughts drifted to Flame, who also has pretty teeth. I don't recall the conversation that followed. I tried to be pleasant, but I felt no vibes whatsoever between us. She was neat, cordial and attractive, but my gut kept telling me she was a boring woman. I didn't pick up any kind of sparkle.

The kind of sparkle that attracts me comes from a place of spirit energy deep inside a person. It naturally overflows and I can sense it. Deanna was smiling, but the smile appeared to be masking insecurity, boredom or desperation. She didn't need a boyfriend. She needed therapy. As a trained counselor I could help her, but not in the way she was expecting. I decided to be cordial and kind without committing myself.

After the palate pleasing lasagna and salad, followed by sweet potato cake, I thanked my hosts and prepared to depart. I sensed a flash of energy passing between Sandra and Deanna's eyes. Deanna offered me her phone number, saying she wanted to know more about the church. "Thank you," I said dispassionately. "Perhaps you can visit Unity sometimes." I admit it was not a sincere invitation. There were already two women in the church who had not gotten the message that I was not interested in courting or marrying them. One of the quickest ways for a pastor to create gossip and discord in the church is to date parishioners. As far as that was concerned, I wasn't going to touch it.

I never called Deanna. Rob mentioned her positive aspects a few weeks later and I told him, "Thank you, my friend, for your concern. I am not interested in a romantic relationship right now." He shook his head, saying "Okay." Deanna never showed up at the church. Thank the Lord. I buried myself in my work, punctuated by excursions with Flame.

More than a year passed without a word from Lila or Henry Lofton. Then, on one of my busy Thursdays, Lila called. Henry had died of cancer. She wanted to have the funeral at Unity. May the Lord forgive me, but my heart skipped a beat.

I arranged a joint meeting with Lila and our music director, Mrs. Warren, to plan Henry Lofton's transition celebration. I simply did not trust myself to meet with her alone. There was something magnetic about that woman, and my usual professional manner was giving way to a surge of passion I had not felt for a very long time.

Henry Lofton's homegoing was a short but fairly upbeat occasion. About twenty people showed up to say goodbye, some of them Henry's old colleagues from the railroad.

Lila's sister and brother, as well as some of her co-workers came to support the new widow. Old Mrs. Carpenter, who attended everybody's funeral, was in her usual spot with her proper hat and gloves. It didn't matter that she'd never met Henry. Funerals were her thing.

Lila's sister, Gwen, sang "I'll Fly Away." Our music director accompanied herself, soulfully singing "Amazing Grace." I gave a short homily, not really knowing Henry very well. This was supplemented by Henry's railroad buddy, Ben, who joked about their adventures on the train. Lila was fairly composed, dabbing her eyes now and then. She smiled at the railroad stories.

The hearse and four cars made their way to the cemetery for a short graveside service. Then, the group dispersed quickly, returning to the Lofton household. I decided it would be best if I returned home. I had no idea if I would ever see any of these people again.

Two Sundays later, as Mrs. Warren played the processional, I walked up the aisle as usual and took my seat facing the congregation. Scanning the room as the processional ended, I saw Lila Lofton enter the sanctuary. I stuck to my prepared message that morning, not trusting myself to ad lib. I could not fathom why this young widow had such a profound effect on my emotions, but I knew I had to rein those feelings in. I vowed to be empathetic but professional with her.

When we asked visitors to raise their hands, Lila and another woman responded. The ushers gave them packets of information about the church and I invited them to join the congregation for refreshments following the service. The other visitor stayed, but Lila slipped out immediately following the service.

That evening, I prayed over what I should do. I got the feeling that I should wait a couple of days, then call Lila to see how she was doing. On Tuesday, I followed through.

After initial greetings Lila said, "Thank you for calling. I enjoyed the service on Sunday. I haven't been attending church lately, and I really needed the lift that I got from your message." I replied, "When you are going through the grieving process, coming to church can give you the strength you need. If you agree, we can put you on our prayer list and ask God to guide you at this difficult time." She answered, "Please put me on the prayer list. I have to get through all the legal paperwork and notices and this feeling of emptiness in my life. I've never done this before." I offered Lila the volunteer services of our recently formed Chaplin support team. I was thinking in particular of Vesta Ellis, who was widowed a year ago. She would know what to do.

With Lila's consent, I called Mrs. Ellis. The ladies met two days later and I felt my work was done for the moment. Lila began coming to church about twice a month and I kept my promise to myself to remain supportive but professional.

Four months later, I received a phone call from Lila. She said, "I need to talk to someone about a problem that has been bothering me for some time. Could I come in to see you?" I replied, "Of course. Could you come to the church this coming Tuesday?" She said, "I get off work at 4:30 PM. I usually take the bus, but I can drive on Tuesday. I can be there by 5:30." I agreed to meet with her at that time.

Lila arrived promptly at 5:30. She had the same indecipherable expression on her face as she had on the day I met her. Taking the seat across from me, she got right to the point. "Pastor, I have a big hole in my life. It's not just because of my husband's death. That just made the hole larger." Then she sighed, paused and bit her lip. Leaning forward, I said, "Take your time." One tear started down her left cheek, and in the time it took me to grab the tissues, she was crying uncontrollably. I handed her the tissues and said, "Just let the tears flow. Whatever you've repressed is coming up to be healed."

Five minutes passed before Lila was able to speak again. She said, "How can it be healed? I have a lost child somewhere, and I have not seen her in two years." I was unprepared for this revelation. "I can see that you are suffering. So during the pre-marital discussion when I asked you and Henry if you wanted to have children, was your negative response somehow connected to this child?"

"Yes," Lila said. "At a time when I was a student activist in the civil rights movement and not giving my little girl the attention she needed, Henry sent her away to live with friends. They were nice people who used to babysit Bessie. Henry gave them temporary guardianship without my knowledge while I was in Georgia. They had no children of their own. We tried to contact them. We looked for them, but apparently they don't want to be found. All I know is that they moved to California and then to Arizona. The husband was in the Army, but he left the service. They could be anywhere with Bessie."

"This happened before you married Henry," I said, trying to put the situation in perspective. "Yes. I almost didn't marry him because of it. Henry had his own way of thinking about things. He thought he was giving me time to get myself settled. He thought I was way off on a tangent with my protest activities."

I said, "You may never know all the factors that motivated him. It won't do any good to analyze that now. You've got one loss stacked on top of another, and that hurts." She said, "I've made such a mess of my life."

"Whoa," I replied. "You're still in the first part of your life. You are still young. I'm going to give you something to think about. There are two things that won't help you move forward. One is blaming Henry. He's gone now. He wasn't perfect, but like everybody else, he did the best he knew how to do at the time. Temporary anger can be part of grief when someone close to you dies. Being angry at Henry long term won't help you. In fact, it will sap your energy and keep you mentally tied to the pain of sad memories. That's not a good place to be.

"The second thing that won't help you is guilt. You were also doing the best you could with your responsibilities at the time you lost your daughter. We gain wisdom because of our experiences. We don't start out being wise. Give yourself some consideration. You're human, so you'll make mistakes. One of our Unity ministers, Eric Butterworth, said 'Guilt is a disorganized state of mind.' You don't strike me as someone who wants to be disorganized. Look, life has hit you with a double whammy, but you're still on the planet. That means you have a purpose to fulfill. It will take some time to work through all this and to get your sense of direction. If you like, I would be happy to serve as your counselor."

In a cracking voice Lila asked, "But what about Bessie?"

"There is a registry where you can sign up with your contact information. When Bessie is old enough to start looking for you, she can find your information on the registry." I wrote down the phone number of an agency that could help Lila with registering. "I know you want to see her now, but that may not be possible. You may connect with her some other way, but at least this provides one pathway to bringing the two of you together. Let's put this in God's hands." Lila nodded, her face still sad.

She agreed to come back the following week, and we met regularly for the next three months. I learned that Lila did not have much family support, so I was happy to be there for her. She appeared to be stabilizing and was beginning to think about next steps in her life. She began attending church every Sunday and even signed up to become a Sunday Celebration teacher. I thought this could provide an outlet for her maternal instincts. She took the teacher training workshop and began working with the first and second graders. She seemed to enjoy working with the children.

One evening, Lila arrived smiling confidently. "I've made a decision," she said. "I'm going to law school."

"Well, that's a surprise. Where did that come from?"

"One of my friends is married to a lawyer. She talks about the pro bono work he does for poor families. I want to practice family law to help other people with problems. I think I'd be good at it."

Laughing, I said, "I know you'd be good at it. From everything I know about you, you are a bright and caring person. There are a lot of people who could use your help."

"I'm going to start studying for the LSAT. I'm a good test taker, so I should be ready for the exam in about two months. I plan to apply to Georgetown Law School. That's a good school. Who knows? I might even become a judge some day."

"What a vision," I grinned. "You've come a long way, Lila. Go for it." She followed her plan to the letter. She took and passed the LSAT. I was happy to write a personal letter of recommendation, and she got accepted at Georgetown Law. After months of counseling, Lila had transformed herself from a sad, befuddled, guilty, angry person to a radiant woman with a clear vision of the future she wanted. I knew she still had some baggage, but she was purposefully moving in the right direction now. Apparently she was capable of supporting herself financially while in law school. I surmised that Henry had left her some money. She was going to be okay.

The next two years were difficult. Both of my parents died within six months of each other. They were in their early eighties. I realize I was fortunate to have them as long as I did, but that did not make the sense of loss any less wrenching. Even though I knew their souls were alive and well on the other side, I missed the loving human personalities that had shaped my life. First my wife left, then my parents. I even felt some anger welling up because the only person still alive in our immediate family besides me was one brother, Herbert. He wasn't in good health. To make matters worse, he had started drinking heavily after his wife divorced him.

I felt like God was erasing my closest earthly connections. As the anger subsided, loneliness overwhelmed me. I was lifted up and sustained by the prayers and loving support of church members. They comforted me as I had comforted them.

Like my personal life, the world was in turmoil. The Vietnam War, which began in 1965, seemed out of control. The U. S. troops were unaccustomed to guerilla warfare and were dying in large numbers. Peace talks were not producing viable results. With 33,641 servicemen dead by April 1969, many frustrated Americans began protesting. With increasing frequency, protestors picketed the White House. This had been happening for several years.

Some of my church members who were peace activists wanted the church to take a stand against the war. We discussed this at a meeting of the Board of Trustees. The Board was divided, with some members feeling that the church should not take an activist political stand. One Board member was among the protestors. The Board concluded that individual members should take whatever action that they felt best. The church would pray for peace and an early end to the conflict.

As an individual, I decided to picket the White House with a group of activists. I knew that we needed to get the attention of those who were making decisions about the war. With my Quaker background, I strongly believed in intentional peace. I recognized the irony of protesting, creating another conflict, in order to get to peace. Still, getting involved with the peace activists shielded me from my personal grief.

I continued to work hard, serve others, ride Flame and focus on my spiritual development. I checked with Lila periodically, as I did with my other parishioners, to see how their lives were going. People went through challenges and experienced blessings. There were births, marriages, divorces, deaths, new jobs, lost jobs, triumphs and disasters. A year later, Herbert died. I was growing weary.

One Tuesday afternoon in May after listening to a litany of sorrows and complaints from some of my members, I needed a lift. I headed for the stables to ride Flame. When I arrived, I couldn't believe my eyes. There was Lila mounting a steed!

"Lila," I called. "I didn't know you rode horses." She replied, "I haven't ridden in years, but I used to ride on the farm when I was a little girl. I heard you make reference to riding several times, saying it was a great way to relax and be in the present moment. I just finished preparing for and taking my final exams, so I thought I would come out here and release all that stress."

"It's a great idea," I said. "I was planning to do some trail riding. Would you like to ride with me?" Smiling, she replied, "Yes, Ezra. I'd like that." This moment was, as they say, the beginning of the rest of my life.

I mentored Lila, sharing what I knew about riding and caring for horses. She was new to the concepts of English versus Western riding, but had ridden bareback as a child. She shared with me stories from her childhood on the farm and her school days. She asked, "Have you ever heard of a school truck?"

"A school truck? No. I've heard of a school bus. I rode one all through school, back in Wisconsin."

"Well, in the country in Georgia, the colored kids rode to school on a truck owned by one of the local farmers. A couple of children rode in the truck's cab, and the rest of us rode in the back. It was bumpy on those unpaved roads. But amazingly, we thought it was fun, even when it rained. We played made-up games. We sang, but not too loud because the truck driver would fuss and make the loudest one sit in the cab next to him. We never realized we were getting second class treatment. We found out later that the white kids rode on a bus." She sighed at the thought. "But today, we're riding together on horseback in this beautiful park. My, how things change."

"Indeed," I said. "A few days ago, I rode Flame alone. Today I'm riding with wonderful company. That's what I call a transformation. A blessing." We smiled at each other and rode in silence for a while. I prayed, "Lord, please let this experience be repeated." Then, I released all thought and melded with the pure energy of the moment.

We both enjoyed the ride and each other's company. I wondered if I could make the transition from father figure and counselor to special friend. Near the end of the ride, I silently asked God to give me a sign if this relationship could become closer. As we approached the stables Lila said, "It's funny. The other night, I dreamed we were riding together just like today."

"That was a prophetic dream," I said. "I've really enjoyed this. I'd forgotten how much fun it is to have a riding partner." I was smiling broadly.

"Could we do this again?" Lila asked. I was surprised but happy at her assertiveness. "Yes. Let's do that. I usually ride on Tuesdays and Fridays." She asked, "What about this Friday? I've learned so much today. This is a sport I could really enjoy."

So there it was. She enjoyed my tutelage, but that might or might not lead to the intimate friendship I wanted. Still, there was that sign, Lila's dream. It was no coincidence that we met at the stables on this day. I know that nothing happens accidentally. God is present and active in our lives. He guides us whether we are conscious of it or not.

Later that evening after my meditation and prayers, I reflected on how these riding "dates" violated my self-imposed policy of not dating church members. Lila had joined the church two years ago. Still, my joy flowing from our riding together canceled out any logical arguments against repeating the experience. I decided to go with the flow while keeping my consciousness awake lest I make a terrible mistake. I spoke aloud, "God, please guide me. I surrender to your guidance." Immediately, the whole room was filled with a golden light and my body felt light as a feather, as though I were part of the golden light. That's how I knew.

Friday finally arrived. Lila and I met at two o'clock on a beautiful day with temperatures in the low eighties and a mild breeze. Again, we chatted and rode the horses comfortably as if we had known each other all our lives. Daylillies were blooming in the park and robins were chirping messages to their friends.

We talked of the contrast between our riding in the park and our soldiers fighting the Viet Cong half a world away. Lila said, "Students at Georgetown are heavily involved in protesting the war. In fact, part of our campus serves as a staging area for protest groups preparing to march to the White House. The school is not that far away from 1600 Pennsylvania Avenue, you know."

"Are you involved in that activity, Lila?"

"Yes. It's like a continuation of my civil rights activism. I picket the White House at least two Saturdays a month."

"I was there picketing last Saturday."

"Oh, I didn't know you did that. I had to study last Saturday for a test."

"Well, our active interest in ending the war is something we have in common."

Near the end of the ride, Lila mentioned that she had cooked dinner earlier that day. She asked, "Will you come over for dinner after our ride? It's my way of saying thanks for helping me improve my riding skills."

I said, "I accept your invitation. My dinner at home was going to be leftovers from my take-out lunch." I sensed that Lila was being cautious, linking her invitation to my riding instruction. I had already been shown that there was more to it than that.

Lila's cooking was wonderfully tasty! She was well acquainted with herbs and spices. It wasn't a down home meal. It was gourmet. She said she used to do good Southern cooking exclusively, but somewhere down the line she enrolled in a gourmet cooking class just for fun. I couldn't have been happier.

So many young women these days don't know how to cook. That's a shame because men never stopped liking to eat a good meal. I support women's rights, but in one way I am old fashioned. I very much appreciate a woman who can cook. That attitude is shared by a number of men who express to me in counseling sessions their disappointment that their wives or girlfriends can't cook. More sadly, these women seem to have no interest in learning. Many young ladies miss out on marriage proposals because of this deficit. Sometimes I yearn to tell them, but I can't.

Some men compensate by learning to cook themselves. Civilization has evolved over the last hundred years, but our digestive systems are about the same. A good meal, pleasing to the palate and to the eye, is a treasure. No matter who cooks it.

Lila's extra special menu included homemade focaccia, chicken cacciatore, roasted vegetables, orzo with pine nuts, spinach salad with goat cheese, cranberries, mandarin oranges and pecans, and for dessert, peach mousse with raspberry coulis. The fresh lemon-lime-orangeade was a real treat. I admit I overate.

After dinner, we sat and talked for a while. Then I offered to help with the dishes. I don't usually do that when I'm a dinner guest, but it felt so natural. Our very mellow evening was capped by a glass of sherry. As I departed around nine o'clock, I thanked Lila and gave her a quick hug. Nothing dramatic. I did not want to do anything to mar the perfect ending of this occasion or the expectation that it could be repeated.

Upon reaching my home, I quickly undressed for bed. I briefly considered starting a journal to chronicle this new turn of events in my life. But this night, I wanted to thank God for my blessings and go to sleep. I wanted to savor the memory of holding Lila in my arms, though briefly. In my mind's eye, she lingered there.

That night, for the first time since I was a teenager, I had a wet dream. I could hardly believe it. Whatever I had been dreaming, I couldn't remember it. But the results were evident. All those years of ignoring my sexual desires and directing those energies into my work apparently had come to an end. My human self was making a statement.

The next day, I took a break from preparing my message to think about my situation. No one at the church must know about my close friendship with Lila. I hated to carry on a secret romance, but this was a dilemma. Maybe I was getting ahead of myself. Maybe Lila wasn't thinking that far into the future. She could just be celebrating the end of the school year. She could have plans for the summer that I don't know about. I thought, "Okay, I'll have to ask her about her summer plans. I don't want to move too fast and ruin this blessing."

I telephoned Lila and left a message on her answering machine. "Blessings, Lila. This is Ezra. I called to thank you for the lovely meal and for sharing the afternoon and evening with me yesterday. I really enjoyed your company. I'll see you Sunday."

That evening, I listened to my messages. There was a telemarketer offering "a great deal" on magazines. Next came Lila's sweet voice. "Ezra, I don't know when I've had so much fun. I fell asleep smiling. Thank you."

Tuesdays and Fridays became regular riding days for Lila and me that summer. Sometimes she cooked afterward and sometimes we went out to dinner. One evening in early August, old Mrs. Carpenter and her sister spotted us at a Capitol Hill eatery. At that moment, Lila and I were holding hands. I knew then that our secret was out. Within a few hours, phone lines among my parishioners would be burning with the news of our relationship. Some of those accounts were bound to be exaggerated. I warned Lila that we would have to face questions the following Sunday.

Up to that point, our dates consisted exclusively of riding and eating. There was no physical intimacy beyond hugging, holding hands, and occasionally a quick kiss on the cheek. Both of us were showing restraint. Henry had made his transition more than two years ago. Still, I didn't want to push Lila. I thought she was satisfied with the way things were.

This woman was enchantingly unpredictable. When I took her home, she invited me in for coffee. As the coffee was brewing, she turned to me and said, "You told me the church members will be talking about us. Let's give them something to talk about." She put her arms around me and pressed her warm lips to mine. I was not slow to respond. Her quick and lively tongue set my imagination spinning. I knew this was just a preview of something spectacular. We kissed passionately several times before I made my way to the door. I had to

124

leave while I still had a modicum of control over my human urges. My dreams showed no such restraint, and the next morning I again woke to wet sheets.

On Saturday, I got a call from Kenneth Whatley, a member of the Board of Trustees. "Ezra," he began, "there is some gossip going around about you and Lila Mae Lofton. Now, I know you are both single and entitled to have a social life. Still, I remember a conversation with you about our former pastor who dated women in the church and caused quite a disturbance. He was secretly dating two of them at one time. I need some reassurance that we are not gearing up for another scandalous situation."

"Thank you for your candor," I replied. "It has been my policy not to date women who are church members. For a long time, I didn't date anyone at all. But, you know, I am human. Lila is very special. I have admired her for some time, so I prayed for guidance. I got the feeling that if we took it slowly, things would work out. When Mrs. Carpenter saw us at dinner, I knew our relationship would be exposed."

"Yes. It stirred up all the old gossip, especially among a couple of women who are sweet on you. I'm just saying it might be wiser to choose someone outside the church."

"I have not known anyone since my wife died who has touched my heart in the way that Lila has. I don't feel that way about any other woman. Lila and I are taking this slowly, just getting to know each other. I won't be dating any of the other women, and I won't neglect my work."

"You know I have to keep an eye on the situation," Kenneth said. "That's my job. I'll defend you if you intend to confine yourself to dating that one woman. If you start seeing any of the others, I can't help you."

"I understand," I answered. "Thank you, Kenneth." This was the first of several conversations with various church members. Some were happy for me and others were jealous. Lila had been a definite asset to the church, working with the children. People liked her. Eventually, the newness of the situation wore off and the church settled for watching Lila and me. In the sanctuary, our decorum was above criticism. It was rare that someone from Unity saw us together outside the church. We were apparently the only equestrians in the group.

After dating for three months, Lila and I went to a Kennedy Center concert featuring the National Symphony Orchestra. Lila planned this surprise in celebration of my birthday on August 21st. The magnificent presentation of Felix Mendelssohn's Symphony Number Four stirred my soul. I had often experienced the melody of that symphony's first movement running through my head while riding Flame. The live music in that concert hall lifted me into such rapture. I was spellbound, yet aware of pent up energy yearning for release. When we returned to Lila's home, my passion overflowed and we entered that intimate place where two join together as one. Afterward, I did not want to leave. I thought, "This is where I want to stay for the rest of my life. I want to stay with Lila. No more going and coming."

Stroking her hair as it lay wildly on the pillow, I confessed what she already knew. "Lila, I love you." She smiled and responded, "I love you too. I love you very much, Ezra." We embraced. Then, I heard a voice deep inside me urging, "Ask her now." I knew what that meant. My guardian angel was helping me to overcome my usually cautious nature. "Lila," I said, "I wonder if you would consider marrying me." Her eyes lit up and her smile beamed. "Ezra, yes! I will marry you." I was overcome with joy and I held her tight against my chest. I stroked her face and kissed her and hugged her again. We absorbed each other's energy. That room was full of joy and light.

I knew that some church member might see my car outside Lila's home, but I decided to spend the night. We agreed to announce our engagement the following Sunday. Henry had given Lila a beautiful diamond. Being practical, she suggested that we have the stone reset and add a cluster of smaller diamonds around it. At first, I resisted this idea, but then I thought about my modest salary as a minister. I couldn't give Lila a finer diamond and she said there was no sentimental attachment to the jewelry at that point. We had a little ceremony that night and "rechristened" the diamond to celebrate our engagement. The next day, we took it to Baker's Jewelers to have it reset.

By Sunday, Lila and I had decided to have a modest wedding in mid-October, four years since the day we met. We would be married following the regular church service on the second Sunday. Peggy Armstrong, one of the ministers who graduated with me at Unity Village, agreed to perform the ceremony. We planned a catered reception in the church hall with all the members invited. Lila's sister and brother said they would drive up for the ceremony, along with her cousin, Mary. Gwen agreed to be the matron of honor. I chose Kenneth Whatley from the Board as my best man.

Lila entered her last year of law school in September 1973. Planning even a simple wedding while studying law full time was not going to be easy for her. I suggested that we use Rosie Stephens, a wedding planner who attended the church. Her father was a wedding photographer and they worked as a team. Lila agreed. The time passed quickly.

On our wedding day, Peggy gave the Sunday message. The church was packed. We had sent out informal invitations two weeks earlier. The date was whispered on phone lines and during coffee hour for weeks before that. We asked that any funds intended to buy gifts be given instead to Africare.

Lila chose a simple beige silk dress for the short ceremony, accented by pearls. Her hair was upswept in a soft but sophisticated style. I wore a black suit and my ministerial collar. I was brimming over with joy, and from the look on Lila's face, I knew she was too. The church was beautifully decorated, both the sanctuary and the reception area. Rosie had outdone herself with flowers and ribbons and lace.

I was amazed at the lavish spread at the reception. Apparently, the Women of Unity had slipped some extra cash to Bettye's Choice Caterers to make the occasion truly memorable. Lila and I intermingled with the wedding guests for an hour before leaving for the airport. We were bound for four lovely days in Aruba.

Aruba is one of my favorite destinations. The beautiful, laid back island is perfect for a relaxing, romantic holiday. Our hotel was luxurious. When we entered our suite, Lila spotted a large Jacuzzi in the bathroom. She suggested that we get in the tub together. I said, inappropriately, "Weijah joined me in the tub sometimes. She washed my back and I washed hers." I immediately realized my mistake, but Lila did not miss a beat. She replied, "I'll get it started." She began running the water into the tub. I thought, "I love this woman. She tolerates my reminiscences and really gives me the support I have been missing for so long. Note to self: Stay in the present."

127

I eagerly stepped into the tub's bubbling warm water. When Lila re-entered the bathroom, she was carrying candles from the table in the dining area. She lit the candles and turned down the lights. She had brought along a small tape recorder and a mellow Miles Davis tape. She placed the recorder on the counter, started the music and joined me in the Jacuzzi.

I was in for the surprise of my life. Lila was no Weijah. She settled into the other end of the tub facing me. I wondered why she was so far away. Then, she started playing footsies with me, stroking my feet with hers. Next, her right foot moved along my leg, stopped at the knee, then retraced its path back to my feet. She repeated this motion, treating me to a gentle massage. She did the same thing with her left foot. No words, but a sweet smile. I felt my body relaxing after the busy day we had. Next, her right foot traveled up to my outer thigh, causing her to move closer. She pulled her foot back, bending her knee. After repeating this motion several times, she switched to the left foot and my left thigh. She had my full attention. I wondered what she would do next.

She moved on to the inner thigh, and then to my abdomen, still gently massaging me with her feet. Then she almost swam through the swirling water, tickling and rubbing my chest in a circular motion with her nipples. By the time she brushed a breast across my lips, I knew I had married a brilliant and multifaceted gem.

When we returned to Washington, Lila had to hit the books. Since this was her last year in school and we were starting a new life together, she decided not to continue teaching in the Children's Celebration Center. There was much to do. We hired movers to take most of Lila's things to a storage facility. She moved herself and a few possessions into the parsonage and we found a tenant for her house. In short order, we began our life together.

Our riding dates were inviolable unless something really extraordinary was going on. Lila purchased a horse at auction, naming her Shug. At sixteen hands, her mare was shorter than Flame. Shug was an ebony beauty with socks on her front feet. Lila was an amazingly confident rider for someone with so little experience.

My work schedule was getting busier as the church membership began growing. We started new music and spiritual dance programs to make the Sunday services more appealing. It's amazing how much the arts can add to a worship service. The performing arts touch people's hearts and make them more receptive to the Sunday message and the prayers.

Outside of church, Lila was busy with a law internship requiring long hours on top of her regular responsibilities. Thank God for the riding dates. That was our exclusive time together. Once in a while, we rode the trail with other people, but not often.

One Friday evening, we were relaxing at home and attending to mundane chores. I shared with Lila that some of the new church members had brought with them ideas that were definitely different from Unity's teachings. "They say they like what we believe, yet they hold on to conflicting ideas they learned in childhood and in churches that dwell on fear, Satan and sin. They seem to fear God more than they love him. I remind myself that everybody moves at his or her own pace. People are exactly where they need to be until they feel ready to take the next step."

Lila quipped, "We can't judge them. There could be growth that we are not seeing. Like you've said, though, the outer is an outpicturing of the inner self. If you look at the way people conduct their lives, you have a view of their innermost thoughts and feelings. When they inhabit an environment, does it blossom or wither or stay unchanged, as if they simply blended in or disappeared? Asking that question is the way I test myself.

"Lila, you pass the test with flying colors. Everything around you blossoms."

"That hasn't always been the case, Ezra."

"You're too hard on yourself. I've watched you grow during the few years I have known you. Almost twice as many children are attending our Children's Celebration Center classes since you got involved. And your idea of starting a spiritual dance group has everyone excited."

"Marty has taken that idea and run with it. She's really responsible."

"Lila, Marty has done a great job of implementing the idea. She's full of spiritual energy and the children respond to that. I love the way you give other people credit for their contributions. I also love the way you unobtrusively suggest possibilities from that creative imagination of yours. Then, you step back and watch the idea take shape around you. You have a special gift, my dear. You are a catalyst for transforming people and circumstances.

"Now, I need to encourage some of the new members to stop hiding their lights in barrels and closets. The world needs their light. They have so much to offer, but they lack confidence. Some of them have been held back by other people's opinions over the years or by old guilt feelings." I sighed and shook my head. "I wish I could get people to stop beating themselves up for old mistakes and start living in the present. That would make such a difference in their lives."

"I know I've done that. Your counseling helped me find my way." Lila responded.

"We all have had guilt feelings from time to time," I said, "but some people have this fear of God's punishment. They don't see the Creator as pure love. They get stuck in fear and guilt, and like a wagon in mud, they can't get out."

"What do you know about a wagon in mud?" Lila asked.

"I grew up on a farm. My parents and my Uncle Presley farmed 140 acres. I happened to be riding in an old wagon with Uncle Presley during a rainy spell. It had rained every day for two weeks. The wagon wheels hit a deep rut in the ground and would not budge. We had to unhook the horse and leave the wagon behind."

"You never told me your parents were farmers. Like mine."

"In their later years, they sold the farm and moved into a nearby town with housing for seniors. Stick around and you'll hear lots more. I've had all kinds of experiences, including riding a camel in Egypt during a vacation one summer."

"A camel? You are full of surprises. I knew you went to England for a semester of your junior year. That's when you learned to ride with an English saddle."

"Yes. You and I should go abroad, if we can ever find the time."

"Let's make it my graduation present."

"All right. You pick the destination."

That night, I heard my beautiful wife crying into her pillow. I moved toward Lila to comfort her. She trembled in my arms. "What's wrong, sweetheart?" I asked.

"Where I really want to go for graduation is wherever Bessie is," she stammered between sobs.

"Baby, you're really hurting. Let's see if the court has any way of tracking the guardianship of that couple that took Bessie. We'll try to find her. Right now, I want you to remember that God is watching over her just like he's watching over you. I'm going to teach you a technique for sending her love and protection. It will help her and help you too. You can do it anytime you feel anxious about her. Okay?"

"Yes. Show me, Ezra."

"Let's close our eyes. Relax and release the thoughts in your mind. Create a feeling of love inside yourself. Feel the warmth of that love in your heart center. Pink is the color of human love. Visualize the love you are feeling as a pink light. See the light spread from your heart throughout your body, then outside your body until you are surrounded by it. Now, visualize Bessie. Get as clear a picture of her as you can. Send a beam of the pink light to Bessie's heart center. Watch the light now spread through Bessie's body and encircle her. She is completely filled with your love and protection. Hold in your mind a picture of you and Bessie, connected by the light which encircles both of you. Hold that image as long as you can. Bessie feels warmed by your love right now. Know that God has made this possible. Thank you, God. Thank you."

When Lila opened her eyes, she was completely at peace. She gratefully hugged me. No words were needed because her sweet smile and peaceful countenance said it all. There was a glow in her eyes, as if she had seen a beautiful vision. I held her in my arms and rocked her gently until she fell asleep.

The next day Lila asked, "Where did you learn things like sending people love?"

"Well, I've read many spiritual books over the years. People share ideas from their own experiences. If I try an idea and it works for me, then I use it. I'm careful about sharing some of this knowledge because many people aren't ready for it."

"I know what you mean. There's something I've never shared with anyone because I thought they'd laugh at me. They wouldn't understand."

"Do you want to tell me about it?"

Taking a deep breath, Lila began sharing with me the visits from her spiritual guide or angel. "She's been with me for as long as I can remember. She gives good advice. Sometimes, a complete thought packet, like a paragraph, will arrive in my head when I'm thinking about something altogether different. Then again, sometimes I actually hear her voice."

"She is contacting you two ways -- by sending energy packs that reassemble as words, and also by mental telepathy which most people have heard of. Have you ever seen her?"

"No. I never have."

"Do you ever wonder who she is? Have you asked her what her name is?"

"No. It's okay if she's a mystery guide. I think of her as Supermama. All I know is she is wise and she loves me."

"Maybe that's enough.

"All these years have passed and you're only the second person I've told about her."

"That's probably a good thing. Most people wouldn't understand. I have a guide, too. Sometimes when I haven't had time to prepare a sermon, I make a silent request, "Help me do this. Thank you." In the pulpit, I speak the words as I receive them in my head. Those have been my most effective sermons. The ones people remember and can recall a year later."

"Do you ever hear your guide's voice?"

"Yes. When the words come as thoughts, I know my listening channel is only partially open. When I hear my guide talking, I know the channel is open wider. No trash clogging it up. Once, I got a visual, but his face was hidden. That was awesome.

"I would love to share these kinds of experiences with the whole congregation, but many people would not understand. Some would call it blasphemy."

"I'm glad we can talk about these things with each other. Apparently, we are spiritually matched."

"And that makes for a strong marriage."

Time passes quickly. Spring of 1974 announced itself in Washington, D.C. with nascent lilies and trumpeting tulips. On Easter Sunday, I drove Lila around the U. S Capitol grounds, adorned with hundreds, maybe thousands of tulips in a rainbow of colors. Our afternoon drive served as a respite from Lila's studies and my church responsibilities. We had conducted and enjoyed a celebratory service that day with guest soloists and violinists. The feelings of joy and love among those attending church were palpable. Christ's spirit permeated the Unity Church Center.

As we left the Capitol Grounds, Lila reminded me, "Two months to graduation."

"Have you decided where you want to go on your graduation trip?"

"Paris. I've never been there."

"Good choice, Lila. I haven't been there either, and I've always wanted to go. Remind me, I have to get my passport renewed. Let's discuss our plans over a seafood dinner at Hogate's. Don't worry. I called ahead for reservations Friday morning."

"Did you reserve extra rum buns to take home? I know how you love them."

"I do love them, but I don't want to take fat clothes to Paris. I need to cut back."

At Hogate's, we sat at a table by the window overlooking the dock. Glistening sailboats served as an introduction to the murky Chesapeake Bay and the blue sky beyond. I said, "We still need to clean up the bay and make it healthy again. How our ecosystem will be passed on to the next generation depends on our consciousness and will. Enough of us have to want to make it happen."

"Another cause, Ezra? Your plate is full."

"Look who's talking. We have to keep each other from going overboard."

Turning from the bay, I studied my wife as she reviewed the menu. Sometimes, I am overwhelmed with gratitude that this smart, caring, gorgeous woman is my wife. The energy of my smile grabbed her attention.

"What are you looking at, Ezra?"

"You, Lila. You look very special today."

"Thanks for my Easter dress. You have great taste."

"Inspired by you."

During dinner, we decided to spend four days in Paris, followed by three days in the south of France on the Riviera, and three days in the

Champagne region. I discovered after our marriage that my wife was very secure financially. Lila had invested her inheritance from Henry wisely and she insisted on paying for the trip. I have no hang-ups about being the main provider. I believe each partner should give what he or she is able to give to make the marriage work.

Over coffee, we agreed to brush up on our French by trying to communicate with each other in that language for at least half an hour each evening. This was going to be either an adventure, or a funny misadventure. We both looked forward eagerly to the challenge.

The weeks that followed were intense for both Lila and me. My wife prepared for her final exams and I worked at managing the transition of our church to a larger, more varied but focused organization. In the new mode, leadership was to be shared at various levels. We formed small group ministries to serve the congregation and the larger community. I had to use my best people skills to ease the fears of folks loyal to the status quo and to calm the jealousies that arose.

The extent to which individuals had assumed ownership of various functions was amazing. Established groups like the active and dynamic Women of Unity were reluctant to release some of their cherished activities to newly formed ministries and teams. The efficient Sanctuary Design Team resisted admitting anyone new. The Camping and Hiking Group had a close knit membership, and wanted to vote on potential new members. They opposed the formation of a Trail Walking Group, seeing the new group as a threat. There were uncertainties and misunderstandings everywhere, the turmoil that precedes a new order.

In the midst of harmonizing these differing views, Lila and I were true to our promise to practice French, although some evenings our sessions were abbreviated. Our riding suffered too, as we seemed unable to get to the stables more than once per week. We were both feeling the need for a vacation. We became short with each other one evening in early May and erupted into a rare and silly argument over clippings out of the sports section of the paper. I knew then that we needed to get away. I persuaded Lila to go with me on an impromptu retreat to Luray Caverns near Virginia's Skyline Drive.

We dropped everything and jumped in the Volvo, leaving all the stress of change and challenge behind. We spent the day walking along wooded, flowered trails and exploring the amazing stalactites and stalagmites in the caverns. In that awesome place, we were able to recalibrate our relationship with the world and with each other. Surrounded by the beauty of God's creations, we rediscovered our center. Before leaving, we had a peaceful meditation in the woods. Growing near the tree stump where Lila sat was a delightful patch of wild daisies. Lila plucked some for her hair. On the drive back to Washington, we felt light and joyful. What a difference a day makes!

For some reason, that retreat opened Lila's heart so that she could share with me thoughts that she had repressed for years. She told me about her past life regression and the prediction that she would have multiple marriages. I am her third husband, so that prediction certainly came true. She also told me about the true father of her missing daughter. I listened with compassion. I knew she was taking a potentially painful risk in sharing this information and I tried to let her know she was in a safe place. We drew closer over the next few days.

On Tuesday evening of the following week, I dragged myself home after a Board of Trustees meeting. Lila looked up from her books, her face full of astonishment and concern. "Ezra, what happened to you? You look awful."

"The Board got into a tangled web tonight. You know we have a lot of strong personalities on that Board. We were discussing outreach to the community and growing the church. Some of them are content with things just the way they are. Others are intimidated by the changes they have already seen. We have more races and ethnicities joining the church, and more gays and lesbians. They are afraid that growing numbers of those "other" folks will destabilize the church. Several times, the discussion got so heated that I had to call a time out and go into prayer."

"But Ezra," my wife responded, "Every Sunday we say that we welcome all of God's children everywhere, because we all have the same loving Creator."

"Well, some take the 'everywhere' part to mean 'not here,' at least for not more than one or two Sundays. Our folks can think of those other folks lovingly while they keep their distance."

"That goes to the heart of Christ's teachings."

"Lila, these are people with an imperfect understanding of who they are in the world. Over and over, I have tried to show that we're here to express God in the world. Every one of us. They just haven't gotten it yet."

"You know what I think, Ezra? I think they are afraid to acknowledge their spiritual selves. They can't imagine actually loving their enemies, or even not seeing people as enemies. That's a leap for most folks."

"You're onto something, Lila. People fear what they don't understand. The name of that fear is *separation from the Divine Spirit*, the part of them that is made in God's image. They are alienated from it. They have unconsciously chosen to embrace the ego, which creates separation, division and categories. When they truly embrace the Holy Spirit, their perceptions will shift to oneness and their lives will change.

"Well, we can't solve that problem tonight, sweetheart. Let's pray." Holding Lila's hand, I began. "God, thank you for the many blessings you have already bestowed on our church. We pray for harmony, clarity and understanding for ourselves, our Board members and others in the church. Let us acknowledge you, listen for your guidance and follow your leading. Increase our faith and strengthen us as we do your work in the world. Let us all understand that the family of man is also the family of God. Remove from us any trace of ego superiority so that we may faithfully serve our parishioners. Through your grace, we affirm the highest and best outcome in this situation. And so it is. Amen."

Lila said, "I feel better already."

"How about a late night snack? I've worked up an appetite."

We made tuna sandwiches and lemonade and Lila turned on the radio. National Public Radio was playing jazz by Miles Davis. As we sat in the kitchen eating and relaxing with that mellow music, I gazed at my beautiful wife. All the emotion and frustration of my evening metamorphosed into a more intimate energy. The top three buttons of Lila's blouse were undone and the open blouse casually revealed a black, lacy bra. As Lila swayed gently to the music, the slight movement in the curvature of her breasts pushing against their lacy restraints entranced me. I leaned over and kissed her. Her response was so electric that we never finished the sandwiches. I led my wife toward the bedroom, but we only got as far as the living room couch. What an evening!

Lila's graduation was fast approaching and she had invited her mother, sister and brother to attend. I had not seen Gwen and Terrell since our wedding, and looked forward to seeing them again. I had not met Lila's mother, but had talked with her by phone. She seemed reserved, and Lila said their relationship was not close. We occasionally shared photographs with the family, enclosed in Lila's letters.

Only Gwen was able to come to the graduation ceremony. Gwen arrived the day before graduation, bringing greetings from the folks back home. I told Lila that whenever she felt ready, I would like to visit the place where she grew up and meet the rest of her family. She said that time would come before long. I sensed that she was struggling with some unnamed fear.

What a happy day when Lila and her fellow law graduates stood to be acknowledged at the large Georgetown University ceremony on Healy Hall Lawn. Gwen and I took pictures and handed Lila an armful of daisies. Lila was ecstatic. She had envisioned this day three years ago, and stayed true to the vision until it materialized. I admire her courage and determination.

Gwen stayed at our home for two more days. There is a special bond between those sisters. I plunged into the work of the church, giving them time to spend with each other.

The next week, we packed for our trip to Paris. I asked a Unity teacher to come and substitute for me for two Sundays. On Wednesday morning at 10:00 AM, Lila and I boarded a plane at National Airport for our trans-Atlantic flight. Normally, my wife is financially conservative. On this day, she surprised me with first class seats, a real luxury! We were off to a fabulous start.

In Paris, we stayed in a small, elegant hotel on the Left Bank near the Notre Dame Cathedral. Before long, we were traveling the subway like native French people, taking in the Louvre, the Eiffel Tower, the bakeries, the restaurants, the shops and even the Moulin Rouge. To put it mildly, we were a long way from the outskirts of Macon, Georgia and Ashland, Wisconsin. We had a ball.

In Champagne country, there were opportunities to visit the champagne cellars. Many of them were located in caves. We sampled a few choice wines, and visited a Gothic cathedral in nearby Reims. We did a lot of walking. Thankfully, we were both in shape from our horseback riding and occasional jogging.

On the beach at Cannes, Lila liberated her wild inner spirit from its box. She bought and wore the skimpiest of bikinis, looking a decade younger than her thirty-three years. You would never have pegged her as a preacher's wife. She promised to donate the swimsuit to the Salvation Army upon our return to the U. S. My wife is a wonder. She is so decorous at church, but underneath a chameleon.

On the trip home, we traded stories about our fanciful trip. With some editing, I could share those experiences in my Sunday messages. Many of the people at church have never been abroad and some have no desire to go. Yet, the stories will stretch them a little and serve to whet the interest of others whose minds are not closed to international travel. Traveling to other lands can erase so many fears and divisions among people, if they go with an open mind.

Nearing the United States, Lila awakened from a nap. After she freshened up, we fell into a philosophical discussion. I was thinking of my change resistant church members. I said, "Some of these folks are going through life like horses wearing blinders. You know the blinders keep a horse from looking left or right. They keep him looking straight ahead so that he won't be distracted and won't wander off the path. When people wear blinders, you might say they are more focused. But focused on what? The same narrow field of vision, that's what. They keep trotting in a circle around the same track until they wear a deep groove into the dirt. Then, they're stuck and have no idea how to get out. It's because they are still wearing the blinders. If you suggest that they remove the blinders and experience a broader view, they panic. Fear sets in. Either they get past the fear and move on with their lives, or they keep plodding around the track year after year."

Lila yawned. "That sounds like a sermon. As much as you'd like to, Ezra, you can't change people. In your heart of hearts, you know that. Don't let them upset you. Just be the change you want them to be. Some will catch on and some won't."

"You're right, of course. What about the choices and changes

138

facing you, young lady? Now that you have graduated from Georgetown Law, where do you go from here?"

"First, I'd like the pleasure of lollygagging for a few weeks. I want to experience life away from the treadmill. I might clean out a closet or rearrange something, but mostly I want to goof off for a bit."

"You'll be bored in no time, knowing you."

"I think I can stand at least two weeks of lollygagging. That way I'll store up enough energy to give you the best back massage you've ever had."

"Lila, I like your plan."

She giggled. "After my leisure period, I'll get focused and study for the bar exam."

"That's my girl. Keep it balanced."

The stewardess interrupted us with beverage service and a snack. Afterwards, I drifted off to sleep and napped until Lila awakened me with the news that we were approaching Washington, D.C.

Lila followed her plan for the next two weeks, including my back massage. Then she began studying in earnest for the bar exam. She enrolled in a prep course to give herself an extra edge. Six weeks later, she took and passed the exam. I was not surprised. My wife sets her mind to accomplish something, and nothing can stop her. We celebrated by going to a little club in Georgetown to hear Nina Simone. What a special evening! Lila and I both love good music.

Lila soon received a job offer from the firm where she did her internship, Walker, Garfield and Rosenberg. The terms were attractive so she accepted the position of associate attorney. She soon settled into a routine. Her hours were longer than I would have preferred, but she managed to leave early most Fridays to ride with me. It meant bringing work home, but riding together reinforced our special bond.

I noticed that my wife had workaholic tendencies because she was so dedicated to her clients. A few gentle reminders kept her conscious of my desire to spend time with her. We both knew that balancing work and home could mean slower progress up the corporate ladder. Still, it was a decision we made jointly. With her sharp mind, Lila was a definite asset to her company.

After four years, Lila was promoted to junior partner. A more ambitious workaholic had made senior partner in the same time period, but he got a divorce in the process. Why is corporate life so brutal?

Lila and I carved out vacations every year, no matter what was going on. We traveled to the Caribbean, to Spain, England and Brazil. I asked her now and then if she wanted to visit her hometown, but she always found a reason not to go. I knew that she would have to go eventually in order to release her painful memories and heal her inner wounds.

I was pleased that Lila no longer seemed to crave a promotion to senior partner. She decided that being at the top wasn't everything and she enjoyed our time together. For this I was grateful. As my church became larger, my own responsibilities became onerous. I asked the Board of Trustees to consider hiring an assistant pastor. After several months of deliberation, they decided to do so. I breathed a sigh of relief. Now I could have some balance between work and home. The next six months were rewarding, as my assistant stepped up to the plate. He was an earnest and hardworking young man.

One September morning, I awakened with a terrible headache. It was worse than any pain I had ever experienced. I had been having headaches off and on for a few weeks, controlling them with Excedrin. Lila had suggested that I see a doctor, but I was stubborn. I thought I could get rid of the pain with a relaxation meditation. It did help, but today's pain was more than I could bear. Lila insisted on driving me to Dr. Gregory's office.

After he saw my agony, the doctor sent me to the hospital for tests. At the hospital, they gave me painkillers that eased the pain considerably. They wanted to admit me, but I insisted on returning home. I did not like hospitals, having visited so many sick parishioners in both hospitals and nursing homes. I decided to wait for the test results in the comfort of my own home. Lila respected my wishes.

The next day, Dr. Gregory called and asked me to come in to his office. I felt well enough to drive myself, rather than disturb Lila at work. I had insisted that she go to work because she was preparing an important brief for an upcoming trial.

Dr. Gregory had a serious expression on his face as he motioned me to sit down. He said I had an abnormal growth on my brain in an area that was inoperable. I was stunned.

When he told me I had two to three months left to live, my ego went into denial. I muttered to myself, "Patients who were told by their doctors that they had only months to live have lived on for years and attended their doctors' funerals." On the drive home, anger began to rise from the place where my fear hides. I thought, "This doctor has handed me a clearly inaccurate diagnosis. I might be going through a rough patch right now, but I'll recover and live into my eighties like my parents. I have so much to live for now." My mind drifted to my precious wife. "I have to be around to protect her. She's already been widowed once."

I decided to get a second opinion. I went to a brain specialist who looked at my test results and reached the same conclusion as Dr. Gregory. It was time to tell Lila.

I finally found the courage as we got ready for bed. "The doctor has handed me a bitter pill, Lila. He says I have an inoperable tumor in my brain. I may have three months left."

Lila tried to be strong, but a tear started down her cheek. "Just when I thought we were hitting our stride, I'm going to lose you? Can you get a second opinion?"

"I already did. I've known about this for a week, but I wanted to be sure before I shared the news with you." She hugged me for a very long time.

"You are so brave, keeping this to yourself. How can I go on without you? You are my rock. We have so many plans for the future. Now, that's not going to happen? I don't know how to handle this." She laid her head against my shoulder.

I told Lila, "I'm dying. You're not. Promise me you won't get bogged down in grief for too long. And don't bury yourself in your work. You deserve to move forward and really live your vibrant life. Pull out all the stops." My eyes searched her face to see if she truly understood me. I couldn't leave her in a hole.

She nodded, and then softly said, "I'll try. It's just that this is the second time..." Then, she burst into tears.

I held her in my arms. "After I'm gone, the memories will come for a while. Bless the memories and allow them to fade over time. Let the new day in. Remember, I'll be on to other experiences on the other side, and you should move on too. When the memories intrude on whatever you are doing or thinking, thank them for coming, and then shift your attention to the energies and requirements of the present moment."

"I know. I know this stuff philosophically, but I'm going to miss seeing you, physically touching you, riding with you, hearing you laugh, even hearing you complain."

"That's normal. Just don't linger in the past too long. Remember the direction you have established. Keep your body strong and fit. That will help you to cope emotionally. Your beautiful soul deserves a healthy body. You still have many miles to go."

"I hear you, Ezra. It's not going to be easy without you, and I know exercise will help me to chase away the blues."

"Do you think you'll continue to ride?" I asked. She replied, "I don't know if I can without you, but I promise to work out and keep myself healthy. You have taught me the value of that."

"You don't have to hang up the reins because I'm not here. Give yourself time to think about it. You look tired. When things seem dark and gray, remember to look for the light. It's always available. I'll send reminders in your dreams." She nodded.

"I'll be listening for you. Because I've seen my own soul between lives, I know it is possible for me to pierce the veil, as they say."

"We won't pierce it unless it's necessary. You need to focus on your life on earth. You have had some remarkable accomplishments so far. Promise me you'll keep going."

"I will."

"Honey, I've called my friend, Jarrett. He and I are planning to go on a fishing trip like we used to do years ago in Wisconsin. I want to have that experience one more time."

"Ezra, that's a great idea. Get all the joy you can out of this life."

"We'll leave next Wednesday and come back Thursday."

"Promise not to worry about me. Just have a good time. I'll be happy knowing you're happy."

"So, Jarrett, that's my story. I hope I haven't bored you. I'm eager to get to that hidden fishing hole you discovered in Maryland. On the way back, you can bring me up to date on your life. Meanwhile, let's listen to some music on the radio.

"Jarrett, this two lane, winding road goes on forever. I admit I was growing impatient when that tractor crawled along in front of us for a few miles. I'm glad that farmer turned off the road. How much longer?"

"About ten miles. We're almost there."

"You think the fish are biting today?"

"Ezra, there's a fifty pound rock fish out there with your name on it."

"Praise God!"

Section Five

Buster Taliferro King

You are the surprise of my life,
The wild card life wouldn't play.

- Patricia Churchill

They call me Long Daddy, but my real name is Buster. When those wild girls in high school gave me that nickname, it just slid in and made itself at home. Right today, I'm comfortable with Long Daddy or Buster, either one.

Dr. Lewis, you say you want my history in this initial session. I never thought I would be seeing a psychologist, but I need help. So here is my story. Being in this business, I guess you won't be too shocked.

I love women. Always have. This is not to say I have to have a lot of them around all the time in a romantic sense. No, but I do like to have a lot of them in my life. You know what I'm saying? Women are good to me. I don't know why, but they love the heck out of me and I love them right back.

Mama Ricks was the first good woman in my life. She raised me. My natural mother, Jessie, was a teenager who didn't know cat from rat. She was just too young. I've gotten to know her since I've been grown, and she's OK, but I love Mama Ricks. She treated me like her own son. She actually never had a natural son, just two daughters who were much older than me. Mama Ricks kept me out of trouble by keeping me involved in stuff. She tried baseball, basketball and the Boy Scouts.

Nothing stuck. Still, the women at church, my teachers and the neighborhood ladies helped to keep me straight. They all prayed for me. Thanks to Mama Ricks, I stayed on the prayer list of the Missionary Society at Mt. Zion Baptist Church.

When I was fourteen, Mama Ricks's brother introduced me to boxing. That lit the spark. Uncle James bought me some boxing gloves and gym shoes, and a passion for boxing fired up my young life. I went on up the ranks of amateur boxing and made the Olympic Team as a middleweight. I came back with a bronze medal which is displayed over my mantel. I considered going professional, but after getting my girlfriend pregnant, I decided to be practical and settle down. Uncle James hired me to work in his restaurant. I got married to Faith and ended up with two children, Stephen and Jasmine.

Honestly, I tried to be a good husband but I had a wandering eye. I flirted a lot, and my wife didn't like it. Some of the women started calling the house. As far as I was concerned they were just friends, but they fantasized that they could get me to leave Faith. I never would have left her. Faith was a good wife and mother. She fulfilled all her duties and was kind to me. She was patient with my immature behavior for as long as she could stand it. Then she walked out.

I went into shock. The excitement had worn off in our relationship, but I thought we were doing all right. My ego was hurt too. I didn't want my male friends to know that my wife had left me. I also didn't want my female friends to think they had a chance to marry me. In fact, being married had put a protective shield around me to keep the women from thinking they could be Mrs. King. At least the rational ones. Faith filed for legal separation, and after a while she divorced me. I kept supporting her and the children while she got herself situated in a job. I used to pick up the children every weekend until Faith remarried and moved to Chicago. Then, I only saw them during summer vacation, but I paid child support until Stephen and Jasmine were grown.

Many times I chastised myself for my thoughtless behavior. I made up my mind that I would never marry again, but just have female friends. I kept my vow for over twenty years.

After Faith, there were a lot of women who entered my life and helped me sort things out in one way or another. I had fun, worked hard, and eventually opened my own restaurant in Washington, DC. It is located on Georgia Avenue about half a block from the gym where I work out. I believe in keeping myself in shape.

My buddy from around the way, T. R., and I usually meet at the gym to keep each other motivated. We were heading toward the treadmills at the gym when I saw this tall sister walk through the door and approach the welcome desk. I nudged my buddy. "T. R., look at the brick house that just walked in here. I feel her vibes all the way across the room." T. R. shook his head. "Long Daddy, you're crazy. A fine woman like that is probably married."

"Well, her husband better watch out. You see those legs. UM-UNH!"

"Man, you're about to get yourself into some serious trouble. Remember, Tanya is still trying to run after you."

"I can't help it. I know what I like when I see it." Just then, the mystery lady went into the dressing room. When she came out, I gave her the most intense gaze of approval, coupled with my dazzling smile. I'm not bragging, but the women say the combination of the sparkle in my eyes and my pretty white teeth can grab any woman's attention. Thank God for mouth guards, or my boxing years could have ruined my smile. Anyway, that's how it all started with me and Lila Mae. She smiled back and I silently shouted, "Yes!"

I navigated over to the stationery bikes just as she was adjusting and mounting hers. Observing her firm butt and shapely legs I thought, "She's got it going on. Not too much…just right." My buddy, T. R., would have seen it differently. He loved women with some serious "back", that is super-sized rear ends. He called them Queens of the Nile.

I opened the conversation lamely with "Hi. I haven't seen you here before. My name is Buster."

"That's your nickname. What's your real name?"

"No. Buster Taliferro King is my real name. My nickname is Long Daddy." She looked at me strangely, and then threw her head back in a throaty laugh.

"Well hello, Buster. My name is Lila Mae Padgett and I don't have a nickname."

I smiled, "In that case, I'll have to give you one." As we rode along our imaginary biking path, I threw out a series of trial nicknames, all of which she rejected. She didn't like Fly Girl, Cute Thang, Miss Legs,

146

Mona Diva or any of the others I suggested. Once I got to know her, I realized that Phoenix was a much better choice. This girl had the guts and determination to rise out of the ashes and face any challenges that were out there. She was made of steel and velvet.

By the time we finished with the bikes, I had invited her to have lunch in my restaurant down the street. She didn't believe I owned the place, but I assured her that I did and that her lunch would be on the house. She said, "I can come tomorrow after class. I'm teaching a class at Howard." I nodded and said, "See you there."

Sure enough, the next day she showed up at Buster's Place. I had been hoping she would come, but thought she might have been jiving me at the gym. I walked over to greet her and she chose to sit at the counter. She asked, "What do you recommend?" I suggested our specialty, a fried fish sandwich with our own secret herbs and a side order of Long Daddy Coleslaw. The place was so busy that I couldn't really carry on a decent conversation. Just as Lila Mae was finishing her food, a Health Department inspector showed up and I was distracted.

When I looked around to find Lila, she was gone. The busboy approached me with a business card. "The tall lady who was sitting over there asked me to give you this," he said. I read her name and title, "Lila Mae Padgett, Esquire, Attorney at Law." Her office phone and fax numbers were listed. Then, I flipped the card over and there was a handwritten phone number. "Her home phone! That's first base. Heaven is smiling on me today."

That evening around seven, I called the girl. The voicemail message came on. "That's all right," I thought. "I can wait. This lady is worth waiting for." Just then, Tanya called and I had to switch gears. "Hey, Baby, how are you doing?" I asked. She went on to tell me about her day. She was a schoolteacher and some smartass kid had given her a hard time. I tried to console her. I liked Tanya, mostly as a friend, but she could be a comfort in bed on nights when I needed someone to hold. I have to say, the girl had a whole lot going on up front. Much more than a handful.

Tanya wanted to come over and spend the night. Normally, I would have been happy about that, but tonight I really wanted to reflect on the charms of Lila Mae. Still, I had no good excuse to give Tanya so I told her to come on over. I was hoping I wouldn't give my secret thoughts away. The image of Lila Mae had taken up residence in my mind and wouldn't go away. Not only that, but in my imagination, her clothes had melted away and there she stood buck naked in all her glory.

Briiing! There was the doorbell. Tanya must have burned up some rubber getting over here. Or was I suspended in time? I thought, "Man, get hold of yourself." I opened the door and saw Tanya's big, sparkling eyes. She floated in and handed me a bag containing my favorite champagne and a bunch of red grapes. I greeted her with a hug as I recalled one very special evening involving champagne, grapes and massage oil.

"You sure know how to stir up some memories," I whispered. "Want to go toesies?" she inquired. "I'd love to," I answered as I headed to the kitchen to open the champagne. From that moment, the girl had 100% of my attention.

Just as things were getting intense, the telephone rang. I knew it had to be Lila Mae, but I needed to seize the moment I was in and revel in the arms that were holding me. I felt like Lila Mae would be a central figure in my life sometime in the future, but the action in the present moment was too compelling to release. Every inch of Tanya's body was sensitive to my touch. The girl was a head to toe erogenous zone. No exceptions.

The phone stopped ringing. I had given up my answering machine just because of these kinds of situations, so I didn't have to worry about Tanya hearing Lila Mae's voice. You learn a few things like that when you are a bachelor with a healthy interest in women.

I was busy licking Tanya's toes while I stroked her legs. Then I moved on up her anatomy. When I gently lifted her left leg and my mouth reached the inside of her thighs, I heard her catch her breath in anticipation. I was glad I had installed soundproofing on the bedroom walls of my condo because I knew the girl was going to holler. When I touched down, an unrestrained banshee scream filled the room. I thought, "Lord, this girl is loud!" But I was enjoying myself too, so my tongue kept going. By the time Long Daddy pushed through the tunnel, the girl had already had one orgasm. Before it was all over, she had three. Soon after my explosion, I fell into a deep sleep.

The morning light peeking through the blinds woke me up. Tanya

148

had showered and was getting dressed. Man, I must have been tired to sleep that long. We chit chatted until Tanya left for work. Then, I dived for the phone and called Lila Mae.

"Good morning, Lila Mae" I began. "Well hello, Buster" she answered. "I called last night and got no answer."

"Yeah. Sorry about that. I turned off my ringer because some prankster was playing on the phone. I'm glad you called. Can I make it up to you by taking you to a movie tonight with dinner afterwards?" She replied, "Not tonight. I've got paperwork to handle. How about Thursday night?" I agreed, and she gave me her address. "Second base!" I thought. Our relationship was off and running.

On Thursday evening, I picked up Lila at her Capitol Hill townhouse. It was an elegant place and it fit her very well. She wore a mauve, silk dress that looked like it cost a pretty penny. She was an upscale lady, no question. I took her to a small, locally owned Italian restaurant in southwest Washington with good food and excellent service.

As we were finishing dessert Lila asked, "Are you seeing someone?"

I answered, "Yes, I have a friend. She's nice and convenient, and she takes care of my needs. I'm not in love with her. She's more or less a habit. I won't lie. I like spending time with her, but I know she's not THE one."

Lila lifted an eyebrow, "So you tend to think of women as conveniences. Does this lady know how you feel?"

"I've never told her that I love her. She knows that I enjoy her company and she enjoys mine. We entertain each other. But frankly, I have been marking time, waiting for the lady I could give my heart to. When I first saw you, something stirred deep inside. It felt ancient and primal, and I'm not talking about sex. It felt like, 'This is the one you've been waiting for.' Straight up."

Lila's eyes rolled up in her head, "Oh, please!" she protested. "That's a line if I ever heard one. How many women have you told that to?" She nervously fingered the fork, her hand trembling a little, belying the controlled look on her face. I looked straight into her eyes and said sincerely, "Just one."

Lila looked at me quizzically as though she was trying to decide whether or not to believe me. She told me months later that at that moment, she felt something stirring in her belly, and the feeling scared her.

"So tell me about you," I urged. "I'm divorced and you know I run a restaurant."

"I'm a widow. My husband died three years ago from a brain tumor. He was a minister. When he died, I had been practicing corporate law for over four years. After his death, I decided to switch to family law. I wanted to help people, and I believe I'm achieving that goal. I have clients on all economic levels and I've done well. I also teach one class at Howard, which I enjoy."

"What do you do for fun?"

"Mmmm. I guess I haven't thought very much about fun lately. I'm just emerging from grieving for my husband. Until the day I joined the gym where we met, my days consisted of going to work, teaching, and taking work home. Once in a while, I'd go to the movies with girlfriends. Oh, and I teach Sunday School. That's about it."

"Are you telling me that you haven't dated in three years? I know the guys have been trying to talk to you."

"I haven't been ready. Healing takes time."

"Are you ready now?"

"I'm ready to spend time with someone. I don't feel ready for a serious relationship."

"How about a fun relationship? You seem like you could use some merriment and happy-go-lucky foolishness in your life. Just for the heck of it."

"I've been told that I'm too serious. When you're trying to help families cope with challenging issues, a sober outlook is a common side effect."

"This adventure called life is meant to lead us to joy. Even dealing with dysfunctional families, you've got to see the humor in it. You've got to have a place in you that can be happy underneath it all. I'd like to help you create that space. Are you willing?"

"Can I take baby steps?

"I won't push you any further than you want to go. Do we have a deal?" I extended my hand. She shook it. "It's a deal," she said. At last, she was smiling that stunning smile, the one I caught a glimpse of at the gym. Then, she turned serious again.

"It's just that life has been rough at times," said Lila.

"Tell me about it. Everybody I know could hold court for a couple of days on the rough periods in their lives, including me. I believe you've had your struggles, but here you are, still beautiful and still moving forward. You're a strong survivor, like that mythical bird, Phoenix. That's worth celebrating. Don't dwell on the ugly stuff."

"Buster, I have a daughter who was stolen from me by people I trusted. I have looked for her for years without success. I have no idea where she is. She's 16 years old now, becoming a young lady."

"If you've done all you can to find her, you can't dwell on it, baby. That sounds cold, but constantly thinking about it doesn't help. Trust that in time, you'll be reconnected. What's meant to be will be."

"What should I dwell on, Buster?"

"The good stuff. Fun. Pure fun. Find something funny or good about everything. Laugh a lot, and don't worry if people think you're silly. Silly can be good."

"You're quite a guy. I've never heard it put that way."

"What strikes you as silly in this restaurant?"

"You," she laughed.

"Okay, fair game. What else?"

"The part of me that wants to resist having fun. That's silly. I think you're calling to the kid in me. That kid has been in a closed cell for a while."

"It's time to let her break free," I said. Lila's smile told me she agreed.

We were the last patrons to leave the restaurant. We had talked until 11:00 PM. The wait staff had been replaced by the cleaning people, while the manager asked for the third time, "Will there be anything else?" Lila and I had been completely oblivious to our environment as we traded silly stories from our youth. For us, time stood still that evening. Finally, we became conscious of the manager standing close to our table, and we realized it was time to go.

When I returned Phoenix to her doorstep, I behaved myself. I kissed her on the cheek and told her, "I'll call you." The next day, I did. I was determined to build her trust. There was something very special about this lady and I did not want to mess up. I knew I would have to do something about Tanya, but not yet.

I thought, "I have to talk to my boys, T.R. and the others. They know I'm seeing Tanya. I may have to get them to cover for me while I'm getting to know Lila.

Lila Mae and I began seeing each other every week, usually on Friday nights. She had a heavy work schedule and she had some church friends she hung out with, so I decided not to monopolize her time. To ramp up the fun quotient, I took her to some of the black neighborhood bars and clubs, especially those featuring local jazz and blues bands on the weekends. I was dumbfounded when she told me she had never been in these clubs. After all the years she had lived in D. C., she had only frequented clubs in Adams Morgan and Georgetown. Those are basically white clubs. I considered it my duty to immerse the girl in the local black scene. It's amazing how you can live in the same metro area and have such different experiences.

One evening, Lila asked me, "How did you happen to open a restaurant?"

"Here's how it started. With Mama Ricks's encouragement, I worked my way through college after my marriage broke up. It was part of my healing process, getting some direction in my life. I majored in business and minored in social science. That prepared me to open the restaurant. Of course, my college experience also involved joining the Omega Psi Phi fraternity, known as the Q's. Although I am not too active in the graduate chapter of the Q's, my buddies always invite me to their social affairs. Do you go to Greek dances?"

"I have never been to a sorority or fraternity dance."

"Unbelievable. You've lived in D. C. all these years and never attended a Greek dance! Didn't you pledge in college?"

"When I was in college, I was married to a guy who traveled a lot. I had a household to maintain, so sororities never came up."

"No sorors tried to rush you?"

"They did, but I never gave it serious consideration. I was involved in the civil rights movement and sororities seemed frivolous by comparison."

"In other words, you didn't know how to have fun."

"If you say so."

"Well, I'm a "Q", and we know how to party.

"When I was a student, I heard about the parties given by Omega Psi Phi. I never attended, but the rumors were legendary."

"Enough with the rumors. You're going to experience this first hand."

My Friday night arrangement with Lila Mae left Saturday nights and assorted week nights for Tanya. I was rolling. I didn't want to turn Tanya loose until I was sure Lila was ready for a serious relationship. After six weeks, she had visited my condo in Silver Spring, Maryland, but I had not yet hit a home run. As you know, third base doesn't put any points on the score board. I needed the euphoria of an exceptional home run.

Finally, I was forced to make a decision. The Omegas were having their major annual formal dance on a Saturday night, and for the last two years Tanya had been my date. Thanks to my bragging, Lila knew I was a Q. One of Lila's girlfriends was going to the affair with her husband and told Lila about it. Lila casually mentioned it to me, saying it sounded like fun. I said I hadn't decided whether to go or not. By then I felt like it was slow going with Lila, and Tanya was a hot potato.

I debated, "Both ladies know about the dance and both of them want to go. Which lady should I invite?"

I asked my buddies over for a friendly game of poker to pick their brains about what I should do. T. R., Smiley and Mad Dog were guys I had known forever. The funny thing about Mad Dog was he used to have a terrible temper. We always had to calm him down. Then, some counselor got him in a yoga class and he turned into a regular peace ambassador. We threatened to change his name from Mad Dog to Smiling Yogi. The new name didn't stick though.

When the gang got to my place, they listened to my dilemma. Smiley said, "Man, is that why you called us over here? We thought we were going to play poker."

"We are, Smiley. Just help me out, my man."

T. R. advised, "Long Daddy, you're at the put up or shut up stage in your relationship with Lila Mae. Don't you know that she knows you're still seeing Tanya? Women have this thing called intuition. If you don't take Lila Mae to the dance, that's probably the end of the road as far as she's concerned."

"On the other hand," Smiley said, "Lila ain't giving up nothing.

Tanya is. Where does that leave you if things don't work out with Lila?"

T. R. responded, "I'll tell you where it leaves him. In the catbird seat. With an incentive like a designer handbag or a three day trip to the Virgin Islands, Tanya will come running back. She may fuss a little to save face, but she'll come back. She'll have bragging rights."

Mad Dog nodded agreement. He is serious about poker and does not appreciate delaying or interrupting the game for any discussion. I beat him the last time, and he was determined to win. We always play for small stakes, but a win is a win.

I concluded, "So you're saying I should take Lila Mae to the dance and let the chips fall where they may?"

Mad Dog spoke up, "Yeah, man. And speaking of chips, let's play." It was his lucky night. I gave up forty dollars. That was pretty cheap for a counseling session with my poker buddies.

The next day, I called Tanya. When she answered the phone, I told her, "Hey Tanya, I'm in kind of a bind. I owe a favor to an old friend who rescued me in a street fight years ago. His cousin needs a date to the Q dance. My friend promised to take her, but he has to go out of town on business. The girl already bought her dress. I told him I had not specifically asked my girlfriend, and he reminded me that I owed him a big favor. Anyway, I decided to balance out the books by taking her."

Tanya screamed, "Long Daddy, do you think I am an idiot? I don't believe a word you're saying. Don't you think I've noticed you're never home on Friday nights? You're seeing someone else, you asshole!"

"Baby, I'm for real. I've been setting aside Fridays to work on revamping the business."

"Yeah, right. Spare me. You think I'm so in love that I'll swallow anything. And just for the record, I already bought my dress too. Since this girl means nothing to you, why can't you take both of us?"

"Baby, I promised my friend…."

"Bull! Nothing you are saying makes sense. Do I really seem that stupid? You think I don't know what's going on? This is it. You've plunged a knife straight through my heart, Long Daddy. Don't call me ever again. Never ever!" She slammed down the phone. That was that.

On the night of the dance, I picked up Lila Mae on Capitol Hill. When she opened the door to her home, I was blown away by her appearance. Her hair was upswept in a sophisticated style, she wore long diamond earrings, and her gold designer dress was stunning. It was backless from the waist up and it fit her like a glove. The Q colors are purple and gold and I knew she would be the center of attention at the dance.

When we walked into the hotel ballroom, one of Tanya's friends approached us. She had obviously been waiting for us to arrive. She whipped out a camera and took our picture. I knew Tanya would be looking at the picture the next day. I explained to Lila Mae what was going on. She was cool about it, very composed. That helped me to relax.

Lila Mae has excellent social skills. She worked the room like a politician, happily greeting the guests seated at the round tables like she owned the room. I walked behind her thinking, "This is her first frat dance and she is totally in tune with it. Her vibes are supercharged. If anyone wants to report back to Tanya, she's giving them plenty to talk about."

We danced many times. Lila Mae still exuded energy when I was ready to sit down. I was glad to have her accept other offers to get on the dance floor. I was seeing another side to this lady. She later told me she had taken dance lessons following her husband's death to release stress.

We left the hotel about 12:30 A.M. and returned to Lila's home. At the door, she said, "Come on in. This has been a very special evening." After that pronouncement, she proceeded to make it even more special. She hit a home run like no other. The ball shot out beyond the Milky Way and formed a new star, *Loveraura*!

I knew then that I was going to marry this lady. My initial impression was right. Phoenix was THE one. In thirty days, I proposed and she accepted.

Neither one of us wanted an elaborate wedding. We decided to get married in Las Vegas in September. Lila had told me very little about her family, but casually mentioned that she wanted to give her old diamond engagement ring to her sister. I was comfortable with that because I didn't want her wearing a ring from another man while married to me.

I decided to sell my condo apartment and most of its contents. Before I could place the property on the market, T. R. offered to buy it.

He said, "I always did like this place. I can take it 'as is' because I don't have a lot of stuff." T. R. had been living with his mother since his divorce. The situation worked out for everybody. We could still meet for poker at the condo.

Being a businessman, I sat down with Lila Mae to talk about our finances. I was amazed at her net worth. She had well over a million dollars in assets, including mutual funds, individual stocks, tax free bonds and rental property. She was renting out a house on Capitol Hill and a four unit apartment building near the Howard University campus. She said she got a great deal on it. Her debts were less than seventy-five thousand dollars. My assets were around three hundred thousand dollars with nearly eighty thousand in debt, mostly business related. We wouldn't starve.

We had a few issues to work out. Lila finally told me that she had had three husbands. I was surprised, but ultimately it made her seem even more fascinating. I told her that I played small stakes poker. She accepted that. I knew she was active in the church. I attended with her one Sunday, but was not particularly drawn to her church. Although I did not attend any church more than twice a year, I preferred the Baptist church where Mama Ricks and the Missionary Society prayed me into a decent life. I do believe in God. Lila said each person has his or her own journey and each journey is different. I was glad to know that she didn't plan to nag me every Sunday about church.

In July 1981, Lila started making room in her house for the items I planned to bring in. We were both busy during that preparation period, but the plan worked smoothly. By the first of August, I had moved my things into her place and signed the deed to the condo over to T. R. The next Thursday, Lila and I flew to Vegas to get the license. We were married Friday evening, August 7, 1981. Amazingly, I never got to a casino. Lila didn't gamble, so I decided to practice restraint. We took in a great show Saturday night. By Sunday afternoon, we were back in Washington. Following tradition, I carried my bride over the threshold.

On Monday morning, we initiated the routine we would follow for the months to come. Lila went to work at the law firm, and I drove to the restaurant. We set up a family night every Thursday to discuss any issues that might be bothering us. This was a great idea suggested by Lila's pastor. No problems ever had a chance to linger and fester. We were both open. We both wanted this marriage to work. Lila had been widowed twice, so she had a tendency to overprotect me. I let her know I was in good shape and close to her age, so she need not worry. Eventually, she relaxed about that. I joked with her a lot to keep the joy factor going. I had long been a secret poet, and I occasionally surprised her with a poem taped to the refrigerator or the bathroom mirror. She loved it.

Time passed quickly. To celebrate our delayed honeymoon, we booked a cruise to the Bahamas. The weather was perfect and the food was great. We reminded each other not to overdo it at the lunch buffet, though we sometimes ignored our own advice. We were so good together, neither of us perfect people, but we were perfect for each other.

Soon after we returned to Washington, I surprised myself by deciding to go to church with Lila one Sunday morning. It felt good. It drew me closer to her. I attended the church again about a month later to see her Sunday School kids perform. After that, I went about once a month. My buddies couldn't believe the change in me. I told them, "It's my decision. I'm a happy man." T. R. said, "I'm happy for you."

Lila said some of the gossips at church had made us their number one news story. She didn't care. She laughed about it. I figured they'd get used to us.

One Tuesday afternoon about six months later, I looked up to see my birth mother, Jessie, strolling into Buster's Place. The lunch crowd was gone and the place was empty except for an old geezer sipping coffee. Jessie had only visited the restaurant once before, on opening day. I used to see her on the street once in a while, but I hadn't laid eyes on her for at least three months.

I strode toward her, "Jessie! Good to see you. What brings you here?" I hugged her, but she pulled away.

"Don't call me Jessie. I never liked that name. If you can't call me Mama, call me by my nickname, Punkin."

"Okay. Punkin it is. Come have a seat and tell me what's going on. By the way, have you been getting the checks from my bank every month?"

"Yeah. The extra two hundred and fifty dollars a month helps out. Ain't you going to offer your mother something to eat?"

"What do you want to eat?" I handed her the menu. "Just pick something and we'll cook it for you." She perused the menu, looking at the pictures. It occurred to me that she might have a reading problem, which I never knew. But she figured it out.

"I'll have the Busterburger with a double order of fries and a piece of key lime pie, washed down with a Pepsi." I gave the order to the cook, and then sat down to talk. Punkin was nervous. I saw worry lines in her forehead. She took off her scarf, revealing gray roots that had grown out since her last dye job. I had to remind myself that she was only fifteen years older than me, which made her fifty-eight years old. Punkin had had a hard life, starting with being born to a fourteen year old incest victim. The last time I asked, she was working as a maid.

She said, "My friend, Re-Re, told me your food was good. I ordered the same thing she had."

"I'm sure you'll enjoy it," I replied. I was back to my theory about her having a reading problem.

"Now, tell me what's going on, Punkin."

"Well, you know you have a brother. I told you about him once."

"You told me he was living with his father in New York."

"Yeah. Was. He fell out with his daddy. He grown, twenty years old now. Two weeks ago, he showed up at my door. I don't know how he found me. He want to live with me until he get on his feet. I only have a one bedroom apartment. He been sleeping on the sofa for the past two weeks."

"What's his name?"

"Mansion."

"Mansion? What kind of name is that?"

"I named him that because I wanted us to live in a mansion like the ones I clean every week."

"Well, I guess that's about as good as Buster."

"Better. I tried to name you something else, but I couldn't spell it. A nurse helped me with your middle name, Taliferro."

"She still misspelled it if you were trying to name me after Booker Taliaferro Washington. But that's beside the point. I've lived with my name all these years and it hasn't hurt me any."

"I wanted your first name to be Messiah, like Jesus was the Messiah."

I was genuinely touched. I said, "I never knew. Thank you for sharing that, Punkin."

"The nurse said God would be mad with me for naming you after His Son. Mama was in the room. She said, 'Name him Buster. I know how to spell that.' I was outvoted, so the nurse wrote down Buster. Your name was suppose to be Messiah Taliaferro King. That's a strong name. That name could take you places."

"You were thinking about my future."

"Yeah. I always knew you would amount to something if I could find somebody to help you. There was nobody in my family, so I asked Mrs. Ricks."

I smiled. "Thank you for that, Mother."

"I like Punkin better. Mother is too formal." I nodded in agreement.

"Oh, here's your food." While Punkin dived into the fries, I looked at her in sympathy. Then, I thanked God for Mama Ricks. I had the feeling Punkin wanted me to rescue Mansion just as Mama Ricks had rescued me. But Mansion was no toddler. He was a grown man whom I had never met. Not only that, but I was enjoying my marriage to Lila and I had the feeling that Mansion would mess things up somehow.

Punkin sipped some of her Pepsi, then got to the point. "I want you to help me with Mansion."

"What kind of help does he need? Has he finished high school? Does he have any skills? What kind of job is he looking for?"

"He got a GED. He had to spend time in juvenile detention for vandalism and the city jail for pimping. He need a fresh start. He don't want to go back to his old life."

"Is he messing with drugs?"

"Not to my knowledge. He talk tough, but he's really lost."

"I need to discuss this with my wife, Lila Mae. Give me your phone number and I'll call you."

"My phone got cut off. I can call you from my neighbor's house."

"How much do you need to get the phone cut back on?"

"Nine hundred dollars. Mansion called me collect from jail. They charge a fortune for them calls."

I sighed. "Bring me the bill day after tomorrow, Thursday, and I'll pay it. Then we'll talk again. That will give me time to discuss this with my wife, Lila Mae. She works in family law so she understands these things."

"She a lawyer? Mansion needed a good lawyer when he went to court the last time."

"Enjoy your food, Punkin. I have to run to an appointment. I'll see you on Thursday afternoon about the same time.

"Bye, Buster. My oldest son sure is tall." I left to get my car inspected. I needed to think about how and when to share this turn of events with my wife.

After dinner Tuesday evening, Lila asked me, "What's bothering you, Buster?" I had tried to joke around, but she could read me like a book. "I haven't seen you look this disturbed since the health department threatened to shut down the restaurant over a minor infraction."

"There's no good way to tell you this. My birth mother, Jessie, walked into the restaurant today. She has a problem and she wants me to solve it."

"Well, for starters, I'd like to meet her. We've been married for over a year and I've never seen her even though she lives in D. C."

"That felt like an attack. You've met my real mother, Mama Ricks. Jessie just brought me into the world." Lila rubbed my back to let me know she understood.

"I'm sorry, honey. I know it's painful for you. I don't blame you for holding back. You haven't met my mother either. You've talked to her on the phone and you know our relationship isn't the best. Forgive me. What is this problem of Jessie's?"

I recounted for Lila my conversation with Jessie a.k.a. Punkin at the restaurant that afternoon. She responded, "We have no idea what Mansion is really like. Obviously, Punkin is feeling burdened by this new challenge. She wants him to get help like you did."

"I feel like I'm about to walk into a quagmire."

"Let's take this one step at a time. When you meet with Punkin on Thursday, I'd like to be there. Who knows? She may bring Mansion with her. If not, we should plan to meet him on neutral ground, not in our home. Not until we get to know him. Let me walk through this with you."

"That sounds like a plan. We need to be cautious. I have a bad feeling about this."

"We'll pray about it. I'm tired. You ready to go upstairs?"

"You go. I'll come later."

"Goodnight, darling. Remember, I'm with you all the way on this."

"Thanks, Lila. Goodnight."

Lila Mae arrived at Buster's Place at 2:30 P.M. on Thursday, vigorously shaking her umbrella at the entrance. The rain outside was intensely washing everyone and everything in sight. Lila had worked through lunch, so I brought her some food while we waited for Punkin. About fifteen minutes later, Punkin came through the door, removing her dripping, plastic rain cape. Right behind her was a soggy, skinny, bearded young man with unkempt dreadlocks. I had never seen him before. He had to be Mansion.

I waved and motioned them over to our table. As they reached the table, I stood to greet them. Lila Mae followed my lead. Punkin said, "Buster, this is Mansion. Mansion, meet your big brother, Buster." We shook hands.

I said, "Punkin told me about you. Let me introduce you both to my wife, Lila Mae. Punkin and Mansion looked her over and shook hands with her.

Mansion remarked, "She's happening."

"Thank you," I said. "Let's sit down. Punkin, first things first. The phone bill please."

Punkin said, "Oh, I don't want to put you to any trouble. Just give me a check or the cash and I'll pay it."

"Punkin, when it comes to business, an agreement is an agreement. Hand over the bill, please. I'll take care of it." She frowned, shrugged, then fished through her purse and produced the frayed envelope containing the bill.

"Now, Mansion, tell us about your situation. What are your plans?" I asked.

"Aaah, really I don't know. I guess the first thing is I need a job."

"Is there any particular kind of work you're looking for?"

"Well, they taught me how to paint and how to sand floors and restore them in prison."

"I thought you were in the city jail."

"I was until I got caught trying to run my business from inside the jail. Pimping. I didn't want my four girls to get taken over by another pimp. I had paid off one of the guards, but another guard heard us making the transaction and they sent me to the state penitentiary. I only served a year though. I got out early for good behavior. I learned my lesson and I don't plan to go back."

It took a moment for all this to register. I looked at Mansion's face. Even though we had different fathers, there was a slight resemblance between us. I thought, "There but for the grace of God go I."

After a spirited four way conversation, we decided that for the time being, Mansion would work as a waiter in the restaurant while enrolling in a trade school program at night. Lila and I agreed to take care of the tuition.

One of Lila's tenants in the apartment building was moving out, so she offered Mansion a furnished efficiency unit at half the monthly rental rate and without a deposit. She told him he would have to sign a month to month lease and abide by the conditions of the lease. This was no free ride, just a hand up. Mansion agreed to those terms.

Punkin thanked us profusely. She was relieved. She slipped back into her own world and I did not see her again until I spotted her on the street almost a year later.

During the next few weeks, Mansion had to be reminded of the work ethic several times. He soon learned that I didn't take any stuff. No excuses. No special breaks. Just do the job. Lila put him on the prayer list at the church, just like Mama Ricks used to do for me. He grumbled occasionally about having to take the bus, but we ignored that. He had a roof over his head and food to eat.

Lila invited Mansion to visit our church on several occasions, but he declined. I appreciated her desire to include him, but I still had an uneasy feeling about getting too close. We fell into a routine and after six months, I invited him to our home for dinner. I wanted him to see what was possible if he worked hard.

Mansion was very uncomfortable from the moment he stepped inside the door. It was like he was entering another world. Lila had set the table in her usual way with a floral centerpiece and glass stemware. At each place, she laid two forks, which I thought was overdone. Mansion was sharp enough to watch what we did and follow suit. He left soon after the meal, and I had a feeling he wouldn't be back.

A couple of months later, I observed a couple of guys dropping by the restaurant to talk to Mansion on several occasions. They looked a little shady to me. Maybe I was getting to be too bourgeois under Lila's influence.

One afternoon around closing time, Mansion's friends dropped by, saying that their car had broken down. They needed to get to a gas station garage about a mile away to pick up a part for the car. They said they had already called ahead to be sure the part was in stock. Against my better judgment, I allowed Mansion and his friends to pile into my Mercedes. I drove them to the gas station and waited while they went inside. In a couple of minutes, I heard an alarm go off, then a popping sound. The three young men ran to my car and said, "Let's go."

"What do you mean?" I asked. "What happened in there?"

"Just go!" Mansion shouted. "We didn't do anything. Some guy was trying to rob the place."

"Where's the robber?"

"He's still inside. Let's go before the cops get here. I already have a record and I don't want to go to jail."

As I started to pull out to the street, I was blocked by a squad car. Another policeman pulled up behind me. A third policeman parked near the door of the garage and stepped inside the building. He shouted to the others, "It looks like we've got a homicide." The officers arrested all of us, read us our rights, handcuffed us and called for a paddy wagon. I was devastated. I asked to call my wife, but they said I had to wait until we got to the station.

The next few hours were a blur. I signed a statement and went to night court. Lila paid my bail. We weren't sure what to do about Mansion, but the law decided for us. It turned out there were papers on him from the New York charge, so he had to stay in jail for violation of probation.

Lila vowed to get me a good lawyer from her firm. She said, "I am too emotionally involved to defend you, although I can help behind the scenes. It should be obvious that you were not an accessory to the robbery and murder, but a lot depends on the judge. Some judges see black men as targets of their discontent."

"Yeah, and I wonder what stories the young men are telling. Hopefully, Mansion will set them straight." I got my cashier to manage the restaurant during the times that I had to prepare for the indictment. Against all reason, Judge McCarthy indicted all four of us. I was about to experience American justice at its worst. A trial date was set.

Shortly before the trial, I ran into Punkin on the street, waiting at a bus stop. She hugged me and said, "I'm sorry. I know you're not guilty. I can't believe my sons, Messiah and Mansion, could both be put in jail. You are my hope, my only hope." Tears started down her cheeks. Then, I felt wetness touch my face, first a drop, then a torrent of rain. It seemed that the angels were crying with Punkin over her failed dreams.

The bus arrived. She released me, climbed aboard and waved through the window, tears still streaming down her cheeks. I stood mesmerized, trying to comprehend the depth of her sorrow.

Prior to the trial, Lila and her colleague tried to get the judge changed. This man had a reputation for trashing black defendants and giving them maximum sentences. There was cause for alarm. My trial dragged on for a week. One of Mansion's friends had testified against me to get his time reduced. Mansion had defended me, but the court wasn't buying the defense. Mansion was shown to have lied in court on several occasions. Incredibly, I was convicted and sent to jail for five years. Lila was distraught that she had helped so many others and was not able to save me. She vowed to keep working on the case personally until I was a free man.

I felt like a piece of vile garbage when that prison door closed behind me. All the people who had prayed for me over the years could not save me. I could not save myself. I was being punished for something I did not do. I sank into depression. A veteran prisoner, sentenced to spend the rest of his life in jail without parole, gave me some advice. He said, "Stay away from depression. It keeps you from being alert, and you have to watch your back around here. It's not all bad, though. Every now and then, you'll find something to make you laugh, or to cheer you up. Even here." He sounded like me giving other people advice over the years.

Lila wrote to me on a regular basis and visited when she could. On one visit she said, "I'm going to defend you myself, even though it will be very emotional for me. Usually, lawyers hire other people to defend their spouses, but this is something I want to do. I won't give up until you're out of here."

"This is hell, baby. I can't be in charge of my own life."

"I'm praying for you and persistently working on your case."

"I don't know how this happened. I used bad judgment trusting those guys."

"How could you know what they were planning? Stop blaming yourself, Buster."

"I know I have embarrassed you, honey. Do your colleagues know about this?"

"Some do. Don't worry about me. God is with me, and with you too."

"In this hellhole?"

"Everywhere."

"Do you still love me, Lila?"

"Of course I love you, Buster. I'll never stop loving you."

"Then help me get my life back, please."

"I will. I'll pull out all the stops to get this injustice reversed."

"It can't be soon enough for me. I have to literally look back at the slightest sound to make sure no one is planning to jump me. Somebody told me that for a fee, I could get some protection in here. It would be well worth it."

"Let me know what you need. We'll make the best of this situation while you're here."

"When you put money in my spending account, I want you to also put money into the accounts of the people whose names I give you next time you visit. That will allow them to buy cigarettes and other goodies. Then, they'll look out for me.

Lila kept her promise. I paid a couple of guards and she put money into the accounts of three inmates to watch my back. After Big Man, Antwan and Mo started protecting me, the watchful fear subsided. I felt sorry for the brothers who had no money. They were easy prey for some of the jail vultures.

Phoenix wasted no time appealing my case. She filed motion after motion, but they were denied. She began collaborating with groups that were working on justice for black men. I know she was working long hours because she still had to handle her regular cases. I had told her to find time to express joy, but where would she find that time now? Not only did I fall in a hole, but I pulled her down with me.

Prison is a nightmare. It's not designed to help people get better so they can bring something good to the table when they get out. It's designed to punish you, to hurt you as much as possible. It's barbaric. All that does is make you want to hurt other people.

I was trying to hold onto hope, knowing that Lila Mae had me on the prayer list at her church. God knows what the church members were saying about her, going from being married to the minister to being married to a jailbird. I don't know how she kept going. I don't know how I kept going.

Just when I thought things couldn't get any worse, I got a work assignment in the kitchen. They placed me there when they found out I had operated a restaurant. In my second week as a cook, I got cut on the arm. It was a freak accident. Gus, the crazy dude working next to me, tried to stop the bleeding with his big sweaty hands. He turned out to be HIV positive. Give me a minute, Doc. Hand me some tissues. I need to collect myself.

I ended up in the infirmary. They said there was only a small chance that Gus could have transmitted the AIDS virus to me through his sweat. The nurse had disinfected the wound within fifteen minutes of the injury. I dismissed the thought that I had any permanent damage from the incident. I never mentioned it to Lila.

On my last day in the infirmary, I received a letter. I thought it was from Lila, but the return address shocked me. It was from Tanya. She had heard through the grapevine that Lila had divorced me. Of course, this was a false rumor. She wrote to pour salt in the wound, to turn me against Lila. She claimed that Lila was embarrassed to be married to a prisoner. "She never loved you like I do. She's not part of our world. We both grew up in the streets. Remember, my brother is in jail. I know how it is." I read the letter several times until paranoia set in. I began to doubt Lila, even though I knew she was working to get me out of jail.

On visiting day, Tanya showed up. I told her she was wrong about Lila divorcing me. She continued to say negative things about Lila. "Why is it taking her so long to get you sprung? She's too busy making money off her other cases to spend time on your case."

"Tanya," I said, "Don't interfere. Let Lila do whatever she needs to do to get me out of here."

"Let me help you, Long Daddy."

"You're not a lawyer."

"I know a few judges."

166

"Tanya, stay out of this. What's in it for you, anyway?"

"She stole you from me. I want to marry you."

"I'm already married. Besides, you're a teacher. Why would you want to marry an inmate?"

"My principal and co-workers don't have to know. It would just be between us. Once you get pardoned, we could tell them. I want to show you some love. You need that. I wish I could come for conjugal visits. Wouldn't you like that? I'll bet Lila isn't making love to you, is she? She's probably making out with one of her lawyer friends."

"I don't believe that. She loves me."

"She loves being high and mighty. I love you no matter what."

"Tanya, you should go. You're messing with my mind. I need to stay focused."

After Tanya left, I kept turning things over in my mind. Suppose Tanya was right? How could I fit into Lila's world again? The church members might be praying for me, but would they really want to sit beside me in the pew?

In my loneliness, I reflected on those exciting evenings with Tanya. I said, "I can't go there. This is driving me crazy."

When you're at your lowest ebb, false ideas can take root and edge out truth and reason. The more I thought about Tanya, the more I doubted Lila. She was free to live her life while I rotted in jail.

Tanya kept writing and taunting me. Finally, I wrote her back and a jailhouse mail romance began. All of Lila's messages seemed dry by comparison. She was working to free me. Some part of me realized that. But Tanya was vividly reminding me that I was loved. Everybody wants to be loved.

One year after I walked into prison to join the other outcasts, Lila filed a motion before a new judge. The old one retired. She had prepared her briefs with the help of seasoned experts, and she secured my release. I walked outside those metal doors and heard them clang shut behind me. Lila was waiting to hug and kiss me. She had never given up. Somehow, I had.

There was much I had not told her. You know that cut that I got upset about a few minutes ago? Well, here's the rest of that story. It happened two months before my release. The guy with the HIV deteriorated into full blown AIDS. That really scared me. I wondered if

I would be next. I did not want Lila to know about it. I felt like I had descended into a bottomless pit without a single ray of light. I didn't want to take a chance on hurting her. I got myself tested, but nothing showed up. Maybe it was too soon.

With my whole dehumanizing prison experience, I did not feel that I could be comfortable in that Capitol Hill townhouse with beautiful Lila. I felt unclean and unworthy. I thought Lila was better than me, and at some point she would remind me of that. Tanya's attacks on Lila had worked. She caught me when I was operating on animal instincts. Tanya and I were both acting like bottom feeders. We were a good match.

In the courtyard outside the prison, I thanked Lila for all she had done. I had already contacted Tanya and she drove up while I was thanking Lila. Tanya ran up and hugged me. I said, "Lila, this is Tanya. This is the lady I was dating when we met. You have been very good to me, Lila. I don't deserve you. You operate on a whole different level than me. I can't come home with you. I'm going with Tanya."

Lila's shocked face spoke more clearly than words. Finally, she found her voice. "Buster, you're traumatized by your experience. You need time on the outside to come back to yourself. You're carrying a lot of baggage that isn't really you. Don't give up now. We've come so far. I love you."

Tanya said, "You're not the only one that loves him. To you, he's just a project to work on. To me, he's the love of my life. He's coming with me." Tanya took me by the hand and I followed like a zombie.

That was two years ago. I divorced Lila, and then Tanya and I got married. I went back to running the restaurant. We settled into a routine. Then last month, Tanya went to the doctor for her annual physical. When the results came back, the doctor told her she had the AIDS virus. I know she got it from me, from that prison incident. I went to get tested, and confirmed that Long Daddy had been poisoned with HIV. So far, Tanya is still with me. She really does love me, but I feel so guilty. I know now that I don't love her the way I loved Lila Mae, yet it's too late to think about that. Regrets don't change anything.

Doc, I've lost my way. Where do I go from here?

Section Six

Lila Mae – Midlife

We dance round in a ring and suppose,
But the Secret sits in the middle and knows.

- Robert Frost

W ell, hello! Fancy running into you on K Street in D. C. I have not seen you since September 1964 when we met in a hotel bar in Atlanta. Let's have lunch together at that sidewalk café down the street while I bring you up to date on my story.

A lot has happened in my life in the last twenty years. I divorced my first husband, and then married three other men in succession. Two of them died and the third is filing for divorce. I'm still in shock over the way my fourth husband, Buster, walked away. He had been imprisoned on false charges. I put all my energy and love into freeing him from prison, only to be rejected. I still think he lost his bearings in that hellish place.

I've had some tough times, but I've also had some joy. Many of my childhood dreams have come true. Yet, I have suffered over seventeen years the pain of not knowing the whereabouts of my only child. My second husband, Henry, let Bessie go to California with a couple we knew, and we never saw her again. I believe Bessie is safe somewhere, but I have missed her terribly. Not seeing her grow up has left an empty space in my heart.

Three husbands ago, Cousin Mary told me I had failed at marriage. She said I had a perfectly good husband in Jimmy and I ruined that marriage. I knew Jimmy was a good man, but he and I were far apart in our views of life. He was a decent, kind, practical, one town person with traditional religious ideas. I shared those ideas at one time.

The problem was that despite my appearing to be a Georgia farm wife, I was really an imaginative world traveler. I was consciously connected to a multi-dimensional universe and an awesome, loving God. The only way our relationship could have worked long term would have been for me to whittle down my true self and pretend to be someone else.

Two of my husbands, Henry and Ezra, started out as father figures to me. I had unresolved issues with my own father, which made these men appealing. Henry had a weird way of handling situations that frustrated him. In a way, he was like a mirror to me, fearfully hiding secrets and making quick, flawed decisions. Still, he taught me an invaluable lesson. If you want to help someone, get to know the person you're helping. Find out how they view things and what they really believe they need. Otherwise, your well intended assumptions might do more harm than good. Listen first, and then serve.

Ezra's spiritual vibes were very compatible with mine. He was the only one of my husbands who fully understood how I was evolving spiritually. His consciousness was open to unity, connection and peace. I found that so refreshing. For his part, he was frustrated that other people could not understand spiritually what he was really saying. He knew that I understood him and I knew that he understood me. The time we had together was precious. I believe I learned something valuable from every one of my husbands, just as they learned from me.

Now, here I am at mid-life, age 43. I am still young looking and physically attractive. I still turn heads among the middle aged set, and some men in their thirties. That hasn't changed.

Yet, I recognize I have a lot to learn, especially about family relationships. More specifically, I have motherhood issues. Some of them were resurrected after I became an active member of Unity Church Center, following Henry's death. I had gone back to school full time and spent my spare time volunteering in the church. Near the end of my first year at Georgetown University Law School, our church women were planning a special Mother's Day program. I found myself out of sync with the others as they discussed the virtues of their mothers. I always loved my mother, but we are such different people. Mama has been shaped by the small Georgia town she has lived in all her life. I think her views are narrow and judgmental. The other motherhood issue is that I never had the chance to raise my own child.

Down in Georgia, Mama and I talked on the phone at least twice a week, but that dwindled down to a brief conversation once a month. I felt like she never forgave me for what happened with JJ. She never visited me in Washington, saying she didn't like to travel. She is who she is and I can't change her. I love Mama at a distance. On the other hand, I only went back to Macon once seventeen years ago, when Daddy was sick. He died while I was there.

My most pressing problem right now, though, is that I have been in a real tailspin since Buster split up with me. I have missed appointments, can't stay focused, and generally don't know whether I am coming or going. Life with Buster was like riding on a roller coaster. He taught me how to have fun, but I now realize that fun is not the same as joy. Fun comes and goes. The joy that comes from the spirit stays in place no matter what is happening in your life. Buster took me to the heights, and then dragged me through the mud. I was so charmed by him and so willing to believe in us as a couple. I had no clue that his former girlfriend was back in his life.

I made up my mind to go into therapy for a while. The way my life has gone, it was probably overdue. My therapist, Sarah, advised me to get involved in some new experiences, not involving romance.

"You need to set a goal and focus on reaching it."

"I'm trying to focus on my work, but that doesn't seem to pump me up anymore."

"How about a hobby? For over a year, you spent hours and hours trying to free Buster from prison. Now that's over and you have dead time in your schedule. It's like a vacuum that needs to be filled."

"Do you have a hobby, Sarah?"

"I'm a runner. That's where the medallions came from." I had seen the medals hanging on the wall, but never inquired about them.

"What are the competitions like? I used to run in high school but not since then, unless you count running on the treadmill."

"Oh, the competitions are tons of fun. You get to meet runners from all over the world at the big races. I'm talking about thousands of people. Some of them live to race, going from one meet to another. Others want to prove just once that they've still got it."

"I'm in good physical condition, but I don't know if I should start running again at forty plus."

Sarah laughed. "Some of the runners are in their sixties, seventies and eighties. You'd be surprised. Think about it. By the way, here are some promotional materials for races that are coming up in the next six months. You could start out by joining a team and practicing with them. Your teammates will encourage you to commit to the practice sessions."

"I'll think about it."

A week later, I joined a team that was raising money for breast cancer research. Jean Foster, one of my colleagues at Howard, had lost a breast to this disease. I had observed her fight to be become a survivor. No one should have to suffer like that.

Halfway through the first practice run of three miles, my legs were feeling it. Running on a treadmill at the gym and running on uneven, hilly streets are two different things. When I looked at my options of running either a half marathon of 13.1 miles or a marathon of 26.2 miles, I chose the half marathon. Even so, I had an arduous road to travel.

Sarah had been right. My teammates were a great support to me, and running required my full attention. When I let my mind wander, my time suffered. I had to be fully attuned to the present. That was hard, since thoughts of Buster kept intruding. I could hear him laughing and challenging me to keep up. "Come on, Phoenix. Move those long, sexy legs." The team practiced rain or shine. It was like milking a cow. I had to milk her no matter what the weather.

During the five months of practice, we took part in two shorter races, one for eight kilometers and one for ten kilometers. I completed both somewhere in the middle of the pack. That was fine with me. My goal at this stage was not to win, but to finish respectably. Which is to say, not in last place.

I'll spare you the recital of all my aches and pains and the knee support I had to wear for a while. The main thing is that I made it through all the challenges. Thanks to my work colleagues, friends and church members, as well as my own donation, I raised three thousand dollars for breast cancer research by race day in June.

I presented myself at 6:30 A.M. at a park near Main Street in

Richmond, Virginia to wait for my wave of the race. I and two of my running buddies were going to run in the third wave, about an hour and a half behind the first wave. The fastest runners were in the first wave, including those who actually had a shot at winning the race. The next fastest group formed the second wave. At least I was ahead of the last wave, the walkers. I couldn't be smug, though. I could end up having to walk the last part of the race. No. Cancel that thought.

My running buddies, Michelle and Tom, showed up at our meeting spot a few minutes after I did, and our coach gave us last minute instructions. We had more than an hour with nothing to do, so I decided to walk around a bit. I scanned the crowd, looking for someone interesting to talk to.

I stopped in my tracks when I spied two young ladies holding hands about fifteen feet away. One was average height with a dark brown complexion. The other one was tall and light complexioned with her light brown hair in a bun. She looked familiar, but I couldn't place her. Then the thought came to me. She looks a lot like I did at her age. It's almost like looking at myself. I had been told on several occasions that I looked like other people so I wasn't too startled by the situation. I decided to go over and meet the young ladies.

As I approached, I said, "Good morning. I was just looking around waiting for my race and I saw you two." Turning to the tall lady I said, "From over there, you looked like a duplicate of me when I was younger. You're very pretty." They both looked at me strangely. The shorter girl put her arm around her friend's waist and said, "I'm Roxie and this is my partner. You wouldn't be trying to hit on her, would you?"

"No," I replied. "It's just unusual to see someone who looks so much like me." They looked at me suspiciously. I casually asked, "Where are you two from?" Again, Roxie answered. "We're from Texas. We decided to come here and find out what the east coast looks like." I said, "I'm Lila King from Washington, D.C., about a hundred and ten miles north of here." The tall girl said, "We're planning to visit D.C. before we go home."

I said, "It's a great place to visit. We have lots of tourists. What is your name?"

She said, "I'm Bessie Ella." I staggered backwards, gasped in amazement, placed my hand over my heart and could not speak for what seemed like a long time. Roxie asked, "Are you all right? Do you have some kind of medical condition?"

The tears came. I couldn't help it. They thought I was a basket case. "I'm sorry," I said. "These are tears of joy. Bessie Ella, I have been looking for you since you were a toddler. I am your mother."

Now it was their turn to look shocked. Bessie stepped back. Roxie edged closer to support her. Bessie spoke. "You're not my mother. My step-mom said my natural mother's name is Lila Mae Lofton. When I looked her up on the adoption finders registry, she had listed her name as Lila Mae Lofton. I even have the street address where she lived then. A friend of mine went there six years ago, but someone else was living there. I'm determined to find her this time."

"Your friend came to my house? I had rented my place out and was living in my new husband's home. I was Lila Mae Lofton. My husband, Henry Lofton, died. I remarried and changed my name. Now, I've moved back to Capitol Hill, back to the house your friend visited."

Roxie spoke, "You and your new husband moved back into your house?"

I said, "I know it's a little confusing. I'll explain all that later. How are the Moores, Bessie Ella?"

Bessie and Roxie looked at me as though I might be spinning a wild tale. Bessie said, "You know them?" I answered, "Of course. I have been looking for them and for you ever since Henry let them take you away while I was in Georgia." Bessie replied, "That's not true. I saw the papers you signed."

"I never signed the papers. Henry forged my name. I'm sure the Moores thought it was my signature."

Bessie and Roxie looked at each other and then at me. Roxie asked, "What is your attitude toward lesbians? Because that's what we are."

"Well, I know they are people. They are children of God like everybody else. That's one more surprise this morning. But I'm not standing in judgment. I'm just so happy to find Bessie Ella. And to see that she's found love."

Turning to Bessie I asked, "May I hug you?" Roxie released her and we hugged. By now, both of us were crying. Then I turned to Roxie, saying "Group hug!" and the three of us embraced. I credit Ezra for teaching me to accept all people, bless his heart.

Bessie shared that the Moores had asked her to move out when she came out of the closet a few months earlier. She and Roxie had moved into a commune temporarily. They were both twenty year old students, thinking of dropping out of school to go to work. I told them I was in a position to help them finish school. They smiled broadly at this news. I was so caught up in the moment that I didn't think anything through. I was still emerging from the emotional whirlwind of Buster's shocking decision.

"When were you planning to go to Washington to look for me?"

"This afternoon," Lila said. "We arranged to stay with friends there. We dropped our bags off at their house."

"I came down here on the team bus. Otherwise, I'd take you to pick up your bags. How did you get to Richmond?"

Roxie chimed in, "We drove down here with our friends. Why don't we go back with them and then come over to your place?"

"That would work. I have plenty of room for you at home. By the way, which wave are you in?"

"We're in the second wave. I see by your ID tag that you're in the third."

"I know you girls are faster than I am. I'd like to run with you, but I'd slow you down or hurt myself. In case we get lost in the crowd, here's how to reach me." I handed her a business card with my contact information, scribbling my home telephone number on the back.

Roxie exclaimed, "You carry business cards and a pen in your fanny pack?"

"Force of habit."

"You stay prepared. Yeah. You're Bessie Ella's mother all right." I smiled.

Bessie spoke, "Wait a minute. I've been searching for you all these years and we're running in separate waves? That doesn't make sense to me. I don't care about my time. I want to run with you, Mom. Do you feel the same way?"

"Yes, Bessie. I do. I'm just flustered right now, but yes. Let's run together."

We decided to run in the second wave. I went back to my teammates to give them the news. When I found them, Michelle asked, "What happened to you?" Tom said, "Your face is glowing like you just fell in love or something." I told him, "I just found my long lost daughter. It's better than falling in love. I'm going to run with her. I'll meet you at the bus." I jogged back to the second wave corral to join Bessie and Roxie.

I forgot about my coach's instructions to stay centered on the race. I felt warm and whole for the first time in years. My body felt free and I ran like the wind. Bessie shouted, "You can run. What were you doing in the third wave?"

"Seeing you again has given me wings."

The girls and I hugged and whooped it up at the finish line. My left knee was starting to ache. Bessie, Roxie and I headed to the refreshment tent for energy drinks and snacks. Someone gave us our unofficial times and we boarded a shuttle bus nearby to head to the parking lot. I felt the pain as I lifted my leg to step up into the bus. Soon we arrived in the area where the buses and cars were parked.

I hugged the girls and said, "Call me when you get to D.C."

"We will. See you, Mom." Bessie and I kissed each other on the cheek and we happily waved goodbye.

I boarded our D.C. team's mini-bus. Some of the team members were already there because they had been in the first wave. We had to wait for the third wave group.

I asked the coach for aspirin, swallowed it down with apple juice, and reclined my seat. Despite the celebratory whooping and singing, I fell asleep. This had been an extraordinary morning. I was barely aware of the engine starting us on our way to D. C.

I awakened with a burst of energy in response to the vibrations of the Capital City as the bus rumbled across the 14th Street Bridge. The Washington Monument soaring toward the clear blue sky was a metaphor for the new direction of my life. Up, up, up! I thought, "Forget the blues, the suffering and the waiting. This is a new day."

After saying goodbye to my teammates, I walked across the parking lot to my black Mercedes. Yes, I finally traded in the Volvo that had belonged to Ezra. On the drive home, painful memories of my dashed plans with Buster were replaced with excitement about having my daughter back.

Nearing the house, I felt doubt creeping in. "I have to be careful. I may not really have her back. I don't want to assume anything. This situation is still fragile. I don't know whether or not she believes I never signed those guardianship papers." Then, from my spirit, a correction came. "Erase those negative thoughts. Delete, delete, delete! God is blessing me now." I learned that from Ezra.

The girls called to say they were exhausted and would come over in the morning. I was tired too. I understood completely. Besides, we all needed to process this happy reunion and think about how our lives would change because of it.

Sunbeams awakened me Sunday morning. Thankfully, only a trace of soreness remained in my legs. I had soaked in a cold bath Saturday night per instructions of my coach, and then applied a heating pad. A good night's sleep completed my body restoration efforts. I don't know how I was able to sleep after all the excitement of Saturday morning. Yet, I had laid down the burden of anxiety I had been carrying for seventeen years, since my daughter was taken away. A glance in the mirror revealed shining eyes and a broad smile. Joy was welling up deep within me.

As I got out of bed, I looked around the room, thinking "Thank God Happy Maids came on Friday. Otherwise, I'd have to rush around cleaning before the girls arrive. And thank God I got a substitute to teach my Sunday Celebration class this morning. I'm totally free to reacquaint myself with my daughter and get to know her partner. They made it pretty clear that they are a package deal. Actually, I'm glad she has a support system. Now, I'll be part of it."

I set the shower head to massage mode and enjoyed the deliciously warm water stimulating my skin. I took my time patting myself dry and rubbing on lotion. Then, I pampered myself with a cucumber masque. I declared this time "Be Good to Lila Morning." I felt a deep sense of satisfaction about the turn my life was taking.

After getting dressed, I headed for the kitchen. As I started the tea kettle heating, the phone rang. I knew who it was. "Good morning Bessie Ella. Oh, it feels so good to say your name."

"Good morning, Mom. We stayed with a friend of Roxie's last night. We've gotten dressed. I don't know if you're up yet or not."

"I am up, dressed and making tea. You should join me for breakfast. Do you have transportation?"

"We're not far from Capitol Hill. We'll take a cab. We can be there in about forty-five minutes."

"I'll be expecting you. Any special requests for breakfast? I have most breakfast foods here."

"Do you have a waffle iron?"

"Oh, I made you waffles when you were a toddler. You loved them then too. Of course we'll have waffles, along with eggs, juice and tea or coffee."

"Roxie and I will be right over."

Memories came flooding back and I had to wipe away the tears for all those lost years. Yet, here was a new day. I pulled the Aunt Jemima pancake mix out of the cabinet, grabbed the mixing bowl and the waffle iron and went into chef mode.

By the time the doorbell rang, the dining table was set with my best china. I lit the candles in the silver candelabras before opening the door. Glancing back, I wondered, "Is the table setting too formal? But at this stage of my life, this is who I am. It's better to be authentic."

I hugged Bessie and Roxie as they came through the door with their suitcases. It hadn't occurred to me that they might be staying with me for a few days. I led them upstairs to my largest guest bedroom. It was sunny with pastel walls, a queen size poster bed, a writing desk and a comfortable sitting area.

"This is a great room," Roxie said. "Yes, I love your house, Mom," added Bessie. I said, "We'll take a tour after breakfast. The waffles are waiting."

At breakfast, we made small talk about yesterday's race and the pleasant weather. Then, there was an awkward silence. I asked, "When did you start looking for me, Bessie?"

"Well actually, I started asking about you and my birth father six years ago. My Mom and Dad, the Moores, were uncomfortable with my persistent questions at first. They had told me all along that I was adopted because they could not have children. I grew up as an only child. Finally, they showed me the guardianship papers and my birth certificate. I saw that I was born in Macon, Georgia. My father's name was listed as Jimmy Lee Jenkins. Since I thought you had given me away, I decided to look for him as soon as I was able to travel on my own."

I swallowed hard. My suppressed truth was about to be exposed to the light. I could not imagine what she was going to say next.

Bessie continued, "I saved up some money from my part time job and flew to Macon, Georgia last year. That was before I got to know Roxie." Here she paused and sipped her peppermint tea. This was not easy for Bessie.

I said, "You are so brave. I know this is hard." I wanted to comfort her, but I thought it best to just wait and listen. How could I begin to explain my convoluted life?

My daughter said, "I found the man I thought was my father, Jimmy Jenkins, in the phone directory. When I called, I could tell he was stunned. He stammered a bit, then agreed to meet me for lunch the next day. He said he worked at the main post office and could meet me at Marie's Barbecue near the Piggly Wiggly grocery store."

The memories came roaring back. I had avoided those places for years. That's where I spent time with Neil Rivers, Bessie's real father, and learned about past life regression. That's where my life took a sharp turn away from the certainties of Macon's settled lifestyles and its rural surroundings. It seemed light years away. Until now.

I had no idea what expression I had on my face, but Roxie was looking at me with real concern. Bessie was staring into her empty cup. I said, "Let me get you some more hot water and a fresh tea bag." I was glad when she nodded her consent. I needed a breather. I asked, "Could I freshen your tea, Roxie?" She handed me her cup. After we were all settled with fresh cups of tea, Bessie began again.

"Mr. Jenkins was waiting when I got to Marie's Barbecue. At first I wasn't sure who he was, but he recognized me. He greeted me nervously, 'Hello, Bessie Ella. You really favor your mother, and you walk just like her.' He recommended the barbecue ribs so we both ordered some. As we waited for our food, he asked me where I lived and what I was doing. Then, he told me a little about himself."

"When I was married to your mother, I was a farmer and worked part time in a feed store. Ten years ago, I sold the farm and moved my family to the city. I'm a postal supervisor and my wife is a caterer. We live pretty good. I've always wondered what happened to you. The break-up with me and Lila wasn't your fault.

"Bessie, I don't know how to say this except to tell you straight out. I met your mother when I was in second grade and she was in first grade.

We were a pair right from the start. We married when she was nineteen and I was twenty. Neither one of us had been anywhere but right in this area. We were probably too young to get married."

"I gasped, 'You were childhood sweethearts!' Mom, I really wondered how you two ended up divorcing. He continued his story."

"Yes. We had been married almost four years when you were born."

"Then he delivered the bombshell. I really wasn't prepared to hear it."

"I thought you were the child I had been waiting for. I loved you. But you didn't look like me at all. When you were about six months old, your mother admitted that she had had a brief fling while I was out of town. She said it was a one night stand with a friend. My name is on your birth certificate and that makes me your legal father. I am not genetically your father. That man had an aneurysm and died while you were an infant. His name was Neil. That's all I know."

A tear ran down Bessie's cheek. She said, "I felt deflated, like someone had just let all the air out of me. I traveled all that way to find out he wasn't my father and my real father was dead."

When I found my voice, I said, "I'm so sorry you had to find out this way. I have had a complex and difficult life, but you are one of the blessings that kept me inspired. I never had another child, and I never gave up on seeing you again."

Bessie gave me a quizzical look, then went on with her story. "By this time, our rib dinners had arrived. I hardly felt like eating although the food was tasty. Have you ever eaten there?"

"Yes. Many times. I loved Marie's barbecue ribs with collard greens and cole slaw."

"That's what I had. Now, it feels like I am walking in your tracks." She smiled through the pain she was obviously feeling.

"You're a trooper, like me."

"Anyway, I asked Mr. Jenkins, 'Where is my mother?' He sighed and paused to collect himself."

Then he said, "Lila Mae left me after telling me I was not your real father. She went up north to Washington, D.C. I've only seen her once since then. She divorced me, and then I remarried and started another family."

"Where in Washington does she live?"

180

"I don't know. I've never been up there. The person who keeps up with Lila is her sister, Gwen. I can give you her phone number and address. She lives around here." He wrote the information in my little address book.

I said, "Thank you. I want to find my real mother. I want to know why she gave me away."

"I didn't know she did that," he said. But the one time she came back when her father was dying, you were not with her. You have a grandmother here too, Lila's mother. She's not doing too well. She and your mother are not that close, I understand."

I told him, "It doesn't sound like she's the person I should talk to. I'll contact Gwen. I guess she's my Aunt Gwen."

"Before you go, Bessie, there is something I want to give you. When Lila divorced me, she gave me her old Buick that she had left here. I sold it and put the money in the bank. I haven't touched that money. It's not a lot, but I'd like for you to have it."

"When we finished eating, he took me to the bank and got the money for me. As soon as I returned to my motel room, I tried to call Aunt Gwen. The line was busy. I tried to call twice. I wasn't quite sure what to do. Finally, I decided to go to Aunt Gwen's house. The sleepy-eyed man who answered the door said she was out of town attending a church meeting. I guess that was her husband. I didn't tell him who I was. I said his wife and I had a mutual friend who told me to look her up while I was in town. I called myself Thelma.

The next day, I flew back to Texas. At least, I knew more than I did before about my father. I waited another year before setting out to find you.

Roxie chimed in, "She kept talking about wanting to find you, so I said 'Let's do it.' As you know, we are both runners and we found out about the race in Richmond. I said, 'That's close to Washington. We can race in Richmond, and then drive up to Washington to look for your mom.' We have friends here who attended Texas A & M with us, so I knew we would have a place to stay for a couple of days."

"Roxie's the organizer. She schedules everything," Bessie said.

"Well, you found me," I said. "It sounds like you and Roxie are a good team. Bessie, I am not perfect, but I do love you and I have always loved you. When I was in college, I didn't give you all the attention you deserved. I was trying to juggle being a wife and mother with my studies and with the civil rights movement."

"I can't imagine juggling all that. When did you have fun?" Bessie asked.

I replied, "It was intense, but I enjoyed what I was doing. I thought I could be a force to change the world. Sometimes, my life got out of balance, though. The sixties were like a whirlwind...really exciting years."

"I've heard about them," my daughter said, "but I guess you had to be there."

I laughed. "You were there, but you were a baby. Janice Moore was your babysitter. She and her husband spent a lot of time with you. Then, Henry let them take you to California. I was devastated. I searched for you. I'm so glad to be with you again."

"I'm glad we found you. We're planning on going back to Texas day after tomorrow. We have to decide what our next move will be. We have been thinking of leaving school for a while to save up some money for tuition," Bessie said.

"You don't have to do that. When I was your age, Henry encouraged me to go back to school. It's the best advice I ever got. Now I'm a lawyer and I'm doing very well financially."

"Is that your Mercedes we saw out front?" Roxie asked. "Yes," I said. "Girls, don't drop out of school. I'll help you. Do you want to finish at Texas A & M?"

They both said, "Yes." They shared that Bessie was majoring in Radio, TV and Film while Roxie was majoring in Business Management.

"I predict that you will end up owning and operating a radio and television conglomerate in a major broadcast market," I said. "The possibilities are endless. I can tell you're both smart. Now you've got a backer. Go for it."

They smiled at each other. Bessie said, "You've got a deal." The girls called their friends and wanted to go out and see Washington. That was fine with me. I needed to spend some time reflecting on the events and revelations of this day. Their friends were coming to pick them up. While they were waiting, I gave the girls a tour of my four bedroom home with its deck overlooking the backyard garden. When the horn honked outside, I gave Bessie a hundred dollars. "Have fun. This is a down payment on all the allowances I never had a chance to give you."

She grinned. "Thanks, Mom." They were off. I danced around the room. There was still so much for us to learn about each other, but we had made a start. "I am a mommy," I announced to the indoor plants, the paintings on the wall, and to the chaise on which I joyfully stretched out.

Bessie Ella and Roxie departed on Tuesday, another sunny Washington day. Their friends wanted to take them to the airport and I didn't object. We were still on the edges of these new relationships. We hugged and kissed goodbye at the door.

Within a few minutes, I also left the house. I enjoyed the manicured flower gardens dotting the Capitol Hill neighborhood as I drove the short distance to my bank. Entering the building, I felt protected by the massive marble walls and granite floor. I asked to speak with the administrator of the trust department. Together with her, I made arrangements to set up a substantial trust fund for Bessie Ella. There was plenty of money since the investment of funds from Henry's bequest to me had nearly doubled in value and my income was more than $200,000 a year. I decided to name my daughter as the beneficiary of the trust and give her the option to share with her girlfriend. Youthful relationships are not always stable.

I gave the bank's trust department sole authority to administer the trust, based on the specific terms of the document. That eliminated my vulnerability to the persuasions and opinions of others. The money was hers and that was that. I knew it couldn't make up for all the years we missed together, but it was something.

After the girls left with their youthful energy, a dullness settled into my home. I had been working so hard for so long that I decided I needed a vacation. I called my sister and said, "Gwen, I need a break. I'm thinking of going to Paris. Why don't you go with me?"

"Paris, Georgia or Paris, France?" Gwen asked.

"Now, why would I want to go to Paris, Georgia?" I asked. "France of course."

"It sound great, but I don't have France money."

"I'll cover your air fare, hotel and meals. You be responsible for your personal stuff and souvenirs. How does that sound?"

"It sounds like a dream come true. When is all this taking place?"

"Well, first you have to get a passport if you don't have one. Let's say in about six weeks."

"I'll apply for the passport tomorrow," Gwen said. "I need to get away too. Meanwhile, you might want to come down here and see Mama. She's getting frail. She never did really bounce back from Daddy's death."

I felt a pang of guilt for letting Gwen and Terrell carry the responsibility of looking after Mama. I arranged to take a four day weekend and visit Macon for the first time in seventeen years. My unresolved past was thrusting through the barrier I had erected long ago. Bessie's visit brought it to the forefront, right in my face.

My plane touched down in Macon on Friday at 12:10 PM. Gwen met me at the airport. On the drive to her home, I told her about my reunion with Bessie Ella. She was astounded, but very happy for me. She couldn't believe that Bessie Ella had visited Macon last year while she was out of town.

"Did Clarence tell you someone stopped by to see you while you were at the church convention?"

"Oh yeah, he told me a white woman came by. We couldn't figure out ... Wait a minute! Was that Bessie Ella?"

"I'm sure that was Bessie."

"Oh, my goodness! Clarence must not have been wearing his glasses."

"Bessie said he looked sleepy. Maybe he was waking up from a nap."

"Why didn't you call me while she was in D.C.? I could have talked to her."

"Gwen, she was only there for two and a half days. I wanted to spend as much time with her as possible, especially since she had college buddies in the area that she wanted to hang out with. You'll get to talk to her the next time she comes."

"How does she look? I know she's pretty."

"Yes, and she's five feet ten inches tall. She looks pretty much the way I did at her age except that her complexion is a little lighter, she is an inch taller, her eyes are hazel and her hair is a lighter brown."

"Henry never did tell you where she was?"

"He didn't know. Dr. Moore left the army and they moved. Henry and I never could find them."

"Girl, you have had yourself some adventures. I love you, but I admit I don't really understand the choices you've made."

"My life is like an appliqué quilt, full of curious characters, funky colors and crazy patterns. Each piece looks like it was cut out by somebody wearing a blindfold. It's quirky, but it keeps me warm and it keeps me going." We both laughed.

"You got that right. My life quilt is pieced together with predictable, repeating patterns. Nice and reliable with colors that match."

"We're both warm."

"And we're together after all these years. I'm always standing by you in spirit. You can count on that."

"Thanks, Gwen. You are there when I need you the most. That means a lot to me."

"Oh, on the way home, I'm going to swing by one of my rental properties. Remember when you advised me to buy property at the tax sales?"

"Yes, that rental income will come in handy when you retire. I've bought a couple of properties in D. C. for the same reason. Do you remember the basic rules I gave you?"

"Of course. Rule one: Location, location, location. Rule two: Strong bones. Don't buy anything where the structure is leaning. Rule three: Don't pay too much. There's the house coming up on the left with the green siding."

"It's very attractive. Did you do a lot of work on it?"

"Clarence and his buddy did most of it, but I helped."

"Congratulations. Should we stop somewhere for lunch?"

"No. I've got lunch made at home."

"Well, thank you. I can't believe how this area has changed. There are so many new buildings."

"Yep. The city has annexed about half of the rural areas. Some of the farms are now housing developments."

We reached Gwen's house. She and Clarence had added brick veneer all around the outside. It was very attractive. We continued to chat over lunch.

"How's Mama? I haven't seen her in years. We talk on the phone now and then, but as you know we haven't been very close. I send her $300 a month to help out. The bank does it automatically."

"I'm sure she appreciates the money, but it's not like you being here, Lila Mae. And by the bank sending the money automatically, it's kind of impersonal."

"I know, but my life is so busy that I didn't want to forget to send it."

"Mama is on a walker now. She started out on a cane, but now she's on a walker. She doesn't drive anymore. Terrell and I take her where she has to go. He helps her take care of her business too."

"I'm glad you're both here to do that. How is Terrell? He and I only talk every three or four weeks and the conversation is usually brief."

"He's fine. His house is across the street from Mama's. He usually cuts her grass and fixes whatever breaks down in her house. He's good with his hands."

"We'll see him when we go to visit Mama, then. If he's not at her house, we'll walk over and spend some time with him and his family."

"Oh, he's expecting you. He'll be at Mama's. I'll call and let him know when we're on our way." After lunch, we started out to see Mama. I told myself to relax and be flexible.

Gwen's car turned onto Mama's street. There, set back from the now paved road, was the gray frame house where I grew up, its tentacles no longer encircling me. It was at once familiar and foreign. There was a fancy new front door with a decorative glass insert. The house seemed smaller than I remembered. Most of the farm land around it had been sold to developers, and there were cookie cutter houses all around it. Only one house across the street was distinctively different. That, Gwen told me, was Terrell's house.

My life had changed so much since I left Macon. I now lived in a different world, but so did my mother. Time and change had moved forward for both of us. This moment, this occasion called for reconnection. A different kind of connection than the one we once had.

As we exited the car, Mama's front door swung open. Terrell bounded out and ran out to the car, encircling me with a big bear hug.

"How's it going, Sis? It's good to see you, foreigner." He laughed. "Welcome home, Lila."

"Terrell, you haven't changed. Still joking around. It's good to see you too."

"Gwen, thanks for picking her up. Come on, you two. Mama's waiting."

As we entered the living room, I saw that it looked almost the same as it did seventeen years ago. A new flowered rug and an armchair to replace Daddy's old recliner were the only noticeable changes. Mama slowly walked toward us from the kitchen, smiling broadly. I moved toward her and we embraced. I was surprised by the tightness of her hug. She was clinging to me and she rubbed my back. When at last she released me, she said "I didn't know if I was ever going to see you again. You're looking good. Pretty as ever."

"Thank you, Mama," I said. "I invited you to come to Washington several times, but you never came. I didn't know you wanted to see me."

"Lila, why wouldn't I want to see my own daughter? I never could figure out how you were thinking or why you did things the way you did. It just seemed strange to me, but I always loved you. And I'm proud of you, a big city lawyer and all. I'm glad you went back to school after you left here. Your Daddy didn't live to see you become a lawyer, but he knew you went back to college. He was real happy about that."

"I'm glad, Mama. It's really good to see you again."

"I want to thank you for sending me the check every month. It really helps out since I stopped working at the health clinic because Social Security only goes so far."

"You're welcome, Mama. How have you been feeling?"

"Some days I feel pretty good, and other days my arthritis acts up. I get stiff and my joints start aching. Just like those people who used to come in the clinic. Yes. Now I'm just like them."

"Have you been going to the doctor regularly?"

"Gwen takes me, but it doesn't do any good. The medicine he gives me for my arthritis upsets my stomach, so I don't take it."

Gwen said, "Mama, you're supposed to take it with food."

"It still makes me feel funny. I'm just getting old."

I said, "Mama, you're only sixty-eight years old. You're talking like you're ninety. Come on. Let's sit down. I want to tell you something."

"And I want to ask you something. Did you ever find your baby girl? Gwen said some people had taken her out west and you didn't have their address."

"Yes. We found each other two weeks ago at a race in Virginia. We're both runners and we found each other out of thousands of people. It was a miracle really."

"Oh, praise God. Well, you always did like to race around. How does she look? She was a pretty baby."

"She looks a lot like me when I was twenty. Her hair is lighter and her complexion is smooth. She's tall and she has curves in the right places. She's a junior in college."

"You never did tell us who the daddy was. I was waiting for you to say something, but you never did."

"Mama, that was so long ago. Let it stay in the past. I know and Bessie knows. That's enough."

"Your husband was in a bad way when you left. Everybody was talking about it around here. That was hard on me and Daddy. We didn't know where you were for the longest time. All we could do was pray for you.

"Well, I'm glad you did that. Everything is turning out fine."

"What about all those husbands? How many have you had now?

"Four. Don't start lecturing me about that, Mama."

"I'm not going to lecture you, but you know, the Lord didn't intend for women to have that many husbands. That goes against God's word."

"Well, the Lord took two of them away."

"You need to pray for forgiveness."

"Mama, you and I have different ways of looking at things. God walks with me every day. I belong to a church that believes that God is our help in every need. He loves and protects us twenty-four hours a day. All we need to do is trust him. God is not as prejudiced and judgmental as human beings. The God in my life is loving and supportive."

"God can also strike you down if you don't follow his commands."

"Mama, I didn't come here to argue. God has blessed me with an abundant life. No life is free of problems and challenges, but he has blessed me so that I can bless others. I thank Him for that."

"Well, I hope you won't be getting married any more."

"I hope you will. You still have some good years ahead of you. Just stop thinking of yourself as old, and take your medicine. Some older gentleman could be looking at you and you don't even know it." I laughed, hoping to lighten the conversation.

"No. One husband was enough for me. When I breathe my last, I'll meet him again in heaven. What a day of joy that will be. Then, we'll spend eternity together. We'll be rejoicing with all the other believers."

"Singing and strumming on harps? It sounds like one continuous party."

"Heaven is a happy place, and only true believers can get in. It's our reward for suffering through this life and keeping God's commandments."

"Mama, what do you do for joy around here?"

"Oh, you know there's not much going on here. I go to the senior citizens center some days and have lunch with my friends. So many of them are ailing and dying off."

"That sounds depressing. You really should take a trip somewhere to get a different view of things. Why don't you come to Washington and let me show you around the city?"

"That sounds like too much walking. I can't walk but so far before I get tired. Yesterday, the doctor told me I have heart failure. I have to take it easy."

Gwen shouted, "Mama! You didn't tell me that yesterday when I brought you home from the doctor's office."

Mama replied, "I wanted to think about it first. Everybody's got to die of something."

I chimed in, "Mama, it seems that you are just waiting to die. What you need is a project of some kind. Something to focus your attention on, other than dying. Are there any classes you can take, like arts and crafts? You can expand your interests."

"What do I look like trying to crochet something or paint something with arthritis in my hands?"

"Do you exercise your hands?"

"I still have to keep the house clean. That's exercise."

Gwen asked, "Mama, where are those little squeeze balls I gave you?"

"Little Greg came over and was playing with them, so I let him take them home." Looking at me, she added, "Greg is Terrell's youngest son." I nodded acknowledgement. "No, I don't need those balls. I don't need to play with toys. They don't do any good."

"Mama, you're in a rut. You're still here, so God must have a reason for keeping you here. There must be something you're supposed to do."

"I might be doing it now -- seeing you again. Now, I can rest easier."

Terrell had been listening intently. He said, "Mama has made up her mind. She has her own routine and she's comfortable with it. She's not looking for any projects or anything new. She's not trying to expand her interests, as you put it. You can't change her, Lila Mae. You and Mama lead completely different lives. She can't be like you."

Mama said, "Wouldn't want to. Like I said, I love you but I don't understand you. I probably never will."

"I love you too, Mama, and I respect your right to make your own choices. Let me know if there's anything I can do to help."

"You already are. Like I said, I appreciate the checks you've been sending. Just pray for me and I'll keep praying for you."

"It's a deal." I kissed Mama on the cheek and she returned the kiss. "So Terrell, when do I get to meet your wife and children?"

Terrell looked at the antique clock on the wall. "Shantay should be home from work in the next few minutes. The kids should be home from school now. That's right. You never met my two sons." He stood up. "Come on and meet Will and Greg."

"Mama, I'll see you later," I said. "I love you. Gwen, are you coming with us?"

Gwen said, "I'll visit with Mama for a while. I'll catch up with you."

I visited with Terrell's family for a little over an hour. That was all I could stand. They were a loud bunch. At thirteen and fifteen, the boys were rambunctious, wrestling each other in the family room. Terrell and Shantay took it in stride. I had not been around teenagers in a home setting in years. I felt out of touch with that raw energy.

The boys thanked me for the Christmas presents I always sent. They didn't believe in sending thank you notes, but they usually called. I could hear their parents coaching them in the background. I told them that from now on, I would send gift cards so they could pick out their own gifts. They liked that idea.

Just as I was wearing down, Gwen came through the door. "Hey everybody!" she called out gaily. "Lila, I know you're tired from the trip. Do you want to go back to my place and get some rest?"

I said, "Yes, Gwen. I think that's a good idea. Terrell and Shantay, Will and Greg, it's been fun. I'm glad I finally got a chance to meet you boys." We hugged goodbye and Gwen and I headed for the car.

As soon as Gwen started down the street, I heaved a loud sigh of relief, "Whew!"

"They are one energetic bunch, aren't they?"

"Yes. My life in Washington is so much quieter. But they seem to really enjoy themselves and each other."

"They sure do," Gwen said. "When I need a little lift, I visit with them for a while. It doesn't take long."

That evening Gwen and I engaged in girl talk, reminiscences and our planned trip to Paris. It was nearly 1:00 AM when I fell asleep. The next day, we took Mama out to lunch. We went to one of her favorite "all you can eat" places. The restaurant featured down home Southern cooking and there was plenty of food. Some of the patrons were piling their plates up like food was going out of style.

I had decided to try to keep the conversation light. Gwen had told me that Mama felt uncomfortable when I started making suggestions about what she should do. I restrained my tendency to criticize and problem solve.

Mama said, "The church members will be glad to see you tomorrow, Lila. They ask about you from time to time. Some of your cousins will be there too. You haven't seen each other in years."

"It will be good to see everybody. Does JJ still go to that church?"

"Oh, yes. He's head of the deacon board.

Gwen said, "Speaking of JJ, he just walked in with two of his sons and his little girl."

I looked toward the entrance and spotted my first husband. He had picked up about twenty pounds since I last saw him. He must have felt my eyes looking at him because he turned around. His mouth dropped open. I smiled. He smiled back and waved.

When his children headed to the buffet, JJ walked over. "Hello, Lila Mae," he said pleasantly. "Hello JJ," I replied. He awkwardly acknowledged Mama and Gwen and asked how they were doing.

I said, "It's been a long time."

"When did you get here?"

"Yesterday, and I'm staying until Monday. It's a short trip, but I wanted to see the family, especially Mama."

"I'm sure she's glad to see you."

"I sure am," Mama said.

"You look like you're doing well, Lila."

Mama responded, "She's a big city lawyer and she owns rent houses up in Washington."

"Mama!" I scolded. Then, "How are you and your family, JJ?"

"We're doing fine. I'm not farming anymore. We moved to the city. I'm a post office supervisor and my wife has a busy catering business."

"She always was a good cook," I said.

Mama added, "Lessie Ann caters for a lot of weddings around here, and she catered for this year's homecoming service at the church."

"Wonderful," I said. Just then, JJ's daughter came over. We all greeted her, and then she pointed at me and asked, "Who is that, Daddy?" I thought, "Uh-oh. This is where the trouble starts."

JJ said, "This is Miss Lila, a lady who used to go to school with me. She lives out of town now. Before your mother and I started dating, she used to be my lady."

The child's eyes widened. "This is your old girlfriend? She's pretty."

At that, JJ said "Lila, this is Jessica. Honey, go eat your food before it gets cold. And I need to get my lunch." He turned to our group and said, "Bye now." We said in a chorus, "Bye JJ."

Gwen, who had been uncharacteristically quiet, now spoke up. "Wait until Jessica goes home and tells her mother about you. Everybody will know you're here. Lessie will call her mother and her mother will call her network. That woman loves to gossip."

I said, "I can't worry about that. I thought JJ handled it very well. If he and I are comfortable with being in the same room, other people will back off."

My mother said, "In a pig's eye."

I reinforced my intention to keep this lunch light and pleasant. I did a quick silent meditation to get centered again. Then, I shifted the conversation to the changes in the area since I last visited.

Sunday morning proved that fear is no match for faith. If I had allowed myself to become upset over the dire predictions of Mama and Gwen, I would have been afraid to set foot in Mt. Carmel Baptist Church on Sunday. They spun tales of people staring and whispering, and of JJ's wife snubbing me. None of that happened. I woke up early on Sunday, sat up in bed and did my morning prayers followed by affirmations. I asked God to take charge so that the whole day would be pleasant and comfortable for all concerned, and that all events would proceed in Divine Order. Then, I meditated in silence for twenty minutes. When I opened my eyes, I was completely at peace. Nothing could ruffle my feathers after that.

The church service was lively, though the sermon was rather long. I have grown accustomed to one hour services at Unity. At any rate, it was a change of pace. I loved the choir with its traditional harmonies. Looking around, I saw many familiar faces. When they asked visitors to stand, I did so and shared that I was a member of the Unity Church in Washington, DC. Some of my friends waved at me. The minister welcomed me warmly and invited me to come to the fellowship hall after church for refreshments.

One of the first people to greet me in the fellowship hall was Lessie Ann Jenkins. She hugged me and said, "Welcome back." She was a class act. I could not view her in the same way after that day. JJ introduced me to their four children and I shook their hands. The oldest boy looked like a replica of a younger JJ.

One of the older parishioners asked about my daughter. I told him she was attending college in Texas. That was all they needed to know. Some of my high school friends wanted to talk about old times, so we arranged for them to visit me at Gwen's house after dinner.

Then, the whole family went to Terrell's house to eat. This time, I was prepared for the high level of energy and noise and made up my mind to have a good time. With every laugh, some of my old resentments melted away. This was a cleansing process, a catharsis of subconscious fear and pain.

When I boarded the plane early Monday afternoon, I was a changed person. I felt closer to my family and felt good about the people of Macon. I still would not choose to live there, but I could be comfortable among them. I invited several old friends to visit me in Washington. Judging from their past pattern of staying close to home, I doubted that they would actually come.

Back in Washington, I played catch-up at work. I began planning the trip to Paris in evening conversations with Gwen. Some evenings, I reflected on my life journey.

I've come a long way. When I first learned my life plan at the age of twenty-one, I was shocked. Now, I've been subconsciously following that plan. The Council of Elders was right. It has been a rough life, but I have been blessed. I need to count my blessings. I have a good career, a stable financial situation, friends, my faith, good health, a beautiful home, and family – even if I'm not that close to them.

The other day, I found a large, yellowing index card in the bottom of my sock drawer where I wrote down all the things the Chief Elder said I was supposed to learn in this life. I need to overcome:

- Selfishness
- Greed
- Prejudice against those unlike myself
- Letting ego control my life

I am also supposed to learn some good habits:

- Willingness to listen
- Openness to spiritual growth
- Courage to take risks for the sake of others
- Viewing of events from the perspective of eternity
- Unconditional love for all of God's children
- Giving service to others

Re-reading this list after so many years made me wonder how well I have done. At age forty-three, my life is half over, maybe more than half. I started out with an overwhelming challenge, and I still have a way to go. I thought, "Two more husbands! They'll have to wait. I need a break. Gwen and I will take Paris by storm. We'll leave our imprint on that city."

I reflected, "This is a wonderful place to be in my life. I feel mellow. I think I'll stay single for a while and enjoy it." I stretched out on the bed to rest. Then, I felt a presence in the room, just behind me in the doorway.

I thought, "Uh-oh, who is this? I haven't had this experience before. I'm not sure I'm ready. It feels like good energy, though. Is that you, Ezra? You talked about piercing the veil." No response, but I still felt loving energy. I asked myself, "Should I look or not? Okay, I've always been more curious than scared. I'm going to look." There in the doorway was a light being in the form of a pretty woman. Her smile was radiant.

"Oh, my goodness! You're beautiful."

"I have been guiding you all your life."

"That voice! You are Supermama. What is your real name?"

"I am Gayla."

"My chief guide?"

"Yes, my impatient one. Your soul reincarnated before I could return from my duties in another mansion. In my absence, you made some tough choices for this life. Once, Ezra asked you if you had ever seen me. When I saw him on the other side, he suggested that I reveal myself to you. I wasn't coming until I saw you reviewing your life plan."

"Tell Ezra this is one more thing I won't be able to discuss with anybody. He was the only one I could talk to about my spiritual experiences."

"I came to encourage you. You are making good progress toward the goals you pledged to meet. You are growing spiritually. There will be many more bumps in the road ahead. Enjoy this period of relative calm. Do some reflecting and gather your strength. Many on the other side are cheering you on."

"Thank you, Gayla. And now I know what you look like."

"Today, I chose an appearance from one of my physical lives. It isn't permanent, but don't worry about it. Just know that Supermama is watching and caring." She smiled and filled the room with warm energy. Then, her appearance dissolved. I had to pinch myself to be sure I wasn't dreaming. Nope. I was wide awake.

The next minute, I thought of the light being who promised to incarnate during my lifetime to lift my spirits and bring hope to everyone. I wondered, "Where is Barama and when will he reveal his human self to America?"

To Be Continued in Book Two

Appendix A

Author's Note

I thank God for giving me the knowledge early in life that I was supposed to write a major book and/or full length play that would benefit human beings. At several stages in my life, I began writing a book. As a student of spiritual matters, I thought I was meant to write a how-to book on growing in spiritual understanding. I began that work, but never finished.

For my senior thesis at Talladega College, I chose a creative rather than a research thesis. I wrote a three-act play, *And the Wind Returns*, which was later performed by the Little Theater at Talladega. It was based on Ecclesiastes and concerned the ongoing cycle of life. I believe this was a practice drama, preparing me for the work ahead. Every experience in my life has served as preparation for the writing of this novel.

The timing of *All My Husbands* was in Divine Order. When I retired after a long career in public education and after raising two wonderful daughters, I was shown that the time had come to carry out my mission. Life events interfered initially. Then, three different people who lived in different parts of the United States revealed that they had received a dream, vision or spiritual message that I was supposed to write a bestseller. They said it was important that I begin the work. I recognized that they were serving as God's messengers. Although the urgencies of life frequently demanded my attention and my constancy sometimes wavered, I was always led back to the task of completing this novel. God has been both patient and persistent.

- Patricia Churchill

Appendix B
Acknowledgements

Many people deserve my gratitude, some for encouraging me to write this book and others for reading the manuscript and offering recommendations.

- My equestrian daughter, Jill Patton, helped me visualize and describe Ezra and Flame's experiences more clearly. She carefully reviewed my manuscript twice.
- My daughter, Tahoma, and her husband, Michael, inspired me by being faithful and committed to their Divine purpose, bringing nine souls into the world and nurturing them.
- My niece, Jessica Okoye, critiqued the novel from a young adult perspective.
- My friend and fellow writer, Jeannette Drake, served as a critical reader/editor.
- Literary critic, Rudolph Lewis, made insightful recommendations to improve the work.
- My brother-in-law, Francis Walker, gave me feedback on the authenticity of my representation of male voices in the narratives.
- My sisters and brothers, Dr. Bettye Walker, Nelson Coleman, Thelma Ozojiofor, Presley Coleman, Elizabeth Coleman and Vesta Gregory patiently waited for me to finish the "mysterious" book.
- The Women of Unity at the Unity of Richmond Church, a great group of supportive women, believed in my success.
- My cheerleaders in the Adult Sunday School Class, especially Doris Marr, Louise Willis, Sue Godwin and Nancy Baker were

curious but patient.

- My friend and fellow writer, William Lucas, inspired me with his own book.
- My friend, Tom Hartman, asked me regularly over a three year period how the novel was coming along.
- My ministers, Revs. Richard and Victoria Bunch and Rev. Joyce Fisher-Pierce from Unity of Bon Air gave me advice and support.
- My friend and fellow creative spirit, Donna Fuller, inspired me.
- Visitors to my web site, www.soundofwisdom.com, encouraged me.
- My mother, Vesta Coleman, was a poet who inspired me to begin writing.
- Penny Gregory listened to my ideas on our long morning walks and shared her practical knowledge.
- My publishers sent regular e-mails and kept me on track.
- A host of friends and supporters sent positive energy.

Last but not least, I must thank the characters themselves. They told me the outlines of their stories in dreams, visions, and auditory messages. I hope you have enjoyed reading what they shared with me.

Appendix C
Chronolgy of Events

Event	Lila'sAge	Year
Lila's birth	0	1941
Married JJ	19	1960
Bessie's birth	22	1964
Divorced JJ	24	1965
Married Henry (1st time)	24	1965
Married Henry (2nd time)	28	1969
Henry died.	29	1970
Married Ezra	32	1973
Ezra died.	38	1979
Married Buster	40	1981
Buster released	43	1984
Reunited with Bessie	43	1984
Reunited with mother	43	1984
Divorce from Buster	44	1985

Appendix D
Recipes from the Characters

Kissing don't last; cookery do.

-George Meredith

- Lila Mae's Egg Salad Sandwich

- Lila Mae's Cornbread

- Lessie Ann's Sweet Potato Pie

- Lessie Ann's Banana-Walnut Pancakes

- Buster's Long Daddy Special

Lila Mae's Egg Salad Sandwich

<u>Ingredients</u>

8 eggs
1 red bell pepper, chopped finely
2 whole scallions finely chopped
1 small carrot, finely shredded
1 tablespoon chopped fresh parsley
1 tablespoon chopped fresh basil

1 tablespoon chopped dill pickle
1 teaspoon honey mustard
2 tablespoons mayonnaise
¼ teaspoon salt
1/8 teaspoon freshly ground black pepper
Ten slices whole-wheat or multi-grain bread
Shredded lettuce, baby spinach or prepared mixed salad greens

Mix all of the ingredients together in a mixing bowl except for the bread and lettuce or spinach. Divide the mixture evenly and spread on five slices of bread. Top with lettuce/spinach and remaining bread slices. Serves five.

Lila Mae's Cornbread

Ingredients

2 cups yellow cornmeal
1 cup all-purpose flour
3 teaspoons baking powder
½ teaspoon baking soda
1 level teaspoon salt
A sprinkling of sugar
¼ cup jalapeno peppers
1 cup homemade or14 ¾ oz. can creamed corn
¾ cup shredded Cheddar cheese
¾ cup buttermilk
2 large eggs
6 tablespoons melted butter (or margarine)

Heat oven to 400 degrees. Grease and flour an iron skillet (or a 9 inch baking pan). In a mixing bowl, combine the flour, baking powder, soda, salt and sugar. Stir in chopped peppers, and cheese. In another bowl, combine the buttermilk, eggs and butter. Whisk these liquid ingredients, then add them to the dry ingredients, stirring until well moistened. Spread the batter into the greased and floured pan. Bake for about 35 minutes, or until lightly browned and firm.

Lessie Ann's Sweet Potato Pie

Ingredients

1 pastry pie shell, unbaked
2 cups sweet potatoes, cooked and peeled
½ cup unsalted butter
½ cup evaporated milk
2 large eggs, beaten
½ cup light brown sugar
1 teaspoon vanilla extract
1 teaspoon ground ginger
1 teaspoon ground cinnamon
½ teaspoon ground nutmeg
½ teaspoon salt
2 tablespoons bourbon
½ cup dark corn syrup
1 cup pecan halves

Prick holes in bottom of pie crust. Bake in preheated 425 degree oven for 12 minutes. Set aside. Mash sweet potatoes together with half of the butter. Let mixture cool. Add milk, eggs, brown sugar, vanilla, spices and bourbon. Beat until fluffy. Pour into pie crust and bake at 375 degrees for 20 minutes.

Mix remaining ¼ cup butter with corn syrup and pecans. Sprinkle over top of pie. Return pie to oven and bake about 25 minutes, or until a toothpick inserted in the center comes out clean.

You may add whipped topping to individual slices.

Lessie Ann's Banana-Walnut Pancakes

<u>Ingredients</u>

1 cup all purpose flour
½ teaspoon salt
2 teaspoons baking powder
2 tablespoons sugar
1 large egg
1 cup milk (regular, low fat or non-fat)
1 tablespoon bacon fat (or melted butter or vegetable oil)
1 mashed banana
½ cup walnut pieces

In a small bowl, stir dry ingredients (flour, salt, baking powder and sugar) together. In a medium sized bowl, whisk together egg, milk, and bacon fat (or butter or oil). Add dry ingredients to wet ingredients in medium bowl. Whisk or stir just until moistened. Small lumps are fine. Add the mashed banana and walnut pieces and stir lightly.

Heat an iron (or non-stick) skillet or griddle over medium heat. Moisten with oil using either a folded over paper towel or a pastry brush to spread the oil over the bottom surface of the skillet or griddle.

For each pancake, spoon about three tablespoons of batter onto the skillet. Cook until the surface of the pancakes shows some bubbles, about one to two minutes. Flip with a spatula and cook until browned on the underside. You may keep pancakes warm by covering them with aluminum foil and placing them in a 200 degree oven. Continue cooking, remembering to add oil to the bottom of the skillet as before. This makes 12 to 15 pancakes. Top with syrup, honey, preserves, or confectioners' sugar.

Buster's Long Daddy Special

<u>Ingredients</u>

4 foot long hot dogs (If not available, use regular length)
½ cup shredded Cheddar cheese
2 Jalapeno peppers, sliced
Spicy mustard
Can of sauerkraut
4 hot dog buns

Grill hot dogs over charcoal heat until well done. Slice hot dogs lengthwise about halfway through. Fill each hot dog with shredded cheddar cheese. Place each hot dog in a bun that has been heated. Spread spicy mustard on top of each hot dog. Sprinkle top of hot dogs with peppers and sauerkraut to taste. Serves two to four people.

Note: At Buster's Place, the Long Daddy Special is accompanied by baked beans.

not new

Printed in the United States
127443LV00001B/3-26/P